GRACE NOTES

Grace Notes

Collected Short Stories

by

Gordon Lawrie

Dean Park Press

First published 2023 by Dean Park Press

An imprint of Comely Bank Publishing

ISBN: 978-1-912365-37-1

Cover art by Comely Bank Design

Text printed in Adobe Garamond Pro
by 4edge

A CIP catalogue record for this book is available from the British
Library.

For Callum, and his unfailing good humour
despite the burden of supporting Falkirk Football Club.

Contents

Foreword

by Don Tassone

Gordon Lawrie is a uniquely gifted writer.

His writing style is breezy, even conversational. Reading his stories, you feel as though the author is speaking to you, and you're happy to be there.

His characters are vivid and memorable. A good number have crazy names. And they're not just people. Gordon can make even inanimate objects come alive, as he does in *Ex Libris*, the magical first story in this collection.

His stories seem light, even whimsical, but they explore important themes — racism and infidelity, for example. Yet there is never a lecture. Gordon's storytelling is too artful for that. In fact, you might not discover the deeper meanings in his stories until well after you've read them.

These things alone would make for great stories. But there is something else with Gordon's tales. There is an open-heartedness about them. They don't just entertain. They lift. That's what grace notes do.

Gordon wrote the 20 stories in this book over nearly a decade. Fortunately for us, he waited no longer to publish them as a collection.

Don Tassone, March 2023

Preface

I can't say I've always wanted to write fiction.

I was a teacher for 36 years. I taught Modern Studies – political science to the uninitiated – in high schools in the Edinburgh area, and for most of that time I was too busy trying to keep my head above real water to be able to imagine drowning in fake stuff. However, towards the end of my time as a teacher, I began to feel no longer part of the future of education, and perhaps I was made to feel a little bit that way, too.

So I looked for pastures new. That's where the writing began, and in 2011, like all wannabe writers, I started at the top, trying to write a full-length novel. It's said there's a novel in everyone, but nobody guarantees it's a good one, and my first was… frankly, awful. But I was determined to grind it out, prove to myself that I could, in fact, put together 100,000 words of fiction, and while I was doing so, I thought of a much, much better idea for the book I'd really like to write. I was like a coiled spring when I set off, and wrote *Four Old Geezers and a Valkyrie* in six months flat.

Four Old Geezers brought me a whole host of new writing friends, but I quickly learned that it didn't bring me a lot of money. Moreover, it was largely going to be up to me to promote my own book. Entering the world of publishing with Comely Bank Publishing, I did author events, joined online writing groups and even ran a couple of writing classes, but I also started to write other shorter fiction to help promote my precious novel. Shortly after that I fell into the role of editor of the online micro-fiction publication Friday Flash Fiction, so I had form at both ends of the fiction writing spectrum. It made sense to have a go at something in between as well.

Writing short stories served two purposes for me. First, all writers experience writer's block – the sudden inability to think of anything new to put to paper – at some stage of their careers, or fear of it at least. One of the less painful therapies is to write something different: a different genre, non-fiction, perhaps an essay, or to write something of a different length. It's often easier to write a short story, because there's no real 'approved' length for short stories. They're as long as they need to be.

The other incentive to write short stories came from trying to market *Four Old Geezers*. The characters were well-received, so it seemed a good marketing idea to write some short stories about them, individually and collectively, in other adventures. Quite a few of the stories here feature Brian/Captain, Fleece, Little Joe, Geoff and the others, and it gave me a chance to fill in a few gaps about Tam as well. You don't need to have read *Four Old Geezers*, though; these are stand-alone tales.

That led to another theme. *Four Old Geezers and a Valkyrie* is about a group of retiral-age guys who jam together, make a couple of home recordings and find themselves with surprise hits. The novel featured some original music, and some of these short stories do as well, including *Grace Notes*, which gives its name to the entire volume. Now and again you'll discover snippets of music tagged on to the end of stories – jingles, annoying pop choruses, a folk melody, an example of 'Rasta-Jock' (read the final story to find out!) and even a song that I'm quietly quite proud of called *The Shores of Caledonia*. But not all of the twenty stories in this collection feature music by any means.

You'll learn a little of my personality from these yarns, too. The things that interest me and amuse me, of course. Some of the stories are inspired by true events, or people I've met. It's said we should write about what we know, so it makes sense to adapt what we know to create our own fiction. All the characters are fictitious, however, and no one should be offended, I hope.

So there's a real mixture. The stories vary in length, too, so please feel free to dip into the book as you like. However you approach the tales in *Grace Notes*, though, I hope you enjoy them. I certainly enjoyed writing them.

Gordon Lawrie, 2023

Ex Libris

J ust to the south of Edinburgh is a small county called Midlothian. Once upon a time it was actually bigger, but that was when Edinburgh itself was part of Midlothian, and I suppose that was quite a long time ago now. I'm not sure if the separation of Scotland's capital from its southern hinterland was a good thing or not, but despite the fact that many people commute to and from the city daily, these days Midlothian is fiercely protective of its independence. Forget Edinburgh, Midlothian does its own thing.

It's not as though the people of Midlothian have a particular sense of 'Midlothian-ness'. On the contrary, its hundred or so square miles really focus on a series of towns and villages, pockets of humanity who compete with each other as much as they can to create any sort of collective county spirit. Midlothian used to be a coal mining area, and despite the demise of the industry across Britain, these local communities have remained strong and distinct. Each has its own local football team, many have 'gala' days in the summer and hundreds of little clubs and associations hold meetings every week or so. Midlothian has its own newspaper and even its own local radio, but both tend to talk about 'news from Gorebridge' or 'news from Dalkeith'.

Local public services – leisure centres, schools and so on – are provided by the local council, and although there's a 'Midlothian ethos' to the way these sorts of things are done, each has its own individual stamp. Nowhere is that more obvious than at its public libraries. Midlothian keeps winning awards like 'Public Library Local Authority of the Year', but the council really lets each library have its head and they each try to provide the best service in the county.

There are ten Midlothian public libraries in all: Dalkeith, Danderhall, Gorebridge, Lasswade, Loanhead, Mayfield, Newtongrange, Penicuik, Roslin and the strangest of all, Meadowfield. Meadowfield itself is little more than an enlarged village, and its library doesn't even open every day, just Tuesdays and Thursdays, plus Monday and Saturday mornings. It has a lovely librarian called Molly, a young woman in her early thirties, perhaps, who despite her relative youth seems to have worked there for years. All the locals like Molly; she's invariably bright and cheery, and is unfailingly helpful to everyone who comes in, even the men who simply come in on wet miserable days when there's nothing better to do. And Midlothian has quite a high unemployment rate, so there's a fair number of those. The older women who come in weekly for their latest crime novel or romantic fiction like to ask Molly about her love life, when she's going to get a man, that sort of thing. Molly plays along happily, not letting on that in fact she 'swings the other way' and prefers women – simply telling her readers honestly about the one young man who, briefly, swept her off her feet before eventually she decided that he, and men generally, didn't quite do it for her. But, special though Molly is, this story isn't really about her. The stars of this story are actually the library books themselves.

You see, in Meadowfield Library, the books are just a little special: they're alive. Only Molly knows that, she's the only one who's seen them, heard them, in action on quiet nights after everyone else has left. You'd have to be exceptionally observant and patient to spot anything if you simply walked in and browsed around, but believe me, the books in Meadowfield are watching you, not the other way round.

The books are absolutely desperate to be read, though, they want to be lent out to some reader, someone just like you, to give pleasure, to do the one thing they were created to do. As you wander round, particular books will start to push out in your direction, reading your mind and your character... well, like a book. They physically edge forward by perhaps a millimetre as you approach – they can tell what sort of thing you like reading, what you're in the mood for, and they want to be of service. The letters on their spine will stand out a little clearer, almost lit up in the shadowy aisles. Sooner or later, it's a certainty that you'll reach out for one, take it to the desk where Molly will scan the barcode, stamp the date that it's due for return on a little sheet of paper on the inside – and you'll be off. If you're a quick reader you might take three or four; the books know what you can stand. Most of the newer, more technically-literate ones even know your diary for the week, or if you're having trouble sleeping. They're always being taken out.

And there's another strange thing about the Meadowfield books. Readers always finish them, and finish them in nice time to return them and take out some more exactly seven days later. The books make sure of that. In turn, the library's readers have come to know each other really well and the library itself has become an important social hub. Molly has won several awards herself, but she knows that she's got the books to thank. Not that she'd ever let on; everyone would think she was mad.

Molly doesn't have to do much putting away of books. She does a little for show during the day, but one evening after closing up, when she'd been working in the library for less than a week, a large dictionary called out to her, 'You really don't need to do that, you know.' Of course Molly got a dreadful fright, hoped she'd been hearing things, but for some reason she asked the dictionary to repeat what it said, so it did. And then some more joined in, and that was that. The books explained that they were happy to put themselves away, thank you, in fact they preferred it because they each knew their place. If there was to be any discussion about any particular book being given special promotion – say, some visiting author doing a talk – they preferred to be consulted, although they would be happy to fit in with any reasonable request that Molly made. She asked to stay behind one night and found herself listening and watching in wonder as the library books discussed all sorts of matters amongst themselves as they wandered around the building.

You can understand that it took Molly a little time to adjust to the situation, but once she'd realised that she could lock up at night and that every morning each book would be back in its perfect position, it was clear that she could concentrate on the important parts of being a librarian. Such as making coffee and being nice to the readers.

It sounds perfect, and it was almost perfect, but there was one cloud on the horizon. Well, there's always a cloud on the horizon in stories like these, isn't there? One of the jobs that only Molly could do herself was to read her emails, and one morning there came a dreaded edict from the council headquarters:

Good morning all,

FRESH NEW LIBRARY PROJECT

You will recall that I wrote to all of you three months ago, explaining that the council needs to rationalise its library stock. This is so that we can create space on shelves for new titles and also make way for new initiatives including computers and other audio-visual material. As a council, we need to be prepared to move with the times and recognise that modern public libraries are more than a store-cupboard for old books no-one wants to read any more.

Accordingly all librarians are now instructed to identify any and all books which have not been borrowed once in the last ten years. These books must be returned to head office where they will be disposed of.

I assume that in the last three months you have been preparing for this clear-out, and look forward to seeing lots of space created in Midlothian Libraries.

Best wishes,
Giles Compton-Watson
Head of Library Services, Midlothian

Molly sat at her desk and stared at the screen miserably. She wanted to cry, but there were already readers in the library and she needed to put on a brave face. But the books noticed.

Of course she'd seen the original email – she'd even acted upon it. Molly knew perfectly well that there were books at Meadowfield that no-one seemed to take out any more, books that had once been loved but now were forgotten. They were old and tired, too tired many of them to push themselves forward towards potential readers, and they were vulnerable, very vulnerable, to Compton-Watson's modernisation edict. But Molly had ideas of her own. She ran two or three book clubs, and she suggested that some of these groups borrowed some of the old books to see how they compared with the modern thrillers, detective novels, and racy romantic fiction. Many of her readers came back to tell her how surprised they were that – once they'd worked their way past the first seventy or a hundred pages – these books were as exciting as any modern one. And most of them were a great deal better written. For all that, The Guinness Book Of Records, P.D. James, Ian Rankin and of course *Fifty Shades Of Gray* remained far more popular.

Nevertheless, Molly's superhuman efforts had by early March managed to reduce the list of vulnerable books to just four: *The Mill on the Floss* by George Eliot, *Moll Flanders* by Daniel Defoe, *Old Mortality* by Walter Scott and *Finnegans Wake* by James Joyce. Now she had just under a month to find someone – anyone – whom she could persuade to withdraw these four, whose very future quite literally depended on her succeeding. She managed to persuade the local church minister to take a local interest in

Old Mortality a telephone call to the local high school's English teacher led to two senior students borrowing *The Mill on the Floss* and *Moll Flanders*. These books were safe from Giles Compton-Watson for another year or two at least. But no-one, no-one at all, could be persuaded to take out *Finnegans Wake*.

If you don't have a clue what *Finnegans Wake* is about, then you're not alone, and that includes almost all those who have actually read it. It's loosely inspired by the Irish folk song of the same name: someone falls off a ladder, breaks his skull and assumed to be dead, then his wake is so drunken and noisy that the 'dead' man wakes up and joins in the whisky binge. But the book then disappears off into ever more bizarre circles, each chapter having its own cyclical structure. Just to top things off, the entire book finishes in mid-sentence and starts with its continuation, so that the book is really just one enormous continuously looping story. At least Molly thought so – she couldn't make head nor tail of it herself.

The Meadowfield copy of *Finnegans Wake* wasn't new. In fact it had been in its collection since 1939, the very year that the library itself opened. And in all that time it had never been borrowed.

That didn't mean the book was easily forgotten. It liked to play tricks on Molly: she would come in of a morning to discover *Finnegans Wake* upside down on the shelf, or in the romantic fiction shelves, or she would find it hiding in the Meadowfield's small music section. She always found it quickly, of course, but *Finnegans Wake* had to have its little bit of fun every now and then. It wasn't Molly's favourite book – *Pride and Prejudice* and a collection of twentieth century poetry filled that spot jointly – but it was close to the top, and Molly loved it dearly. *Finnegans Wake* was actually her favourite 'male' book.

You see, the other thing about the books at Meadowfield Library is that they have genders, male or female. By and large, those written by men are male, and those written by women are female; collections, reference works, poetry and so on could be either. But when Molly speaks, she can hear their voices, and they aren't all the same. When *Finnegans Wake* spoke, it spoke with a high sing-song Irish lilt, as if James Joyce himself was speaking. Perhaps he was.

Meanwhile, she wasn't sure if *Finnegans Wake* quite realised he was in mortal danger. He had a habit of singing to himself quietly, mostly Irish folk songs, and in particular the folk song '*Finnegans Wake*'.

'We need to get you borrowed, James,' she said. She called the book James, its author's name, rather than by its title.

'I know, I know,' *Finnegans Wake* broke off his tune to reply. 'Do what needs must. I trust you.' The words came out as 'most' and 'trost'. Then he drifted off into a yet another rambling tale about a fishmonger, a priest and bag of cement. He could talk like this all day.

The *Guinness Book Of Records* – whom everyone knew simply as 'Guinness' chimed in, 'Have you seen one of those shredders, Jimmy-boy? They can crush a book your size into solid lumps of shredded paper in seconds. Next thing you know you're on sale in B&Q as MDF.'

Some of the more sensitive souls, such as the poetry collections and the computer manuals, shuddered at the thought.

'What are we going to do?' Molly asked. 'I've run out of ideas for James.'

'He's his own worst enemy,' *Wolf Hall* said. She was a new kid on the block, and everyone else hated her. 'Anyway,' she added, 'what's he for? He really is taking up space that new books could use instead.'

It was an interesting question coming from a book, and Molly didn't immediately have an answer. She tried to give a philosophical defence of reading in general, but *Wolf Hall* pointed out that it really didn't matter then if one or two particular books were lost so long as there were always more books around than anyone could possibly ever read. She went on to support her point by saying that even she, *Wolf Hall*, would eventually be fit only for the scrap-heap. Molly replied that, in Meadowfield Library at least, there always seemed room for more books, although privately she wasn't quite sure how long that could last. It was just part of the 'Meadowfield Mystery'.

The following day was a Wednesday. The library was supposed to be closed but Molly went in anyway for a council of war.

'Ladies and gentlemen,' she began, clapping her hands to get attention. The crime fiction section was mainly female at the moment, and their voices were the last to come to order. 'We need to do something for James, here.'

A Hercule Poirot novel called out that *Finnegans Wake* had never done anything for anyone else, and anyway he talked rubbish all the time. The Agatha Christie books all tended to stick together, in fact, and in no time there was a babbling of discontent against *Finnegans Wake*. Most of the other crime novels were more understanding, though. A Rebus novel, *Black And Blue*, wanted to lead a revolution against Headquarters in Loanhead. Three P. D. James books reckoned they'd devised a perfect murder plot to dispose of 'this Giles bloke'; all they needed was explosive, detonators, a lot of help from Molly, and the 'Giles bloke' in question to be stupid enough to be in the wrong place at the wrong time. Molly calmed them down, pointing out that murder remained illegal, even in Midlothian, although she wasn't sure what charges could be brought against conspiring paperbacks.

In the end, helpful ideas came from a surprising source – the magazines. Usually, the books ignored what the magazines had to say because they were just temporary residents, but of course the magazines understood only too well how tenuous life could be for any publication. Some of them were even produced on recycled paper themselves, and, deep within, scars of past encounters with the shredder were etched into their very fibre. One such newspaper was the *Midlothian Gazette and Star*, a new publication in direct competition with the *Midlothian Advertiser*, and as a result likely to put both out of business in no time.

'Can't we hide Finnegan?' she said. 'Just lose him under a pile of old magazines like us?'

Molly smiled. 'It's a lovely idea, but' – she stopped, then said – 'listen, can you hear him?' *Finnegans Wake* had returned to singing to himself. Clearly it was going to be hard to conceal a book that wouldn't be quiet, and couldn't understand the seriousness of its situation.

'Do you have any ideas, Molly?'

'Not really. In fact the problem might be more serious than I thought. It appears the Head of Library Services is personally going around each library this month, just to pay us all a visit.'

'That's this 'Giles' bloke?'

'The very same. Normally I'd look forward to showing you all off, but everyone knows that what he's really doing is to look for any signs of wastage in any of our libraries. Get rid of anything useless and create space for new stuff. That applies to staff, too. Mr Compton-Watson reckons he can get rid of one or two librarians and replace us with computer games experts.'

Her words were greeted with gasps of horror. Then, slowly at first, Molly could sense a rumbling sound in the shelves, not loud in the beginning but getting louder, then louder and louder still until soon the bookshelves let out one vast mighty roar: the library was angry. Naturally they were there to help each other, but a threat to Molly and her friends was not to be countenanced.

'We really need to show Mr Compton-Watson that all the books are read,' Molly said again. 'Including *Finnegan*. Everyone has to help.'

But despite her best efforts, *Finnegans Wake* remained unborrowed for the next ten days. The book seemed blissfully unaware of its danger, whistling tunelessly here and there, singing the odd song quietly, sometimes even '*Finnegans Wake*' itself. Molly tried to promote it as best she could, placing it on display right at the front of the library; she even created a little competition around it. However, although the book was picked up and studied more than it had been in the previous twenty years combined, no-one seemed interested enough to take it out – on the contrary, a casual glance within simply put readers off.

By the last day in March, a Thursday as it happens, Molly was all but resigned to losing her eccentric Irish friend. Giles Compton-Watson was due to appear at

Meadowfield, the last of his 'state visits', and she knew he'd be asking how well she was implementing his 'Fresh New Library' policy. Giles was actually quite a nice man, she believed, even if his sense of humour could sometimes be a little hard to find. She'd only met him once or twice, so when he walked in from the car park she was a little surprised to see that the man at her desk was both taller and thinner than she remembered.

'Hello, Molly,' he said, shaking her hand, 'and how are you?'

Molly, slightly off guard, replied 'fine' a little hesitantly. She offered him coffee, which he accepted, black, and they sat down together at the front desk to allow Molly to deal with the occasional enquiry while they exchanged small talk. The desk was quite busy, actually – Giles remarked how impressed he was – so Molly was once again caught off guard when he suddenly said:

'How are things going with the Fresh New Library project?' Molly looked slightly bemused, so he repeated, 'The Fresh New Library Project? Our spring clean, if you like, to create space for the next generation of reader needs? You remember?'

'Oh yes,' Molly replied. Yes, she remembered. That's the great requirement for senior staff in any organisation, she thought, the ability to convert the English language into gobbledegook that only other senior staff can understand. 'Yes, yes, I remember.'

'Well? Can I see your list of books to go?'

'The list?' Molly asked, nervously.

'The list,' Giles said quietly.

'There isn't one,' Molly blurted out.

'There isn't one? Didn't you get the emails?'

Molly hesitated. 'Yes… it's just that… well there is a list, but it's blank. There aren't any books on it.'

Giles raised his eyebrows. 'No?'

'No,' said Molly, flatly.

He looked at her hard. 'Are you trying to say that there are no books surplus to requirements?'

She tried to look defiant. 'None, Giles.'

He smiled. 'Molly, tell me, hand on heart, that nowhere on your library shelves is there a book which hasn't been borrowed in the last ten years.'

'I can honestly say that every single book on those bookshelves has been borrowed at least once in the last ten years.' Molly didn't like lying, but *Finnegans Wake* was sitting on the front desk beside her; it wasn't a lie.

Giles wandered across to look at a couple of other likely victims: *The Silver Darlings* by Neil Gunn, and *The Seven Pillars of Wisdom* by T. E. Lawrence. Their most recent date stamps showed them each to have been borrowed twice within the last five years. He chuckled, shook his head, and returned to his seat by Molly at the counter. An elderly woman wandered across with three books to take out. As Molly scanned their barcodes and stamped the date they were due for return, the woman correctly sensed that this man beside her was 'from Head Office' and launched into a paean of praise for the library and 'its wonderful librarian'. Molly was only slightly embarrassed.

'OK, you win, Molly,' Giles eventually conceded. 'You seem to have a little space for the new stuff anyway.' His eye drifted casually to the counter again, where *Finnegans Wake* still sat, and, picking it up casually, said, '*Finnegans Wake*. Well, well. I tried to study this briefly at university, not that I could make anything of it, mind you. But I still loved it –

there was something mysteriously fascinating about it.' Giles opened the book. 'Hang on,' he said, 'this hasn't been taken out ever, has it? There are no date stamps here at all.'

Molly panicked. 'No, no, I was just putting a new sheet for the date stamps in. That's why it's out here.' OK, so that was a lie. Nobody's perfect.

Giles flicked through *Finnegans Wake*. 'Can I borrow it, for old times' sake? See if I can understand it second time around?'

Molly could hardly believe her ears. 'Em.. do you have your reader's borrowing card?'

Giles felt in his pocket. 'As it happens, I do.'

Molly, her heart pumping loudly, scanned the barcode and stamped on the return date, just as if Giles were any other ordinary member of the public. Meanwhile, Giles seemed to have forgotten the original purpose of his visit. Rising, he set off for the exit.

'Well, thanks for the coffee, Molly,' he called back to her. 'It's been a very fruitful visit,' he added, waving his book.

'See you soon.'

Giles was right at the library entrance, just about to leave when suddenly he stopped, turned around, and said:

'Molly?'

'Yes?'

'Do you hear… singing?'

Finnegan's Wake

Tim Fin-e-gan lived in Walk-in' Street. A gen-tle-man Ir-ish migh-ty odd, He had a tongue both rich and sweet, And to rise in the world he car-ried a hod, But Tim had a sort of a tip-pl-in way, With a love of the li-quor he was born, And to send him on his way each day He'd a drop of the crai-tur ev-'ry morn. Wack fol-de-dah, will ye dance to yer part-ners, Welt the floor yer trot-ters shake. Was-n't it the truth I told you Lots of fun at Fin-e-gan's wake!

One morning Tim was rather full
His head felt heavy which made him shake
He fell off the ladder and he broke his skull
And they carried him home his corpse to wake
Well they rolled him up in a nice clean sheet
And they laid him out upon the bed
With a bottle of whiskey at his feet
And a barrel of porter at his head

Well his friends assembled at the wake
And Mrs Finnegan called for lunch
Well first they brought in tay and cake
Then pipes, tobacco and brandy punch
Then the widow Malone began to cry
"Such a lovely corpse, did you ever see,
Arrah, Tim avourneen, why did you die?"
"Will ye hould your gob?" said Molly McGee

Well Mary O'Connor took up the job
"Biddy" says she "you're wrong, I'm sure"
Well Biddy gave her a belt in the gob
And left her sprawling on the floor
Well civil war did then engage
T'was woman to woman and man to man
Shillelagh law was all the rage
And a row and a ruction soon began

Well Sean Maloney raised his head
When a bottle of whiskey flew at him
He ducked, and landing on the bed
The whiskey scattered over Tim
Bedad he revives, see how he rises
Tim Finnegan rising in the bed
Saying "Whittle your whiskey around like blazes
T'underin' Javuns, do ye think I'm dead!"

Tam

et's be honest about it now: the early 1970s wasn't exactly a golden era in the history of pop music, was it? The sixties were a hard act to follow, sure, what with the Stones and the Beatles, to say nothing of the Beach Boys on the other side of the Atlantic. Then there was all that wonderful bluesy rock stuff, Cream and so on, and the Californian marijuana-based music; and Dylan. But by the seventies, bands seemed to feel the need to shout to get themselves noticed, either literally, by turning the volume up seventeen notches or so, or metaphorically, by dressing up in silly costumes and outrageous make-up. The act became more important than the music itself, and old-fashioned 'pop music' simply went out of fashion.

Not that producers and record labels didn't try. No-one was quite sure what singles would sell, or indeed if singles would sell at all; this was the heyday of the album, particularly the themed concept album where half a dozen numbers of varying quality could be padded out with electronic mash, strange noises, and little poems, packaged together in some sort of dreamy-looking cardboard sleeve full of photographs, more poetry, a list of every conceivable individual remotely connected with each track, and of course the obligatory lyrics. A single? Singles – and those who sang on them – were for *Top Of The Pops* and for the musical interlude in whatever variety show was on television that particular Saturday night. Already, singles were more likely to be bought not by teenagers but instead by their parents, trying to keep up and not doing a very good job of it.

Tam Cantlay's band, the Hot Flushes, played at discos in the central Scottish town of Falkirk and its surrounding parts: Grangemouth, Denny, even the odd visit to Bonnybridge. Mostly, they played covers of songs they'd picked up from their own record collections, but a couple of the band fancied themselves as songwriters, too, and they liked to slip the odd self-penned number into their act each night. Tam was the front man, played rhythm guitar and sang lead vocals, and in addition organised all the bookings, which he was able to do without difficulty at the same time as his day-job, working as a clerk in an insurance office.

The Hot Flushes had made a couple of demo tapes in a local Falkirk recording studio. One day, and without consulting the others in the band, Tam decided to send some tapes of the band performing two of his own personal songs to a handful of recording labels. To his great surprise, one of them, Jupiter Records, got in touch with him to ask when they would next be playing, which as it happened was to be at a Falkirk youth club that very Saturday. Tam decided not to tell the rest of the band because – well, he said it was in case they got stage-fright, but really it was because he wasn't sure if they'd be pleased or not. In the event the Hot Flushes were only average, but Tam gave one of his best-ever performances.

Afterwards, a man, clearly from Jupiter Records because he was actually wearing a suit at a disco, approached him quietly. Wearing sunglasses, although it was nearly pitch dark where they stood in the hall, he said, 'Not bad, son, we might be able to use you. Can you make it to Grahams Road on Tuesday?'

Tam, of course, was delighted. 'You want us there on Tuesday? Great! I'll go and ask the others. What do we need to bring?'

'Don't bother with the others, son, it's just you we're interested in. We can make something out of you.' He handed Tam a business card'.

Charles Carter
Jupiter Records
Grahams Road
Falkirk

'There's a studio there where we can do a decent demo tape – a professional one – and we'll take it from there.'

*

So Tam phoned in sick to the office that Tuesday, and he turned up in his best suit at Grahams Road in Falkirk, for the demo tape anyway. But Tam was also wearing another other important item of clothing: a pair of leather boots sporting incredibly high cuban heels. These were no fashion statement, it was simply that Tam was tiny, under five feet tall in his stocking soles, and he wore cuban heels to lessen the effect, at least he hoped it might. In practice, though, the way he strutted around in the cuban-heeled shoes only served to draw attention to his height. Not that it seemed to matter to the people in the studio.

There were a number of staff in the recording area. There was a bass player, a guitarist who sat down to play, a keyboard player, and two drummers who looked as though they might be twins. There was a sound engineer, and two other men in suits. Another was Carter, the dark-glassed character who'd watched him in the Falkirk youth club.

'Ever cut a track before, Tam?'

Slightly startled by the 'cut a track' reference, Tam stumbled over an admission that he hadn't.

'The trick is to pretend you're singing to a crowd of thousands. Imagine we're not here, and the band is at your command.'

'Right, Mr Carter. I'll try my best.'

'Oh, and don't call me 'Mr' Carter. It isn't cool, Tam. Call me Charlie.'

'Right, Mr... I mean Charlie. Which of my songs do you want me to sing?'

'Oh sorry, didn't I say? It's not one of your songs we want, it's a song one of our resident writers put together. It's called 'I'm Gonna Make It Big With You.' It's a kind of novelty song, it's not hard. We just need a singer and we can put it out.' As he read through the lyrics, it slowly dawned on Tam that his big chance owed very little to his singing ability after all; the record company wanted someone small, someone very small in fact. To compound the humiliation, Jupiter Records absolutely insisted that Tam be known as 'Long Tom Cantlay', inviting anyone watching to burst out laughing when they set eyes on him.

When he was being totally honest with himself, Tam admitted to being just four feet seven inches tall. Growing up, there had naturally been concerns that there was something wrong with him, and he had had numerous visits to hospitals for tests. But after exhaustive investigation, the medics had eventually decided that Tam was just small, in the same way that some people are very tall. Putting a positive spin on things, the doctors pointed out that he was only fourteen inches from the average height, whereas many basketball players had to put up with being around seven feet tall. They noted that Tam's parents were both very small, too – indeed Tam's mother was only an inch taller than he – and the general scientific consensus was that small people and tall people were simply the result of natural selection. Because all of his family were small, Tam never felt too bad about his height, while his job as a telephone operator meant that the public at large were completely unaware of his appearance.

Only when he was out with his mates socially did Tam ever feel his lack of height. Girlfriends might have been hard to come by, but because he was basically a decent guy and tried to be cheery all the time, his chums looked after him. On the very rare occasions when he found himself in a fight, either at school and once on a Friday night when he was eighteen, Tam could hold his own long enough for bystanders to intervene on his behalf with a 'go and pick on someone your own size' to his adversary – a very effective putdown.

But for someone – even a record executive seemingly offering Tam a golden opportunity for stardom – to deliberately play on Tam's height, or lack of it, that was pretty hard for Tam to swallow. He was too stunned to offer any complaint for the moment, but he learned there and then that the pop music industry was actually a dirty, dirty business. Which two could play.

Tam put his heart and soul into *I'm Gonna Make It Big With You*, and he was impressed by the session musicians drafted in to back him: a huge heap of beard and hair called Dave Norman played rhythm guitar; an Irish chap called Malone played bass, keyboards were played by someone called George; and, memorably, a pair of identical twins played drums. Actually, they weren't that memorable – Tam could never remember either of their names. But they were good. Unfortunately the song was simply awful, and everybody knew it. It turned out that the songwriters, who wanted released from their contract, were engaged in a feud with Jupiter Records and their means of escape was to write such bad songs that Jupiter would eventually give up and let them go. Jupiter's response was to record the songs and release them in an attempt to ruin the songwriters' reputation. This was the last, and worst, song in the battle.

Tam was a quick learner, however. Recognising that all records need a B side, that the songwriters didn't have any more numbers, and that Jupiter certainly wan't going to waste one decent ones of its own from another of its writers, he came up with a suggestion. He'd come prepared to sing one of his own songs anyway, and he produced a little ditty called *Any Way You Want Me You Can Have Me*, which was quickly recorded by the same musicians and added as the B side.

As everyone predicted, *I'm Gonna Make It Big With You* by 'Long Tom Cantlay' was a monumental flop, charting at number 1278. At its peak. Jupiter Records effectively abandoned the record, deciding that anything spent on promoting it was merely throwing good money after bad. The singles sat in warehouses, forgotten and unloved for several months and Tam himself returned to his day-job of helping phone customers connect with friends, family members, difficult-to-find businesses and – occasionally – emergencies. In the meantime, he was forming a plan.

Tam followed BBC's Radio One keenly, and one of his friends suggested sending his single to some of the DJs prepared to play less mainstream music. But Tam's plan was not to promote *I'm Gonna Make It Big With You*, but instead to get them to play his own song from the B side. In addition, Tam's accompanying letter to Annie Nightingale, John Peel, Bob Harris and others portrayed himself as a victim of a corporate recording system that had plucked him off the street then abused and demeaned him. It was a plan that bore some fruit; his own song *Any Way You Want Me You Can Have Me* started to receive a little play time late at night on some of the minority programmes. In time, *Any Way You Want Me You Can Have Me* made some inroads into the Hit Parade at the second attempt, eventually reaching No. 23, and 'Long Tom Cantlay' even appeared on Bob Harris' late-night cult TV programme *The Old Grey Whistle Test* – which Bob was only too happy to preface with Tam's sad story of the 'midget abused by the system'.

It was at this point that Tam's played his little trump card.

Jupiter had been so engrossed in its fight with the songwriter that it failed to take its usual care with the B side of Tam's single: it forgot to acquire the rights to Tam's song *Any Way You Want Me You Can Have Me*. When the royalties started to flow in for Tam's single, Tam let it run for a little while, then gently enquired where his share was. Jupiter were furious, of course, and even tried to say that the rights were actually theirs, but Tam was having none of it. He took legal advice and threatened court action. Despite the likely costs to Jupiter of contesting such a lost cause, the record company reckoned it could grind Tam into the ground, or at least it did until a series of headlines – each a variant of Little Guy Takes On Giant Bullying Corporation – appeared in the tabloid newspapers. From then on, there would be only one winner. Tam's dues were paid in full.

But of course he paid a heavy price. Not only did Jupiter terminate his contract immediately, Tam found that no other recording company would touch him either. It was clear that he'd been blacklisted, and there was little he could do about it: his recording career was over almost as soon as it had begun.

Tam went back to working as a telephone operator, and even patched up his quarrel with the Hot Flushes, so that he found himself back on the wedding reception and birthday-party circuit in Falkirk – although now, of course, they invariably finished with their 'big hit' *Any Way You Want Me You Can Have Me*. Tam also began to develop a love-life of sorts, mostly slightly older women who felt sorry for him, wanted to look after him, that sort of thing. Tam was grateful for their attention, but as he became older himself, he found the women who wanted to be near him were starting to be in their sixties and even seventies. In the meantime, his career in the telephone industry was starting to stagnate, too, until finally, in 2002, he was made redundant.

Tam wasn't destitute. He was old enough and wise enough to have salted away some money for a small pension, and – never short of grand ideas – he had other plans, too. Over those three decades years, he had got to know most of the music, comedy and dance talent in the Falkirk area, and now he set himself as a musical agent called The Real Deal, operating out of a small office in central Falkirk. Tam's speciality was to listen to up-and-coming groups and 'discover' them, set them up with a few gigs or a small recording deal, then to pass them on to what he called 'the big boys' to take them on to the very top of the tree. For Tam this was a win-win idea. First, he charged more than most agents, explaining that he needed to recover his costs quickly before 'the big boys moved in'. Secondly, he was spared the grief of working at national and international level, employing extra staff and so on; frankly, Tam knew he'd be out of his depth. Finally, although his acts didn't know it, he received a healthy commission for handing over his charges to 'the big boys'. His first big success was an electronica group called The Maplins, who moved on from him to the giant Limpet Agency, but retained an affection for Tam for ever after, grateful for his help in their early years.

Tam liked to remind everyone of his former glories, or to be precise, his former glory with *Any Way You Want Me You Can Have Me*. Anyone making a telephone call to The Real Deal was forced to listen to three choruses before being allowed to speak to anyone. Tam was the only employee; the muzak was mere vanity. But he had a surprisingly kind heart. In 2010 he stumbled across a young man called Evelyn Kerr – fresh out of Falkirk Young

Offenders' Institution, having been released having served five years for killing his father. Tam quickly established that Evelyn wasn't actually genuinely violent, but his father was – Evelyn had hit his father on the head with a heavy pan in order to stop him killing his mother, with fatal results. Prison, of course, had turned Evelyn into a real hard man but now he was desperate to escape the clutches of the local gang and start again. He'd little or no chance of finding a job, of course, so Tam came up with an idea. Calling on three other young singers and dancers on his books, a young lad of Indian descent called Jimmy MacGregor, a student called Quentin Hickmott, and Omar Thompson – whom he'd actually worked with briefly before both were made redundant – Tam formed a boy band called the C-U Jimiz. The C-U Jimiz did covers of boy-band numbers, and because each of them in their own way was attractive, they were remarkably popular at teenage discos, pub evenings, and especially with hen nights, after which needless to say the four unattached young males were invariably in considerable demand. Even Tam himself sometimes benefited – there was often someone older, perhaps an office colleague or even a mother, present as well. But for the most part, Tam's finest years as a sex object had passed.

The internet was also proving a fruitful source of talent and Tam scoured YouTube and other for any local bands who recorded themselves. A year after forming the C-U Jimiz, he took on a small amateur Edinburgh band who had recorded themselves in a home-made studio – an arrangement which at first proved chaotic until Tam combined them with his new boy band. It was a success of sorts – but not for Tam himself, who accidentally upset some of the Falkirk locals in the process. They made it clear that if he stayed around to collect any money due to him, his very life might be in danger. One night, on the brink of his greatest triumph, he suddenly decided to disappear – indeed it was agreed all round that if it was best if he simply *did* just 'disappear', Tam himself being given some input into the decision. His enemies even gave him enough money for a one-way ticket to somewhere in the Middle East, plus a small compensation for his loss of earnings from *Any Way You Want Me You Can Have Me*. Anything to get rid of him without fuss.

And amazingly, Tam did exactly as he was told, although sheer terror probably accounted for that. No one ever saw him again in his native land, and although strange rumours of a very small man in cuban heels were occasionally to be heard, that was as far as it got. Sadly, no one even seemed to miss him; his parents had both died, he'd long fallen out with his only other relative, a sister in Canada, and, well… he didn't seem to have any close friends either. Tam, like his song, became a footnote in history, a pub-quiz question too obscure even for Trivial Pursuit. It was a bit of shame, really, because even although he could be utterly untrustworthy and irritating, almost everyone he met gained from the experience; only Tam failed to prosper.

Then... many years later, something strange happened: a small firm based in Malawi called Little Tones latched onto the market for ringtones for mobile phones. The firm's office and factory converted music of all styles, and proved to have a magical talent for finding music that would make brilliant ringtones – it's not as easy as you'd think – and furthermore it gained fame across the country for employing pygmies, amongst whom the unemployment rate was especially high because of job discrimination. The Malawi government was delighted, but not as delighted as the firm's owner who had realised that selling ringtone downloads for just fifty pence per tone was a sales winner; people just bought them, used them for a bit, then bought another. Little was known of this strange recluse, although it was understood that he, too, was a pygmy, although not a local one. In addition, the owner also let it be known that his own favourite ringtone – and by far the most profitable one for Little Tones – was a version of *Any Way You Want Me You Can Have Me*.

Any Way You Want Me, You Can Have Me

Thomas Cantlay

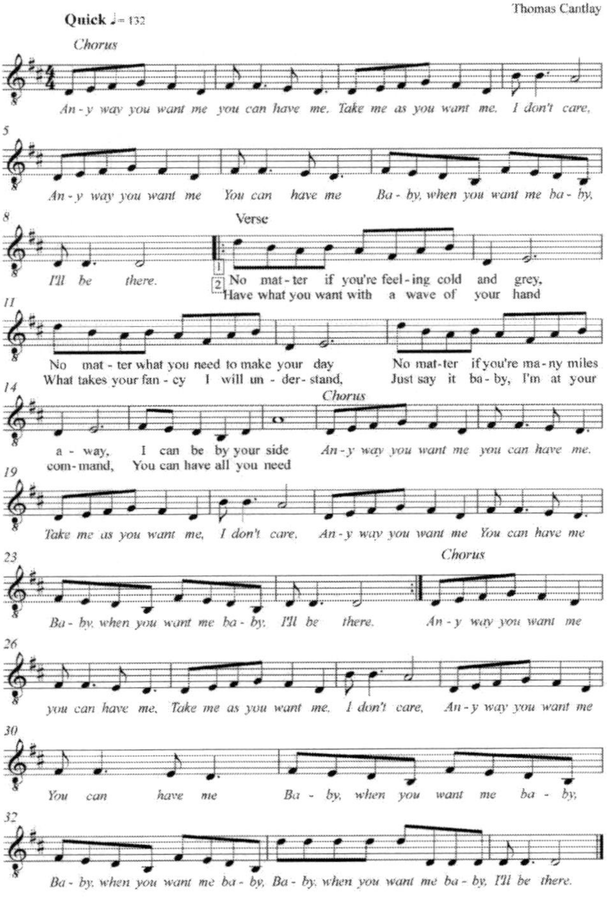

Favour for a Friend

What would you have done? Really?

In the beginning, Trish was really Diane's friend. They'd known each other since the start of secondary school where they'd immediately helped each other cope with the brand-new surroundings, then it had grown into sharing makeup, music tastes, even books... and of course eventually there were boys.

I was one of Trish's 'boyfriends'. We got off together at a Saturday night youth club at the start of sixth year while my friend Danny Marwick – who was even more hopeless with girls than I was – was left with Diane. We went out as a four twice but Danny and Diane were simply not meant to be. In no time Danny and Diane were back at the Saturday night cattle market, but separately. Not that Trish ignored her bosom buddy; she insisted that we went along, too, to make sure that Trish was 'all right'. We needn't have worried.

Actually, I wasn't worried about Diane at all. I was a typical seventeen-year-old boy with testosterone to burn and my instincts drove me to want to explore Trish's lovely body. She was shortish, five-five at the most, shortish dark hair with a simply dazzling smile. She wore calf-length coats over jeans and tee-shirt. She wore trainers. She didn't look like a model, she simply looked... naturally sexy and sexily natural. I wanted Trish. I was desperate for her. Either her or something quite similar.

Our 'romance', if it ever deserved that name, happened over the summer months so that when we found ourselves on our own, Trish and I would do what kids of that age do – snog. Each time, I almost invariably tried to go just a little further, a little easier to do when there are fewer clothes to get past in the first place. Trish resisted – not totally, mind you – and kept her virginity, no thanks to me. Gradually we went from gentle kissing in more intimate areas to some full-on activity around her breasts and between her legs, although for some strange reason she never went anywhere near as far to please me as I did for her. But I did see Trish naked more than once. What would have happened if she'd ever said 'Yes' to the big one, I shudder to think. I never had any thought of 'taking precautions', of course, I'd seen machines in public toilets but I'd never had the nerve to put the coins in the slot.

Our little dalliance didn't last long, just until early September as I recall. Trish had insisted that we look after Diane, even taking her along occasionally to things we did – a concert, perhaps, or a Chinese meal. Diane's presence curtailed our sexual activities as well, of course, not that

Trish seemed to mind. I did, though, and I could see that Diane felt a bit uneasy about constantly playing gooseberry, but we got to know each other quite well and I even felt able to share some little secrets and to ask for advice. Diane became my friend as well. She was attractive, too, but in a different way. She was taller, a little ungainly even, but she had a friendly smile that opened up once you got to know her. She was a decent athlete – a very good high jumper, in fact – and an excellent tennis player. I didn't play tennis but she was always threatening to teach me.

Then one Friday night, Trish dumped me out of the blue. It was a complete thunderbolt, all the more so when she announced that she'd been seeing someone else for weeks and wanted to be 'a bit more serious' – which meant end of me. Or 'us', at any rate.

I was devastated. I remember spending the next day in my bedroom in tears, totally wiped out by Trish's betrayal, brazenly cuckolding me. Then around four, my Mum knocked on my bedroom door to say that there was a young woman on the telephone for me. At first I didn't want to answer it, then I wondered if Trish had changed her mind, then I simply picked up the receiver. But it wasn't Trish, it turned out it was Diane, wanting to find out how I was and offering to take me out for a drink in the nearest bar prepared to serve drink to not-quite-eighteens. The hotels were always the best for that.

And from there she and I started to become not only friends, but very good friends, then eventually lovers and –

after a couple of brief on/off moments while we were both students – husband and wife. Along the way we kept vaguely in touch with Trish, perhaps only once or twice a year even although we lived in the same city. Trish went through a string of men, but each relationship in turn seemed to stutter to an end and she would tell us about them over tapas, a drink, or perhaps a simple mug of instant and a chocolate biscuit. Somehow, though, a permanent relationship with a man never quite came to pass.

Diane and I had been married for almost ten years – I'm certain that both of our children had started school – before she let me into the secret. There had been no 'other man' that Trish had thrown me over for. She'd simply stood aside for her dear friend Diane, who it turned out had fancied me all along. I was Trish's gift to Diane. But Trish had made Diane promise that she'd never tell me the truth, so I in turn was sworn to secrecy as well. Trish must never know that I knew. But you can understand that from then on I realised Trish was as much my friend as Diane's.

*

One night, fully twenty years later, Diane received a call from Trish. It had been quite a while since we'd last met and, listening to Diane's end of the conversation I'd expected a long chat. Pretty quickly, though, Diane's tone turned from 'how nice to hear from you' to one of shock.

From then on, Diane asked the odd question but mostly simply listened. At the end, she simply said, 'Of course, Trish, I'll certainly do that. I can take the day off easily to be there.'

The call ended and Diane sat silently for a moment before saying, 'I think Trish is dying.'

Obviously, I'd worked out that something serious had happened, but I wasn't ready for what I'd just been told, so I asked her to repeat what she'd said.

'That was Trish, as you've guessed,' Diane said. 'It seems she'd been feeling a bit funny and went along to her GP, who did a couple of routine blood tests. Next thing she was up at the hospital's haematology unit getting a whole load of further tests done and it looks like she's got some rare sort of leukaemia.'

'And it can't be treated?'

'Treated, perhaps, but not cured.'

'What does 'treatment' mean? Did Trish have any idea?'

'Things to make her feel better, that's all. Steroids, apparently. Some painkillers eventually.'

I had to ask. 'So... did the hospital say... how long?'

'They don't know for sure. Could be a year or so, but more likely a few months. Could be even less.' She stopped. 'That's what's happening on Wednesday. Staging – a whole series of tests and scans that take most of the day. It'll show how far things have advanced. I said I'd go with her and keep her company.' Gradually the shock was turning to tears. 'We're losing her, Robbie. We're losing her.'

As Diane wailed and I held her, I found myself crying for my fading friend, too.

*

Wednesday's news turned out not to be good. Three months, perhaps four at the most, was the best Trish could hope for, although they could promise her good quality life for almost all of that. Her decline, they said, would be sudden at the end, but in the meantime they advised Trish to go away and enjoy the time she had. A psychologist had been particularly insistent on the point, suggesting that Trish try to cram in as much to what remained of her life as possible: a holiday, perhaps, or something bizarre like a flying lesson. Trish had apparently replied by suggesting that she might do a parachute jump and not bother to pull the rip-cord, thus solving two problems at once. The psychologist didn't take it as the black joke it was intended to be.

Afterwards, she and Diane came back to our house and we all ate together round the table – I'd prepared a huge dish of macaroni which I knew Trish was particularly fond of. Our kids had picked up on something and were asking quite a lot of questions; I'd tried to put them off but Trish wanted to be reasonably upfront. She told them she'd be going away soon but would see them some day. Later, while Diane had been clearing up in the kitchen and the kids watching some television, Trish quietly confessed that one of her regrets in life would be that she'd never had any children.

Just at that point Diane returned. 'I heard that, Trish,' she said, putting her hand on her friend's shoulder.

'What other regrets do you have?' I asked. 'It's a bit late for family but is there anything else you fancy?'

Trish laughed. 'You mean a 'bucket list', Robbie? 'Fifty things to do before you die?'

I shrugged my shoulders. 'I suggest you leave the parachute jump to the end, though,' I said, which made everyone laugh. To tell the truth, the conversation was never maudlin, and a couple of bottles of wine once the children were in bed helped to ease the atmosphere, too. Trish got hold of a piece of paper and a pen from somewhere and began writing: a weekend in New York; climb the local hill; eat in a nice restaurant; an all-over aromatherapy body massage (preferably by George Clooney, she added); attend a football match; try cannabis. I was quite surprised by that last one, as I'd seen Trish as a little bohemian in her younger days and likely to try anything. Then we lay back and talked about the past, about how Diane and I had got together through Trish, and how grateful we were.

'There was me, an adolescent trying to get inside your knickers and it turned out Diane was the one who fancied me,' I said.

'Every boy seemed to want into my knickers then, Robbie,' Trish replied.

'I think it's a 'boy thing', Trish.'

'I let you get further than most, Robbie. I always liked you.'

I chuckled. 'But you dumped me.'

There was silence for a moment, then Diane said, 'I told him, Trish. Robbie knows.'

Trish sat up. 'You promised!'

'She did, Trish,' I said, 'but she was right to. It's why I know you're such a good friend.' For some reason I felt quite emotional, and Trish immediately leaped across to hug me and kiss me.

'Stop it, Robbie. I've no time for this. But seeing as I've not much time left I want to put on record that I always fancied you. I always found you attractive, and handing you over to my lovely friend Diane was just about the hardest thing a horny seventeen-year-old girl could ever do. Fortunately, Diane's not let me down. She's loved you even more than I ever could have.' Then she picked up the pen and paper and added something else to the bucket list. "One afternoon in bed with Robbie." She sat back and slugged the remainder of her wine. 'There. I've said it.'

She must have seen the looks on our faces, but Diane and I recovered our composure as quickly as we could.

'After all these years, I didn't realise you still held a candle for me, Trish,' I said, trying to make light of the situation. 'Given that Diane and I are married, would you settle for a dozen red roses instead?'

Trish laughed. 'I don't want flowers, Robbie, I want sex.

If you prefer it more directly, I want to fuck you.' She pointed to the bucket list. 'It's down there – fifty things to do before I die.' Then she added, 'Don't worry, I didn't expect you to agree, but you'll forgive a dying woman for trying.'

Diane had said nothing up until this point, but now she spoke up.

'Trish, you're my oldest friend. You know I owe you so much, and in particular I owe you for Robbie. If Robbie's up for it, I'll not say no.' She shrugged her shoulders. 'I can't refuse you, Trish, you know that.'

'Yes, you could,' Trish said. 'So could Robbie. Still.'

I was completely speechless. Here I was being passed back and forwards like property between the most important woman in my entire life and her best friend.

'What am I supposed to say here?' I said.

'Yes?' said Trish.

I looked at Diane for help, who once again just shrugged her shoulders.

Trish looked at the pair of us. 'Look on the bright side,' she said, 'I'll be dead by Christmas.'

'Jesus,' I said.

Meanwhile, for Diane this was all too much, who moved across the room to embrace her friend.

'I mean it, Trish. I owe you everything. Right now, you can have whatever I can give you. Even Robbie, if he'll have you.'

'I owe you everything, too, it seems,' I added. I was

sitting facing Diane, but Trish for the moment had her back to me. I looked at Diane for help, who simply nodded.

'OK,' I found myself saying.

Trish spun around with that broad smile. 'Thanks, both of you.'

Trish did the trip to New York first, then she went on a steam train trip up the west coast of Scotland for a couple of nights. Then Diane answered the telephone one night.

'Hi Diane, it's me, Trish.'

'Hi there,' Diane said. 'How are you?'

'Oh, same old, same old. The football match was fine, but I really don't see what the fuss is about. Even watching a tennis match is more fun.'

'Fuh-nee,' said Diane. Trish was always teasing Diane about her love of tennis, playing and watching. 'When are we going to see you?'

'Well, that's just what I was going to talk about… Is Robbie there?'

Even across the room, I could hear Diane's breathing stop momentarily. She passed the handset over to me. 'Trish.' Taking it, I looked at her, and she nodded her consent.

'Hi, Trish. How are you doing?'

She told me about her state of health, which it seemed wasn't bad, and about some of the other bucket list activities, then she moved on.

'Are you and I still going to… get it together, Robbie?'

This time I noticed that Diane had left the room.

'I think so, Trish. What did you have in mind?'

'How about tomorrow afternoon? Could you take time off work?'

'Not tomorrow. I've a meeting. The day after, if you like.'

Trish paused at the other end of the line. 'You don't sound very happy, Robbie.'

'No, no, Diane and I have discussed it.' And we had, although not extensively. I think both of us felt it was too tender a subject. 'It's a favour for a friend. Diane feels she's repaying the one you did for her all those years ago.'

'And you?'

I checked that Diane couldn't hear me. 'Unfinished business, Trish.'

'Come round to my flat on Thursday afternoon. Not too late, Robbie.'

When the call ended, neither Diane nor I discussed it.

*

I rang Trish's doorbell just before a quarter to two, bearing gifts.

As she opened the door, Trish greeted me with a huge smile. 'How lovely! A dozen red roses – what an old romantic!'

Following her into the kitchen gave me a chance to note that she was dressed in jeans and sleeveless tee-shirt, and was barefoot. Already, I wondered what else she was wearing.

Trish laid the roses down on the kitchen drainer and turned around to face me. Without a word, she pulled the tee-shirt over her head: nothing underneath. She reached forwards to take my hands and place them on her breasts.

'Take you back, Robbie?'

I laughed. 'Memories are made of this. It all seems so long ago, doesn't it?'

In no time at all she was naked from the waist down as well and removing my own clothing.

'I don't really have time to waste on roses, Robbie. I'll deal with them later.'

She led me through to her bedroom. We made love almost straight away, Trish explaining that she had to be on top because apparently my weight was capable of doing her a lot of damage. For the first time, I noticed that she had some significant bruises, which she said weren't sore but were simply symptoms of her illness. I don't like to share details of my sex life with anyone, but I will confess that what happened felt like we'd been kept waiting for decades. Which I suppose we had. Afterwards we lay together and I managed not to fall asleep for once, kissing her all over, before eventually we made love again, this time more slowly, then shared a shower.

As it happened I was home at almost exactly the same time as I would have been had I been coming from the office. I hadn't actually said anything to Diane about the arrangement, but she knew, somehow.

'How was Trish?' she asked. On the surface, such an innocent question, but on this occasion with multiple meaning.

'Fine,' I said. No more.

Four months later we were at Trish's funeral. As the doctors had said, she'd been fine until very late on, when she'd taken a sudden downturn. Diane and I stood together but not holding hands, more acquaintances than lovers; she might have been dead, but Trish stood between us.

The other mourners didn't spot it, though.

'She was such a good friend, wasn't she?'

'Gosh, how we'll miss her.'

'So full of life, taken too young.'

'Not an ounce of badness in her body.'

'Such an unselfish person.'

Throughout, Diane and I made small talk with others but not with each other, and we sat silently in the car on the way home. The silence wasn't really a reflection of our grief at Trish's death, silence had simply become the norm in our lives. Diane and I simply couldn't find anything to say to each other, anything meaningful at any rate. A wall had developed between us, and it was as if we were afraid to break down the barrier for fear of what we might each find out about the other.

Later that day of the funeral, we sat quietly through our evening meal, before watching some television, in the same room but not really sitting together. Diane went to bed before me, long before me, but when I came to bed she was asleep instead of reading a book and ready to take me in her arms. And that's how it continued, not just in the coming weeks, but in the coming months and years, until one day, once the kids were properly settled in their own homes, we simply decided to live apart. Diane and I are civilised in our separation, and very grown up. Neither of us had any need of a divorce, so our explanation to the children was simply 'these things happen but we still love each other.'

If we do, though, it's a strange kind of love. And I still don't know what either of us did so terribly wrong.

Gorilla Warfare

The first time James knocked on the door, there was no reply. He tried again, then checked his watch, then studied the printed form in his hand to make sure that the date and time was as agreed. He knocked again: still nothing. Finally, he tried the handle and discovered that the door was unlocked, and so he peered tentatively inside. Sure enough, David 'Call-Me-Dave' Robertson was sitting at his desk.

'Yes?' Robertson said abruptly. He was busy reading through some papers, making the odd note here and there.

'Mr Robertson, it's me,' James said quietly.

'Make it quick, please. I'm expecting someone any minute.'

'I think you might be expecting me, Mr Robertson.'

Only now did Robertson look up, his face a picture of confusion.

'I've come for my Annual Review, Mr Robertson.'

Robertson sat up. 'Oh – oh, yes of course, em…'

'James. James Wilson.'

'Ah yes… we haven't bumped into each other all that much recently, have we?'

'Not since my Annual Review last year, actually, Mr Robertson.'

'Oh please – call me Dave, Jim – or do you prefer Jimmy?'

'I prefer James, actually, as I think I mentioned last year.' James could have added, *And the year before, and the year before that*, as well.

'Well, Jim, I can call you whatever you prefer,' Call-Me-Dave said, looking up at James, who was still on his feet. 'In the meantime, please make yourself comfortable, take a seat. I just need to finish something here and I'll be right with you.'

Instead of sitting, James opted to wander towards the window. The Bird League rented third-floor office space in a modern block which it shared with a newspaper and seventeen other operations of varying sizes. An outsider might have assumed James was admiring the magnificent view, gloriously lit today by the June sunshine. In truth he was watching 'Dave' in action: doing precisely nothing, he was just keeping James waiting for the sake of demonstrating his authority. It was a game he played every year, and James had come prepared, which was another reason why he hadn't yet sat down – he'd only take a seat when he, James, was ready. And he'd make sure that was some time after Robertson was ready. Two years previously, the entire Annual Review had taken place standing up, neither man prepared to give in by being the first to accept the lower position.

Eventually, Robertson sat back. 'Thanks, Jim. I just needed to finish that off.' The language was grateful, the tone was irritated. 'Now, your Review.'

James continued to look out of the window for a little longer than necessary before slowly making his way over to the desk. Again, he chose a slightly unusual angle for his seat position, slightly in the shade.

'It's a lovely day out there,' he said. 'Lovely view of it, too.'

'Thanks, Jim, privilege of office, I suppose.'

'Of course,' James nodded. One of many, he thought to himself.

Robertson sat up and forced himself to smile, looking more business-like. 'Shall we do this properly? Keep a record?'

'I think we're supposed to, aren't we?' James said, studying the Bird League's Director. It never ceased to amaze him how a man could spend so much on clothing to so little effect. Today, Robertson was wearing an Armani dark charcoal suit with very thin blue and gold stripes, which meant it must be Tuesday. In contrast he wore the Bird League tie, a red and pink horror-show adorned with motifs of penguins, eagles, kingfishers and parakeets. To be fair, James himself had dressed up for the occasion: an open-necked shirt and blue chinos. By chance, he was wearing his newest and therefore least-worn shoes. Very unusually, James had brought a light jacket too, although he carried that over his arm.

As Robertson was completing essential information at the top of the Annual Review form, James reached into a jacket pocket and pulled out his own little notebook and pen.

'That's fine, Mr Robertson. I think we should record the details of this discussion and we can compare notes afterwards.' James smiled innocently. 'Agreed?'

Robertson grunted. 'Agreed.' Then he remembered his manners. 'But call me 'Dave' please.' James nodded. 'Thank you for your Peppa, by the way,' Robertson added.

Wilson was a little mystified. 'Peppa?'

'PEPPA – Your Preparatory Electronic Personal Pre-Appraisal form.'

'Of course. Good, you received it.'

'It was very helpful.'

It was a copy of this very form that James had brought with him, although it was well hidden now. He'd filled in all the blank spaces with runners and riders from the day's racing pages, knowing full well that no one, least of all Robertson, would notice. Previous PEPPAs had featured football results, a Winston Churchill speech, and the Terms and Conditions from the Bird League's own website.

Robertson was about to start asking a few questions when James – well prepared – suddenly interrupted.

'Of course, Dave, you'll be aware that the Annual Review is my opportunity to discuss my place in The Bird League, bring forward any issues that I might have, and to review the directions my career might develop in the coming year.' Robertson was about to butt in, but wasn't given the chance as James charged on.

'Accordingly, it falls to me to lead the conversation. You'll be aware that I've been a Development Officer with The Bird League since the charity began eighteen years ago, and I'm now Chief Development Officer for the area covering Scotland and the North of England. It's a very responsible job and it's one that I believe I do well.'

Robertson was about to interrupt, but James simply ploughed on.

'I knew you'd agree with me. After all, in the last twelve months I've overseen the establishment of six new conservation areas and two new visitor centres, one in Fife and one in Mull. In addition, I've brought in four major sponsors. And I'm a man of considerable experience.' He took a breath. 'I think I'm due a considerable pay rise. Twenty percent, anyway.'

At last, Robertson found himself obliged to say something.

'The thing is, Jimmy, we're having to watch our finances here at The Bird League. Life is tough everywhere at the moment, but particularly so in the Fifth Sector.'

'Fifth sector? What's that – I thought we charities were 'third sector'.'

'Third sector? That's so old hat now, we've moved on. New millennium, new decade, new definitions. That's the trouble with you dynosaruses – your so stuck in the past.' This was the one feature of the Annual Review that James looked forward to – Robertson's frequent misuse of the English language. 'Anyway, there's no money,' the Director added.

'None?'

'What are you paid at the moment – forty grand? That's a good salary. I don't think you should be complaining. You'll be aware that The Bird League is currently reviewing its expenditure.'

Now were approaching the heart of the contest.

'The real problem is that we're not hitting our targets, Jimbo.'

'Targets? I thought our core purpose was to protect birds and promote their welfare.'

'Oh goodness me, Jimmy-boy, but there's so much more to it in than that,' Robertson said. He was on more secure ground now. 'Our most important task each year is to secure our choir funding.'

'Sorry?'

'Our choir funding. The bird lovers will pay to look after the birds, but who will pay to look after us, the workers? Without us there would be no Bird League.'

James already knew that 72% of all Bird League expenditure went on staffing costs. It wasn't a figure widely shared with the public.

'So is our choir – I mean, core – income dropping?'

'In short, Jim-lad, yes. We've had a disaster on the Fluffy Puffin from – normally we look to sell over a quarter of a million each year, but this year we only sold 90,000.'

'Oh dear.'

'Same story with the Kingfisher Keyrings. Only 8,000 units sold. And the new range of Plastic Poo-Dropping Herring Gulls proved a complete flap.' Robertson adjusted his tie, then leant towards James. 'You could say that the Herring Gulls are a bit of a dead duck,' he said, winking and grinning inanely. On the whole, James preferred the serious version of David Robertson.

'Why don't we diversify?' James suggested. 'Wind-up snakes? Cuddly gorillas? Pedal-power tortoises?'

The Director looked a little blank. 'Do any of those actually have wings?'

James had to admit that they didn't. He was reminded that the Director's own higher education background might have come up short in the wildlife field: he'd trained as a joiner in a technical college that had later become a university. Call-Me-Dave had a degree in Joinery Skills.

But James had made enough of a mistake to allow Robertson back onto the front foot.

'Anyway, you'll see that, rather than increase our staffing costs, we really need to look at cutting them a bit. Especially here, in head office.'

The two men sat in silence. Eventually James said, 'I suppose our management structure is quite costly.

'I'm glad you see it from The Bird League's point of view, Jim-Bob. We need to lower our wage bill in the management division.' Robertson sat back.

'Are you looking to make me redundant?' James would have been happy to accept redundancy, but he didn't think that was quite what the Director had in mind.

'I'm not sure whether The Bird League can afford the financial imprecations of redundancy payments in the current financial year.' There followed a pregnant pause before Robertson continued, 'So, what are your plans? It was your birthday recently – how many's that now?'

Here we go, James thought. 'I was 63.' Then he added, 'I hope you're not connecting those two matters, are you?'

'In what way?'

'I'm sure The Bird League would never allow itself to be accused of age discrimination.'

'Oh no, no of course not, Jay-lad. Perish the thought.'

James decided to fight fire with fire. 'Out of interest, how much are you paid?'

Robertson smirked. 'Is that really relevant to this meeting?'

James sat back. 'I was only trying to gauge the relative values of our salaries in terms of…'

'In terms of budgerigary impact, you mean?'

James suppressed a smile. 'If you care to put it like that.'

Robertson shrugged. 'I'm paid a reasonable salary, I suppose. In line with the industry average.'

'Go on.'

'Why should I share my salary details with you when it's your Annual Review?'

'Because it's my review and I'm asking the questions… Dave. Look on it as part of my in-service training.' James added, 'I can find out under a Freedom of Information request anyway. And I'm sure that the top salary will be filed for public viewing at the Charities' Commission.'

The Director picked a non-existent piece of fluff from his jacket, sighed, then a smug smile came over his face. James knew what the smile meant: *I'm going to tell you exactly what I'm paid so that I can rub your insolent nose in it, you inferior piece of trash.*

'Two hundred and nineteen thousand pounds.'

James just about managed to cover his shock. Now it was his turn to sit back and smile.

'Well done, you. But why don't you take a salary cut yourself? It would be so good for staff morale.' James waited for his boss's face to turn a slightly darker shade of purple before adding, 'Can I suggest a cut of around £40,000?'

The Director didn't reply, instead choosing to stare, unblinkingly, directly at James. James would have been intimidated had it not been that every previous Annual Review had ended up going the same way – although this one had got there a little quicker.

'It's just a suggestion.'

'So was my retirement suggestion.'

'Well, then, that's two suggestions that have emerged from this meeting,' said James, brightly. 'That's good, isn't it? Except that one of them was legal and the other wasn't.'

'You're not going to play that card – '

'Shall we call it a day at that? Till the same time next year? I'll write up my version of the meeting and you can write yours. Don't forget each of the suggestions.' James got up to leave.

'Don't be silly,' the Director said sharply.

'No, I mean it,' James said again. 'I think it should be a true and full account of everything we discussed.'

'It'll be your word against mine.'

'True… but you wouldn't want to be seen to be falsifying the records, would you?'

'As I said, it'll be your word against mine,' Robertson said firmly.

'Sort of…' James said. Then he reached into his jacket and drew out a small electronic recorder.

Robertson looked in disgust. 'Is that a dicksaphone? Have you been recording this all along?' When James nodded, the Director went on, 'You're not allowed to record conversations without permission. It'd be thrown out in court.'

James said nothing, but instead replayed from the very start…

– Shall we do this properly? Keep a record?
– I think we're supposed to, aren't we?

    — *That's fine, Mr Robertson. I think we should record*
      the details of this discussion and we can compare
      notes afterwards. Agreed?
    — *Agreed.*

'So you see, I did try to warn you,' James said.

'Warn me? You were simply being disingenius!'

'I'm not sure that's the word most people would have used.'

Robertson looked on the point of exploding. 'Bastard.'

'Unfortunately, I've switched the recording off, so I missed that.'

'What do you want?'

James went returned to his seat for a moment. 'As I see it, you have three choices... Dave. Either we just carry on as we are, or you can give me full redundancy payment – a year's salary – and then I simply retire and you're rid of me for good.'

'That's only two choices. What's the third?'

'I go public. Sure, I'd lose my redundancy payment but I could still retire. You'd have to resign. Does that appeal?' He offered his hand for a handshake but Robertson declined.

Two weeks later James left The Bird League, complete with 18 months' salary as redundancy payment – Robertson discovered that the cost of obtaining the recording was a further six months' salary. The Bird League held a small farewell event for James, but Robertson himself was mysteriously unwell that day and had to go home before it took it place.

Fishermen

Rab **looked down** at Dale, smiled, and shook his head. The boy was four now, and to Rab's great joy and amazement they were out together and making their way along the canal tow-path. Barely four weeks earlier, Dale would settle for nothing but his grandma's attention, often screaming for several minutes if he couldn't get his way. Too often, Rab supposed, they'd given in and Grandma had indeed gone to him when probably it would have been better to take a stand; but that's not what grandparents are for, is it? Grandparents are for ice-creams, days out, and chocolate biscuits, particularly the latter when Mummy and Daddy aren't looking. But today's adventure wasn't to be about chocolate biscuits.

'Where are we going to, Grandpa?' Dale was asking.

'We're going fishing, son. You'll see.'

'Will we be trying to catch fish? Like Peppa?'

Rab had read many Peppa Pig stories to Dale but couldn't recall any about fishing. He took the easy option.

'Yes.'

'Will we be going in a boat? Peppa and George are in a boat when they're fishing. Have we got a boat, Grandpa?'

Rab realised that Peppa Pig's involvement wouldn't be as straightforward as he'd imagined.

'We're not going in a boat, Dale. We'll be fishing at the canalside. Are you looking forward to it?'

'So we're not going in a boat, Grandpa?'

Rab could sense the disappointment in the boy's voice, but knew all about 'spin'. 'It's much easier to fish if you're not in a boat, Dale. Oceans have a lot of water in them and it's harder to find the fish.'

Dale didn't reply. He was only four, after all: working that through was enough to keep his mind occupied for the moment.

Meanwhile, Rab was leading them to a place just beyond the Slateford aqueduct. Rab was carrying all of the equipment: two fishing nets, two empty jam jars and a stick; on his back was a small rucksack. The stick had been Dale's contribution to the fishing trip – it was his 'fishing rod', picked up shortly after arriving at the towpath but then passed over to Grandpa as soon as he'd realised that he needed a piece of string and a hook to make it complete. Rab would given the lad a jam jar to carry but his daughter Lisa, Dale's mother, wouldn't have been happy with her son being responsible for looking after anything made of glass. Rab understood, but wondered at the same time if kids weren't sheltered too much from life's risks.

Rab didn't have to say much. Dale was acting out some action-hero scene he'd been watching on the television that morning.

'Batman zings The Joker kerpow kerpow!' having to be saved by Rab from falling into the canal as he performed a complicated spin. Even Batman makes the odd false move. Meanwhile Rab wondered at the miracle that a child could grow from Peppa Pig to Batman in the space of just a hundred yards or so.

'Grandpa, will we be able to have tonight's fish for tea?' Dale asked.

Rab explained patiently that they were hoping to catch minnows, and that they'd need an awful lot to make a decent meal even for one. Anyway, he added, they weren't going to kill them, these were nice minnows that deserved to live, even if it was only in a jam jar for a little while.

Eventually they reached a spot where the path widened quite a bit, and where the grassy slope down towards the canal wasn't too steep. Rab took off his backpack and laid it on the ground, then sat down and instructed Dale to sit beside him. Then they each removed their socks and shoes and Rab introduced Dale to the pleasures of dangling feet in the cool canal water; it was a hot summer's day and it wasn't too hard to persuade the young man to try it for size.

'Cool, Grandpa!' Dale said, and of course, it was.

Rab leant down and filled each of the jam jars with water before laying them to the side. 'We'll need them later, hopefully,' he said.

'We're going to catch fish!' Dale said, excitedly kicking his feet in the water.

Rab patiently explained that the fish were likely to be frightened away if he splashed his feet in the water. What was needed was patience. He knew that four-year-olds generally don't have a lot of patience, but it was worth a try. But Rab could hardly blame the lad: after all, cooling his feet in the canal had been his own idea.

Reaching behind, Rab now brought one of the little fishing nets forward. Gently, he leaned forwards once again and laid the net into the canal. He could see some minnows swimming under the surface and reasoned that they should be quite successful. Upstream, however, there was competition.

'Look up there,' Rab whispered very quietly to Dale. 'We've got company.'

Less than thirty yards away on the opposite bank, a heron was standing in a slightly overgrown area of reeds. Rab hushed the boy to be quiet.

'That big grey bird is looking for its lunch, Dale. Can you see it?'

Dale, of course, had no idea at first what he should be looking for, but even a four year old boy can spot a grey heron given enough help.

'Do you know what that bird is called, Dale?' Rab asked him.

Dale thought for a moment, then said, 'Leonardo?'

Rab smiled. 'No, it's not one of the Ninja Turtles, Dale.

It doesn't have a name like that. I wondered if you knew what kind of bird it was.'

Dale tried again. 'A pigeon?'

Again, Rab held back a laugh; the boy was doing his best, and the colour was right. These were rewarding moments with a grandchild. He explained that the bird was called a grey heron, and it was fishing for the same fish that Dale and Grandpa were after. In the short time they watched, the heron caught five fish; Dale watched captivated as it slowly swallowed each one.

Then Dale turned to more important matters.

'Can I have a biscuit now, Grandpa?'

'You can have a packet of raisins soon.'

'Can't I have a biscuit?'

'No, Dale. Mummy said no biscuits today, especially chocolate biscuits, and I promised. We must keep our promises, mustn't we?'

Dale didn't reply. Dale was fed up with raisins, even although they wee better than nothing. The heron flew off.

'Shall we see if we've caught any fish?' Rab said. They looked down: the net had been in the water unmoved for a while and a shoal of little fish were swimming, unconcerned, in and out of it. 'Let's see if we can catch some now.'

Rab moved the net slightly to and fro; several minnows and a couple of other little things were inside. With an adept flick of his wrist, he made sure they had all escaped.

'Oh dear,' Rab said, 'I wasn't very lucky there, was I, Dale? They all got away.'

'Bad luck, Grandpa.'

Rab played the same trick again, then reached behind for the other net and said, 'Suppose you try, Dale. You might have better luck than me.'

Rab held the stick with Dale and they lowered the second net into the canal together. The boy was tense and the net waved about underwater, frightening all the nearby fish away. Not realising what he was doing, Dale was simply happy enough to see evidence of fish. They sat together for a little while; Rab doing nothing with his net, Dale catching nothing with his.

Eventually Rab said, 'Well, Dale, do you know what all good fishermen do when they don't catch anything?'

'No.'

'They have something to eat. Would you like a packet of raisins?'

'Yes.'

'Yes what?'

'Yes, please.'

From the rucksack, Rab produced a little packet of Sun-Maid raisins and a paper plate. Carefully, he laid them out, counting them one by one as he did so for the boy's benefit. There were forty-one. Meanwhile, Rab himself took a swig from a bottle of water. He offered the bottle to Dale, who had a swig, too, just the way all fishermen do.

They turned back to the canal and resumed fishing. Rab

told Dale some old fishing stories – the one about Superman going fishing, the one about Spiderman going fishing and of course the one about Batman going fishing. Dale told his grandpa a joke.

'Grandpa, what did the lion say to the elephant?'

'I don't know, Dale. What did the lion say to the elephant?'

'Arrrrrrgggghhhh!!!!!' said Dale, and they both laughed out loud; their laughter could be heard all around as it carried in the still air.

But Dale wasn't finished.

'Grandpa, what did the tiger say to the elephant?'

'I don't know, Dale. What did the tiger say to the elephant?'

'Arrrrrrgggghhhh!!!!!' Dale said again, falling backwards at the same time and letting his net slip into the canal. The lad was momentarily distraught, but of course the current was so slow that Rab was quickly able to rescue the situation, reaching across to fetch it back.

Just before midday, Rab pointed out that there were fish in Dale's net – Dale hadn't noticed himself. Guiding him gently, Rab helped his grandson lift its contents out of the canal and into one of the jam jars, which Rab had previously labelled with a waterproof marker 'DALE'. Dale was thrilled to be the first to catch anything.

'You're obviously a better fisherman than me, Dale,' Rab said. Then Rab allowed himself to catch a net-full – deposited in the jar marked 'GRANDPA' – and then they each had one more catch before Rab decided it was time for lunch. He peered down into the backpack.

'Guess what's for lunch, Dale?'

'I don't know. Cheese sandwiches?' It was a decent guess. Dale's lunch had been cheese sandwiches every day for each of the past two years. He loved cheese sandwiches, but he was a creature of habit, too.

'Well guessed, Dale, my boy! Grandma has made us cheese sandwiches. But first we have to wash our hands. The canal water will be dirty.'

Dale wasn't so keen on washing his hands, especially using the antibacterial gel that Rab had brought with him, but Rab insisted that real fishermen always used gel before eating and Dale reluctantly joined in. They each ate a cheese sandwich, then they had some grapes. Dale washed his down with water and a little carton of apple juice from Sainsburys; Rab drank from a flask of coffee. Then it was time to catch some more fish, then they lay back on the canal bank and Rab suggested that they look at the sky.

'What colour is the sky, Dale?'

'Blue, of course. Silly Grandpa.'

'Do you see those clouds?'

Dale vaguely pointed upwards. 'Up there, Grandpa?'

'Those are the ones, yes. What colour are they?'

'White?' Dale said. For some reason he was doubtful.

'Yes, they're white. Clouds aren't always white. Sometimes they're grey, even dark grey. But those are thin clouds, aren't they?' Rab pointed to some in the distance.

'Those ones over there, they look like cotton wool, don't they?'

'What's cotton wool, Grandpa?'

Suddenly, Rab realised that Meteorology Lesson One was in danger of going pear-shaped, so he cut his losses.

'Well anyway, when the sky is blue and the clouds are like the ones above us, it means it's not going to rain for a while. We don't need a coat or anything.'

Dale wasn't too impressed with Meteorology Lesson One.

'Did we bring a coat, Grandpa?'

'Now that you mention it, no. I reckoned that if it started to rain, we could probably just run home.'

Dale didn't say anything for a while. Then he asked, 'Have we finished fishing?'

'I suppose so,' Rab said. 'Do you want to go?'

'I wish I could have a chocolate biscuit.'

'I told you, Mummy said we weren't to have any chocolate biscuits. But… oh you'll not be interested.'

'What, Grandpa?'

Rab delved into his rucksack and produced another carton of apple juice.

'Like some?'

'Yes, please, Grandpa.'

Then Rab produced his trump card: a bar of Cadburys Dairy Milk chocolate.

'Would you like to share this with me? Fishermen eat chocolate.'

'Is this chocolate, Grandpa?'

'Yes, Dale, but it's not a biscuit. It can be our little secret.'

They shared the chocolate squares, broken off one by one, while Dale drank some apple juice and Rab the rest of his coffee.

'Good, son?'

'Yes, Grandpa, thank you.'

'My pleasure, Dale, my pleasure. Remember, though, it's our little secret. No one must know.' Then Rab sat up. 'Now I think you'd like to go home wouldn't you? You can tell Grandma all about your adventure.'

'Yes. Can we take the fish home?'

'No, son, the fish belong here in the canal. They need to get the chance to grow up, just like you'll grow up.' Rab omitted to mention that the minnows were probably full-sized already, and prayed that Dale had forgotten that the heron would probably eat half of them. He poured the contents of his jam jar back into the canal, then held Dale as he did the same.

'You should be very proud, Dale. Well done.'

They meandered back home. Grandma was in the kitchen preparing some food for the evening meal and she was delighted to hear Dale retell the entire story of the day spent fishing with Grandpa, how Grandpa was hopeless at fishing but that he, Dale, was a champion fisherman and had caught hundreds of fish although they'd had to put them all back and that they'd had cheese sandwiches and grapes for lunch and that he'd told Grandpa a very funny joke about lions and tigers and elephants.

Grandma suggested that he draw a picture for Mummy, who would shortly be calling in to collect him on her way home from work. That kept Dale amused for a bit; children's television did the rest.

Around half past five Lisa appeared.

'Had a nice time with Grandma and Grandpa today, Dale?'

Dale was too busy concentrating on the Ninja Turtles to do more than grunt an 'Uh-huh'. To be fair, he was a bit tired anyway.

'What did you do?'

Suddenly Dale was quite animated. He told his mummy all about the day fishing with Grandpa, in particular how bad Grandpa was at fishing and how he'd shown Grandpa how to do it. Some of the fish had been huge, but they'd put them all back. They'd had a lovely lunch of cheese sandwiches and grapes by the canal.

'That's wonderful, Dale,' said Lisa. 'Did you say thank you to Grandpa?'

'Thank you, Grandpa,' Dale said.

'It's a pleasure, Dale,' Rab said. 'Thank you for the nice company. I really enjoyed my day.'

'Can we do it again?' Dale asked.

'Oh yes, I'm sure.'

'Can we go tomorrow?'

'Well, maybe not tomorrow, Dale, because you don't come here on Thursdays. Only on Wednesdays. But soon.'

Lisa thanked her mum and – especially – her dad again for looking after her son.

'OK, Dale,' she said. 'Shall we go? Get your stuff.' Then, as an afterthought, she said to him, 'Which bit of the fishing was the best bit?'

Dale fought for a moment, then said, 'Chocolate.'

Embarrassed, Rab said, 'It wasn't a biscuit, Lisa.'

Lisa screwed her eyes up in mock anger at her dad. then laughed and said to Dale, 'Your Grandpa's a bit naughty, giving you chocolate.'

'Mummy,' said Dale. 'All the best fishermen eat chocolate. Don't you know that? Grandpa said so.'

Lisa chuckled. 'Well, Grandpa should know, I suppose. He's the one who knows all about fishing.'

Dale looked at her. 'Apart from me, Mummy?'

Rab smiled. 'Apart from you, Dale. Apart from you.'

Grace Notes

J ust the other day, I stumbled on her box again.

For a man in his late seventies like me, the days can sometimes seem a little long, as if the sun's journey across the city skies from east to west is slower than it was when we were all younger. Perhaps I just have more time to notice it in my twilight years. I'm in decent health, my doctor tells me every year, or at least 'not bad for a man of my age', whatever that means. I suppose it means he doesn't see any reason why I should 'be taken before my time', to use that quaint old phrase.

Taken before his time – taken before her time, I should say – that's what this is all about, of course. My daughter Imogen was taken before her time, you see, just over ten years ago, and, well, you'll understand that things were never quite the same again thereafter. Imogen was our only child. My wife Heather, a diabetic, was advised only to have the one and even carrying Imogen caused problems; her eyesight was never quite the same thereafter. Naturally it meant Imogen was the most loved, most cherished child on the earth, and nothing was too good for her. Not that she was spoiled, or at least that she behaved like a spoiled brat. Sure, she could have her tantrums, and in her teenage years the hinges on some of the doors needed a little tightening following some 'grand slams'. But she more than made up for it, much more, in so many other ways. She attracted lots of nice friends, many of whom we got to know quite well. She was academic; she was a decent athlete and played tennis for the university team; and she was musical. She had a lovely voice, and I used to adore listening to her playing the piano. Even her practice seemed musical. Heather liked when she played Chopin, Mozart, Beethoven, that sort of thing, but to please me Imogen would also throw in a little Cole Porter or Duke Ellington. Now and again I'll put on a CD of *Night And Day* or *In A Sentimental Mood* late at night and memories of those times will flood back; it's perhaps as well I'm alone then, you'll understand I get a little emotional.

Imogen was just thirty-eight. A few years previously, she'd met a young man called Seth – they were 'Seth and Im' – and they'd fallen in love. This all happened while she was working in Manchester, so we really never got to know Seth very well. It's an unusual name, Seth, at least in this country, but it seems his grandfather was from New Jersey, had come across here to serve with the US airforce during the war, met a local lass and settled. Somewhere in East Anglia, I think. Anyway, it was a family name on that side. Heather and I were delighted that Imogen was so happy with him. She'd not actually had so many boyfriends over the years – her career as a company lawyer seemed to be more important. We'd even wondered more than once if she was lesbian, not that it would have mattered of course, we'd just have been glad to see her happy, but you know it makes things a bit more complicated, doesn't it?

We'd met Seth a few times, but most of their time together was naturally down there in the north of England. They each held on to their own flats for a year or so and then moved in together into a huge modern flat in a very nice area. Cotton Street, it was called. Both of them had good jobs, and they could afford it. We visited them a couple of times at weekends, but you're aware these young people are so busy, aren't they? They work so hard nowadays, after all. We saw them up here slightly more, but not often, so as Imogen's relationship with Seth developed, we simply saw less of our daughter, something that made me sad, and Heather bitter. Many an evening I'd spend listening to her bemoaning the distance – geographical and emotional – that she felt was growing between mother and daughter, and no amount of my trying to reason with her seemed to make any difference. In fact, more often than not, Heather would end up turning on me, sullenly departing the room to go to bed early without so much as a 'goodnight'.

It was actually at this time that I first discovered that I could connect with Imogen by listening to recordings of piano music I could associate with her, music she'd learned to play herself when she'd lived with us. I told Imogen herself about it once, quietly, although I'm not sure what she made of me. I'm not sure children really understand how much their parents depend on the little points of contact, photos, a telephone call, some mention in the newspaper or television. I think that perhaps that children only start to grasp that notion when they have kids of their own, and even then only sometimes.

Anyway, it was in July that year that it happened. Imogen called to say that she and Seth had some news for us, and they were coming up. We wondered if it might be a time for wedding bells, but it turned out that it wasn't as simple as that. Sitting over dinner, Imogen explained that she and Seth didn't really see a point in spending vast sums of money on a large family wedding, money that would be better spent on the family they hoped to start within months. So their plan was to get married while they were on their honeymoon, not before it, and that this wonder honeymoon would be the holiday of a lifetime in Brazil – Rio, of course. They had plans to get married simply on Copacabana Beach in the shadow of Sugar Loaf Mountain. The local hotel, it seemed, could arrange such things at short notice.

Heather, of course, was desperately hurt. Actually, I need to be fair here, we both were, but Heather really didn't make much effort to hide her disappointment that we wouldn't be invited to our only daughter's wedding. I mean, no matter what, you really should pretend you're happy, shouldn't you? But that wasn't for Heather, I'm afraid, and it soured the whole visit. Seth – who was a personable enough young man, actually – just kept his head down, but between Imogen and her mother it was like the Cold War. And of course Heather and I fell out, too, not because I agreed with Imogen, more because there was nothing to be gained by fighting over it. I suppose, though, Heather always felt that she'd risked her health having Imogen and that should count for something special between them. In the event, Imogen and Seth left on the Sunday afternoon with barely a hug from Heather, and a promise to send us a postcard from Rio.

We never saw them in person again.

They were due to leave for Brazil on a flight on a Tuesday some five weeks later from, of all places, Newcastle Airport, where a low-cost carrier had some amazing deal. They'd set off very early, so early that it appears likely that they decided to take a detour into Durham, perhaps for a bite to eat. and I'm told that road, the A167, has a really bad reputation. Seth liked to drive – too fast said Heather, of course – and he had a very fast Audi sports car of some sort. We'll never know what happened for sure, but their Audi was on the wrong side of the road, apparently. I just feel bad for the people in the other car, they never had a chance and the police reckoned they just happened to be in the wrong place at the wrong time. The papers said it took the Fire Service hours to cut them all out, not there was really any hurry, I suppose.

Human beings aren't programmed to outlive their children. Our friends made consoling noises, but there's little consolation to be gained from words. All you feel is emptiness. Heather simply cracked up, most days taking to her bed for long parts of the day and relying on anti-depressants for weeks, then months. Left alone in the living room, I found myself listening to those CDs of piano music that allowed me to connect with Imogen, and for sure she was better company than Heather. One day I came home from doing some shopping to discover that she'd taken some fearful cocktail of any pills she could find, washed down with any alcohol she could find – and she found quite a lot. Fortunately, she would say unfortunately, I found her in time, barely alive, but medical help came quickly and somehow they managed to pump her stomach just in time.

Not that Heather was grateful. For her, it was the last straw between her and me, I'd betrayed her one final wish in life; she never wanted to see me again. The doctors reckoned she'd be better off in hospital under medication until she was fit to go home, but of course she didn't want to go home, and she was never deemed fit to leave anyway. She refused to let me visit. I went to the hospital several times, but she screamed whenever she saw me, and when they moved her to a long-term psychiatric institution a couple of months later, I was told there was little point in my coming any more. The doctors were actually very nice about it; they said that they were concerned for my welfare as well as for Heather's. But it meant was that in the space of less than six months I'd lost the two most precious people in my life.

Quite a lot of my time was taken up with sorting out Imogen's affairs – some of Heather's, too, of course – and one benefit of not having to visit Heather was that friends and relatives started to get me back into the normal routine of social life. For me that meant the bowling club and the golf club, although I couldn't bring myself to go and play bridge anymore on Tuesday evenings. Each night, I'd listen to a piano CD, waiting for the small snippet that Imogen tried to play. Eventually, I came to pretend it really was her playing, despite what the label said, not only the pieces that I'd heard her attempt when she was alive, but all the other tracks, too. I just shut my eyes and pictured her at the upright across the living-room from me.

Then one day about a year later I discovered that I, too, had lost more of Imogen than I'd realised. I was happy enough to listen to her play in my imagination, but in focusing on her piano playing, I'd forgotten Imogen the woman. I had photos of her on the mantelpiece – yes, Heather, too, of course – but I couldn't remember her voice. I remember the exact moment when I noticed it. I was on the sixth green at the golf club, playing well in a monthly medal competition, and I was trying to hole a five-foot putt for a par four. I couldn't hear Imogen's voice, I'd forgotten what she sounded like. I holed the putt, actually had a good score, but I'd have traded something well over a hundred to have Imogen's voice back.

I rushed home, put a couple of CDs on again, but her voice wasn't there. Instead, the pianists seemed to be mocking me, asking me how on earth I could be so careless as to lose the memory of my daughter's voice. My friends were actually quite understanding, more than one pointing out that they couldn't remember what their own mother sounded like any more. I was amazed that we didn't have any recordings of Imogen, though, considering how everyone has video cameras on their mobile phones these days; but we had Imogen just too early, we didn't have any of these things and although we had plenty of stills, we didn't have any movie footage at all. The nightly CDs seemed less attractive after that. I went back to watching television or reading a book at night.

I spent a lot of time pottering about around the house and in the garden, and I'm sure I grew a lot older-looking then. Eventually, a couple of years later, three after Imogen's death, I decided it might be a good idea to think about moving to somewhere smaller, somewhere with less painful memories. It was Imogen that I missed more than her mother, partly because Heather and I had discussed a few times what might happen if one of us died – well, you have to, sometimes, don't you, and Heather was always well aware that her diabetes could well cause lots of complications in later life.

I realised that selling our family home would mean I'd have to clear a lot of stuff out first, and I began with some of the books in the spare room, and then the garage.

Heather's stuff was difficult. I knew she was never coming home, but I didn't feel I had her permission to throw anything out. Eventually, there wasn't any alternative to it; I had to take on the job of clearing Imogen's old room.

Imogen's 'room' was no longer the old room she'd had as teenager. Even the protective Heather had been sensible enough to realise that Imogen would a need a double bed if she arrived home with a boyfriend – or even a girlfriend. Imogen did indeed bring home a girlfriend one time and shared a bed, which had both of us guessing. It was none of our business, though, and personally I suspect it was simply a matter of their deciding that her double bed was also the two most comfortable single beds. Mostly, though, it was one of the boyfriends.

She was pretty tidy, but when you go through a modern young woman's bedroom who's not a chance to clear up behind her, you're likely to have your eyes opened a little. Hair straighteners, make-up, her contact-lens stuff and one or two other things which are best left private. I also found a diary, which I haven't yet read; I'm not sure if it's right to.

I'd no difficulty throwing out her piano music. It was too painful to see and feel material which had caused her so much grief, and anyway much of it turned out to be simply photocopied scraps of sheet music provided by piano teachers, with their markings, not Imogen's.

The hardest part was throwing out Imogen's clothes. They weren't things she wore any more, but they were things we'd seen her wear when she'd been younger; often, they were associated with events, such as the school prom, or her twenty-first birthday, or her cousin Robyn's wedding. It all went either to the charity shop or else to the city's recycling plant.

One morning, when the room appeared to be cleared, I decided to clean it thoroughly, dusting and hoovering everything. It took more than two hours – I'm not very good at housework – and it was just before lunchtime when the hoover bumped into something at the furthermost corner under Imogen's bed right up against the wall. Getting right down on the floor, I could see a light brown object, and with some difficulty I dragged the double bed away from the wall to reveal a cardboard box about fifteen inches square and eight inches deep, all complete with a well-fitting lid. On the top – in her own handwriting – was written simply: 'Private, Imogen. NO ENTRY!'

I shook the box first. But I couldn't resist opening it.

Inside, there were letters, lots of them, tied with ribbons. I looked cautiously to see who they might be from, and indeed they were from a variety of boys and girls, but by far the biggest group seemed to come from Seth himself. I probably shouldn't have, but I found myself browsing Seth's loving words, realising that their relationship had been far stronger, far deeper, and had begun far earlier than Heather and I had ever realised. Yes, some of the stuff was intimate, but it was so genuine, and at last I knew for sure that our daughter, whatever we'd thought at the time, had died in the company of the right man, two lovers whose lives had intertwined for good.

But that wasn't all that was in the box. There was a handwritten piece of sheet music there, piano music that I'd never seen before, in Imogen's own handwriting. In all the years she'd played, I'd never known her try to write anything herself, but here it was: 'Consolation in A Minor, by Imogen Clark'. And there was a cassette tape.

It had been a long time since the cassette deck on my music system had been called into action, but I couldn't wait to hear what it contained. Sure enough, after some clunking of microphones, there was a sigh – yes, Imogen's – followed by the sound of our upright piano being treated to *Consolation in A Minor*. It probably wasn't anything special, but for me it was glorious, and I don't mind telling you it brought tears flooding to my eyes. It had a simple enough melody, perhaps best described as romantic in style with a touch of Chopin or Rachmaninoff, the composers she'd always liked listening to herself, and it contained soaring runs alternated with quiet, contemplative moments. A critic would probably dismiss it, but I thought it was the most wonderful thing I'd ever heard. I think I listened to it eleven times eventually that day.

It was just Imogen playing, I thought. But then, after the piece had ended, she sighed again, and I could hear her rise from the piano, presumably to switch off the cassette recorder, and as she approached I could clearly hear her say to herself, 'I wonder if there are too many grace notes?'

It was her voice, my Imogen's. I had her back.

Consolation in A minor

Imogen

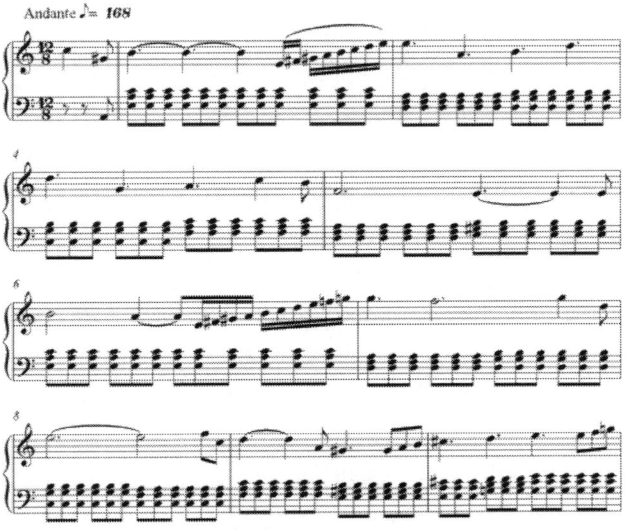

Bridges Burned

Outside, snow is falling heavily. It happens often enough in January, particularly in the Borders near Innerleithen, where Duncan and Zoe McIntyre have their second home. Duncan, you'll recall, is an Edinburgh solicitor and a partner in the prestigious law firm Marsden McKinlay McIntyre Bell, although he's not the McIntyre of Marsden McKinlay McIntyre Bell, it's simply the reason why he invested rather more than he perhaps should have to buy into the practice. His clients all think that he's the original 'Mr McIntyre', whereas the real original McIntyre actually popped off over fifty years ago.

Zoe loves the cottage, which she and Duncan refer to as 'The Lodge'. When they bought it, it was called 'Stank Cottage', a local reference to the stream and pond at the bottom of the garden, but at Duncan's suggestion they renamed it 'Deer Lodge'. And indeed there are deer about, as there are in almost every moor in Scotland and a lot of other places besides. But the 'Lodge' still looks like a large cottage which has been extended a couple of times; which is exactly what it is. It has two floors with lovely coom ceilings - the Scottish word for sloping ceilings - in the upstairs bedrooms, and a staircase which so low that even after twelve years Duncan still regularly bumps his bald head on the ceiling as it turns halfway up. Today, he's actually wearing an Elastoplast on his shining pate, the result of an unfortunate clash first thing in the morning as he was making his way down for breakfast.

Snow in January would be fine, and indeed Duncan now takes a little time off from work each January to enjoy any snow or icy weather that happens to come along; they love the isolation and the lovely walks, and in any case they always have their four-by-four to get them to local shops if they need to. The trouble is that this isn't January, it's late October, and the snow is completely, utterly unexpected.

Into the bargain, Duncan and Zoe are not alone. In a weak moment, Duncan has invited a couple of friends to stay; more particularly Zoe has suggested that 'it might be nice to invite them, Duncan', and Duncan has given in. One of them isn't even a friend.

As it happens, the McIntyres have invited Josh Mackay, aka 'Fleece', to visit them for the day, and as Fleece is currently 'seeing' someone called Jen, then Jen's along for the ride, too. It's their first ever visit. Fleece and Jen have arrived in Jen's BMW five-series, which is a very nice car - to go with Jen's very well-paid job - but Jen is looking out of the enormous triple-glazed patio door at the ever-whitening scene outside with some concern. BMWs, of course, have rear-wheel drive, all except those BMWs that claim to be 'Minis' but actually look more like playground bullies on the streets. Jen's car looks less thuggish but is entirely hopeless in snow and ice.

'This snow is heavy,' Jen observes. 'Very heavy. I hope we'll be all right.' Jen is small - five foot three, blonde with a little help, and petite. She also never smiles except to impress; observers of the smile in question are left feeling less than impressed. In her job, she has risen far beyond her talent level, and she is known as a thoroughly unpleasant woman, even to an extent by Fleece. But she and Fleece have one thing in common: they both need each other physically because no-one else will have them.

Poor Fleece. He's a large, overweight, coarse, generally slovenly, bearded monster. He's decidedly un-dapper. Apart from that, he's a top class guy. Women like Zoe feel sorry for him, but they all stop short of actually being his close mate unless they themselves have as little to offer as Jen does. Jen is a power-dresser - even dressing casually she wears riding jodhpurs and tight-fitting jumpers to show off her figure - and she could be attractive if only she could sign up for a personality transplant.

'Bugger me, that's snow,' Fleece says. 'That's snow.' Fleece repeats much of what he says, probably to remind himself that he's said it.

'Nice and warm in here, though, Fleece,' Duncan replies.

'Nice cottage, right enough, Walnut. Nice cottage.'

Fleece never calls Duncan by his Christian name, it's always 'Walnut'. It's an obscure homage to Duncan's Walnut Whips that used to be made in the Canonmills area of Edinburgh back in the 1960s. Duncan hates being called Walnut but he's long ago given up the unequal struggle against Fleece.

'It is a lovely cottage, Walnut,' Jen agrees, screwing her mouth up as she says it. She has no idea that Walnut has any other name other than 'Walnut' because Fleece simply hasn't thought to tell her. Jen continues, 'It's called 'Stank', you say? That's an unusual name.' Fleece likes to wind Walnut up, and he's set Jen up.

Walnut knows Fleece is trying to goad him. 'No, Jen, we call this 'Deer Lodge'. We changed its name when we bought it,' he explains patiently.

Fleece roars with laughter. He does that a lot, too. 'So you reckon it doesn't stink, Walnut? It stank, but it doesn't any more? That right?'

Zoe watches this with concern. Like so many men of his age, Walnut has high blood pressure, and she knows it's getting an upward push at the moment. 'Don't wind him up, Fleece. We love this place, and we love its new name.'

Fleece is just about enough of a gentleman to back off at a woman's request.

'We're guests here, after all, Fleece,' Jen points out.

'Ah, Walnut doesn't mind, does he?' Fleece replies. 'Walnut doesn't mind. But for Zoe's sake, I'll give a bit of a rest. Maybe a minute or two,' he adds, roaring with laughter. Then he suddenly stops laughing and looks out of the triple-glazed patio door again, adding, 'Christ, that's heavier than ever.'

'I'm sure it'll pass over,' Walnut says, more in hope than expectation. The skies outside are a dark, purplish-grey colour and look ready to dump enough snow to start ski runs all over the surrounding hills.

Fleece is captivated by the white scene outside. He's still wearing his outdoor fleece, a maroon one that he's very attached to.

'Bugger me, Jen,' he says, 'look at your car. There's almost a foot of snow on it already!' Jen's says nothing but simply purses her lips. Turning to Walnut, Fleece blunders on. 'Jesus, Walnut, the way things are going, you're going to have put us up for the night!' Fleece thinks it's hysterical.

It's a thought that has occurred to Walnut, too, and he doesn't think it's hysterical, anything but. 'I'm sure it'll pass over, Fleece. It's only half-past-two, you know.' Jen is not amused, and makes no attempt to hide her distaste for her predicament.

Zoe keeps her own counsel. Instead, she offers a cheery smile.

'How about a nice cup of tea and some gingerbread?'

By seven o'clock, nearly two feet of snow have fallen, and it's getting dark.

Having succeeded in dragging Walnut outside, Fleece has spent the afternoon building a series of snowmen across the driveway, which he compares with the Chinese

'Emperor's Warriors', the terracotta army discovered back in 1974. Then Walnut is subjected to a severe snowballing, descending on him like mortar shells so that even his four-by-four gives him no cover.

Inside, Jen has spent the last few hours pretending to look interested in Zoe's collection of magazines. This is an art she's perfected; in fact, she *is* interested, but wants to pretend she isn't because she's above reading magazines, and then she wants people to think she's pretending to be polite. What is very clear to Zoe - who's had to watch this pantomime all afternoon - is that Jen would rather be anywhere but Deer Lodge.

Zoe, meanwhile, has - unaided - prepared a fabulous meal, starting with chestnut soup, then a venison pie, and then finally a tiramisu, a tour-de-force involving an obscene quantity of marsala. Like a mother calling to her children, she's had to summon the men in from outside at six o'clock, with instructions to her husband to offer drinks and nibbles to the guests.

Jen requests a soft drink because she's driving, but Fleece has no such inhibitions. Indeed it's the main reason he manoeuvred Jen into driving the BMW in the first place.

'What can I get you then, Fleece?' Walnut asks, hopefully. 'Red wine? I've got some cold beer in the fridge.'

Fleece goes straight to Walnut's soft underbelly. 'Walnut, I assume you still have some of your thirty-four-year-old Macallan?'

Walnut's heart sinks. 'I have a little left. Not much.'

'How little is little?' Fleece insists. 'I don't want to take your last drop.'

'Well - ' Walnut sets off for the 'special' walk-in cupboard, only to discover to his horror that Fleece is following him all the way.

'Fuck me!' Fleece yells. 'There's at least twenty bottles of fantastic whisky here. And look - what a wine cellar!' He drags a bottle out from an array, beautifully set out in wooden racks. 'Christ, Walnut, you need to dust these.'

Walnut attempts to grab it from him and return it to the rack. 'These were being laid down, Fleece. You've just disturbed the sediment. It'll be undrinkable for months, now,' he sniffs.

'OK, if the wine's off, I'll settle for the whisky.' He squints at a green bottle with an obscure label. 'Jesus, that's the Bowmore stuff that costs over three grand a bottle. Did you pay that?'

Walnut looks embarrassed. 'What if I did?'

Fleece looks amazed. Then he pretends to drop it, nearly does, then catches it at the last minute. 'Had you worried there, Walnut, had you worried there!'

Walnut wants to replace it, but Fleece will have none of it. 'Come on then, you old skinflint, share with yer old pal Fleece, eh?'

'Fleece, it wasn't what I intended - '

'Come on, Walnut, come on. Are you planning on just letting it sit in the cupboard there, in an unopened bottle, till the day you die?' Walnut looks even less comfortable than before; Fleece knows he's winning. 'Come on, Walnut.'

Fleece is a bit of a juggernaut in these situations, and there's no doubt who will prevail. Less than a minute later, Walnut has breached the prized bottle of malt, although he might as well have been a glove puppet being operated by his bearded guest.

'Christ, smell that, Walnut,' Fleece roars. Bear in mind that they're both still in the walk-in cupboard, but Fleece can be heard in both the upstairs bedrooms nevertheless. 'Smells of Germoline. I can smell it from here.'

'Perhaps you'll settle for the smell, then, Fleece?' Walnut tries to make light of his predicament, although in truth Fleece has placed himself in the cupboard doorway and there's quite literally no escape for him. Fleece doesn't reply, but instead he merely intensifies his bearded grin. He's doing his impersonation of Blackbeard again, and like the legendary pirate he intends to pillage for all its worth. Walnut wordlessly passes him a dram.

Fleece studies the glass, then holds it out again. 'Come on, Walnut, you're the host and I'm the guest. That means you give me a generous measure.'

Walnut adds a little. The glass stays held out, so he has to add some more. Then some more. Eventually, he has an idea; in fact it's a brainwave.

'Jen, would you like some?' he enquires, barging past Fleece so that at last he can resist Fleece's demands. And Jen doesn't let him down; her face is already curled up in distaste.

'No thank you, Walnut,' she replies. 'I don't like whisky. Anyway, I'm driving, so I should stick to water.' She looks out of the window and adds, 'I hope. The snow seems to be piling ever higher.' She is not happy.

Eventually, the four sit down to enjoy a drink together, although in truth only Fleece seems to be genuinely enjoying the situation. Walnut reckons his precious bottle has taken too big a hit tonight, so he and Zoe are on chilled chardonnay. Zoe tries to engage Jen in some sort of small talk.

'So, have you been busy at work lately, Jen?'

'I don't like to talk about work when I'm off duty.' Jen doesn't offer any sort of apology. Instead, the inevitable apology travels in the other direction.

'Sorry,' Zoe says eventually, more than a little hurt inside, although she's good at hiding it.

Walnut and Fleece discuss football, which only Fleece is interested in, and then rugby, which only Walnut really enjoys. Fleece actually plays a form of rugby, but does so because his doctor ordered him to take some exercise, and for the genuine pleasure of delivering surreptitious uppercuts to opposing second-row forwards. But visits to Murrayfield for Scotland internationals are really only for the hospitality: Walnut's, of course.

Come seven o'clock, Fleece is successfully parted from his hundred-pound-a-nip glass by the arrival of the homemade chestnut soup, which has appeared on the table in the open-plan kitchen-diner. It's a simply fabulous Zoe McIntyre speciality in which her very best chicken stock is combined with a tin of chestnuts and some cream. It's muddy brown, but it tastes much better than it looks. To help the appearance, each plate has a further swirl of cream and some parsley in the middle. The guests are instructed to take their places.

'Ah, fantastic,' Fleece declares, leaning over the plate to take in the aroma. 'My favourite, Zoe.' He turns to Jen, 'Take a shuftie at that, Jen, take a shuftie at that.'

Jen's lips are pursing, her nostrils are twitching.

'Did you say 'nuts', Zoe?'

Slightly taken aback, Zoe replies, 'Well, yes, I suppose so, it's chestnut soup, Jen. Is that a problem for you?'

'I'm somewhat allergic to nuts,' Jen replies. She looks repelled by the very idea that chestnut soup is being thrust upon her.

Fleece looks incredulous. 'You're somewhat allergic to nuts? You're somewhat allergic to nuts? What does that mean?' He's too shocked by Jen's announcement to remember that he hopes to lull this woman into sharing a bed with him tonight when they get home. He's too shocked even to swear.

'It means, Fleece, that I become ill if I eat nuts.' She's still looking down her nose at her plate as if she were wearing reading glasses, although in fact she doesn't need them. (Needless to say Jen's vanity has required her to spend a fortune on having her eyes lasered into shape so that she can see perfectly well.)

'But Jen,' Fleece says desperately, 'they're not real nuts, like peanuts or cashews. And by the way, you were tucking in to those nuts on the coffee table earlier.'

'They were fruit and nuts. I was only eating the fruit. It's better for you anyway.' Jen looks at Fleece with distain. This is clearly the reason for the difference between their body shapes, that Jen only eats dried fruit, leaving Fleece to gobble up the cholesterol-soaked nuts.

Fleece is struggling to cope with this new discovery. 'Sorry, Jen,' he says, 'I just thought you had a sweet tooth.'

Zoe stands up to intervene. 'Jen, I'm sorry I didn't know you had a problem with nuts. What a pity. Can I get you something else? I could make you up a quick salad. There are some tomatoes and some mozzarella in the fridge. Or there's feta, too - I could mix it with some olives. How would that be?'

'It's all right, thank you,' Jen insists. Actually, it's anything but all right; how could these stupid people be so insensitive as not to be able to read her mind and know she doesn't eat nuts?

'Are you sure?' Walnut asks, rather bemused.

'Yes, thanks, it's all right. I'll be fine,' adding as an afterthought, 'I could do with losing some weight.'

Nobody knows quite how to reply to that, and the silence which follows gives Fleece to come up with exactly the wrong thing to say.

'Oh well that's great, then!' he roars. Then he adds, 'You get to go on a diet, and I get to have your helping as seconds!' He's laughing, but he's the only one and he hasn't yet noticed. Zoe and Walnut sit in embarrassed silence while the sound of one man laughing echoes around the large room. To avoid conversation on dangerous subjects, Walnut invites Fleece to talk about his work as a civil servant, even although he works in the Department of Work and Pensions and is entrusted with the task of stopping benefits to the deserving poor. It gets them through the chestnut soup, while Zoe sits in silence, hoping the evening will soon be over. Jen sits studying the pattern on her table mat. Suddenly she looks up, clearly still irritated that her needs haven't been catered for.

'I presume Fleece mentioned that I'm vegetarian as well.'

Walnut and Zoe look at each other in horror. Fleece just looks embarrassed, which for him is a rare experience.

'Em... I forgot to mention it, Jen.' He tries to suggest it's funny. 'Sorry,' he adds, with a fixed smile that's meant to crack the icy atmosphere, although it'll take more than that.

'So you won't eat venison pie, either?' Walnut growls, giving Fleece a dirty look to say *could you not have warned us?*, to which Fleece responds with a shrug which says *I really don't understand it either, Walnut.*

'No.' A pause, then, 'Maybe some vegetables.'

Fleece can't understand this, and demands an explanation. 'Jen, explain this to me. Why don't you eat meat?' Actually he's heard the answer many times, so he's obviously up for debating the matter.

'It's a moral thing,' Jen replies icily. 'All creatures on this earth need to be respected.'

'Even salmon?' Fleece loves fishing and has even been known to catch a salmon. He maintains that the very fact that even he can catch them proves that salmon are stupid.

'They make wonderful journeys out into the oceans and back. For what?' Jen spears, 'for what? Just so that we can be caught with fishing hooks in their mouths, bashed over the heads, and have their guts ripped out, all so they can be dumped onto your plate?'

Zoe tries to pour oil on troubled waters by seeming to support her. 'Jen's entitled to her views, too, Fleece.' She starts to rise to find what else is in the fridge.

Fleece is amused by the turn this debate has taken, but is clearly game for it. 'I like the idea of salmon having their guts ripped out, Jen. It's like Wallace in *Braveheart*. Proves they're Scottish.' He yells this sentence out at the top of his voice, but his laughter is greeted with a contemptuous sneer from Jen.

'I could do you a nice feta salad, Jen,' Zoe says, peering into the fridge. 'There are both black and green olives here, too.'

Jen is starting to bubble with rage, and not so far under the surface that it isn't clearly obvious to all. It takes her a moment to be distracted enough to reply.

'No - no, Zoe, no, thanks. I'll be all right. Just a few vegetables will do when the time comes.' Actually, she means, *please can I go home? These people have no idea.*

For the next ten or fifteen minutes they work their way through the venison pie. Fleece praises the pie, announcing that it's the best he's ever tasted. Zoe brightens up at the compliment, at least she does so until Fleece reveals that this is the first venison pie he's ever tasted.

Walnut asks Jen about her work.

'I work in the education department,' she says. 'Currently I work in the headquarters in strategic management - you know, recruitment, hiring and firing, disciplinary issues, that sort of thing.'

'Sounds interesting,' Walnut lies.

'It's not. Most of the time you meet or have to deal with poor sad, useless, miserable unemployable morons who shouldn't be let anywhere near a school.'

'And that's just the heads!' Fleece roars.

Again, the joke misses Jen completely. She simply ignores him.

'I'm bored with it all, in fact,' Jen says to Walnut. She might be talking about her job, but Zoe and Walnut guess, probably correctly, that she's talking about life, Fleece, and her company right now. 'I've only been doing it for a month, but I'm ready to move on already.'

'What did you have in mind?' Walnut inquires.

'I don't know... something in the media, perhaps, journalism or something like that. I'm sure I could do TV. Better than that dreadful women that's on at the moment.'

'The one on *Reporting Scotland*? I rather like her,' Walnut replies.

'You just like looking at her tits, Walnut,' yells Fleece, again embarrassing Walnut. 'You said so yourself the other day.'

Walnut stammers, 'Well... she is a nice-looking woman, but that's not why I like her. I just like her style.' He's blushing, which brings a scowl from Jen, a chuckle from Fleece, and a surprisingly tender touch on the back of Walnut's hand from Zoe, who understands perfectly well what love is all about. Deep down, it's what she and Walnut have in spades, and it gives them strength. Strength they're going to need this evening.

Ten minutes later, events have progressed to the tiramisu.

'Looks lovely, Zoe,' Jen says, trying to be polite.

'Thanks, Jen.' Zoe sees light at the end of the tunnel. This is one of Duncan's favourites. Jen is still reminding herself that Duncan equals the person she's been told is called 'Walnut' when she realises that Zoe is giving away the recipe secrets, mentioning the words 'plenty of marsala'.

Abruptly, she stops and asks, 'Sorry, Zoe, did you mention marsala?'

'Yes, there's quite a bit. It makes all the difference.' Then Zoe feels a cold seeping through her bones as she suddenly senses there might be a problem.

'If I'm driving, Zoe, I really shouldn't have any alcohol.'

Fleece is outraged. 'Aw cummon' Jen, that's not drink! That's pudding!' It's an interesting debate, but not one he's going to win.

'I'm sure you'll pass a breathalyser, Jen,' Walnut suggests.'

'And Walnut'll get you off for free if you don't!' Fleece adds unhelpfully. 'Anyway, it's snowing, you might not be able to drive home at all!'

This is a hideous prospect for all except Fleece himself, who still harbours dreams of more of Walnut's whisky, but he's right; the snow is falling harder than ever.

Zoe says it first.

'The roads are bad here, but they'll be worse further down, actually. There's a stretch between here and the main road which will be impossible already.' She pauses. 'We were expecting heavy rain, not this. Perhaps... would you be able to stay? It might be safer.' She's getting dagger looks from her husband, horror looks from Jen. She stumbles on, looking at Walnut, 'We can put them up in our spare room, Duncan. Couldn't we?'

Walnut takes a long time to reply, but eventually says, 'I suppose we could. How do you fancy that, Jen?'

Jen fancies that not one little bit, but realises she is cornered. 'I'd rather we went on our way,' then she adds grudgingly, 'but I suppose we've little choice.'

'We can give you each a toothbrush of course,' Zoe says, 'and... I'm sure I could find a nightie for you, Jen, and - ' she's about to offer Fleece some of Walnut's sensible pyjamas when she realises that there's a slight size discrepancy between the two of them that might cause a problem. But Fleece is to rescue her, after a fashion at least.

'Oh that's all right, Zoe my dear, Jen and I sleep naked, don't we?' Jen looks less than impressed that this little detail of her private life has been revealed, but Fleece is in full flow. 'Children of the sixties, Jen and me, flower-power, free love and all that, eh Jen?' Jen doesn't reply; instead she wriggles a little nervously on her chair.

Once again there's an awkward silence as each of the four present allow their minds to contemplate a later scene in the spare room. Surprisingly, it's Jen who asks the next question directly.

'Zoe, Duncan, I assume you don't mind if Fleece and I share a bed in your house?'

'No, Jen, of course,' Zoe says, 'I think we're all adults here.' She smiles reassuringly; Walnut's eyebrows are raised, even although he's known that - somehow - this relationship between Fleece and Jen is physical.

Fleece is laughing. 'Of course they don't mind, Jen! They're grown-ups. Fuck me!' he says, laughing even louder.

'Later, Fleece,' Jen replies in a low voice, adding a low cat-like growl for effect.

Fleece roars with laughter, while Zoe and Walnut are speechless as Jen - for the first time all day - can be seen to have a sly smile across her face.

Eventually, Zoe manages to compose herself.

'I'm sure you'll manage some tiramisu, then, Jen?'

*

Fleece, Jen and Zoe are sitting in the living area of the cottage. It's a huge open-plan area with windows on all sides, so they can carry on conversation with Walnut as he tidies up the last part of the meal and prepares coffee. Zoe goes to pull the curtains, but Fleece suggests they should be left open to allow him to keep an eye on the weather. Instead, she is to instructed to put her feet up.

''Well, that was great, Zoe,' Fleece repeats once again. His meal is repeating as well, as he blasts out gusts of wind in all directions.

Jen has succumbed to some wine; first some dessert wine with the tiramisu, then on to some amarone. It transpires that it doesn't take much to make her 'mellow' - mellow enough even to use the opportunity of helping with loading dishes into the dishwasher to get 'close up and personal' with Walnut. Much to Fleece's amusement, she even caresses Walnut's rear as he bends over, cooing a vaguely sexy 'Hmmm' as she does.

Walnut's attempts to discourage this takes things in a new direction.

'So now we're all here for the night, what are we going to do with ourselves?' he asks. 'Trivial Pursuit?'

Jen doesn't look interested anyway, she's only interested in more wine, but Fleece puts his foot down.

'I'm not playing Trivial Pursuit with you, Walnut. Never again after the last time,' he says. 'You knew all the answers.'

'Is that not the idea?' Walnut asks, innocently. However, even he would accept that he's got an exceptional memory for irrelevant facts. It's what makes him such a good lawyer, of course.

'OK, then, how about Monopoly?' Walnut suggests.

'Not a chance,' Fleece insists again. 'My old dad always said, never play money games with a solicitor. So it's one of my rules. Remember I used to be one once.'

Walnut bridles at this slur on his profession, but knows it's intended as a joke. 'You were never a solicitor, Fleece, you failed.'

It's the opening Fleece is waiting for.

'Yes, I failed! I was too honest!' he says, roaring with laughter. Walnut simply rolls his eyes in despair.

Then Zoe says, 'How about a game of cards? Something simple like Racing Demon? Or Switch?'

Once Jen has had the basics of these two games explained to her, she says, 'Actually, I can't really be bothered with silly card games. I do play bridge, but that's more like chess, it's not really a card game if you know what I mean.'

Zoe and Walnut look at each other, then Walnut says, 'Actually, Zoe and I play a lot of bridge. Do you fancy a rubber or two? Fleece, do you remember the rules? I'd play with you, if you want.'

Fleece is having none of it. 'Of course I can play bridge, Walnut, and I resent the insinuation that someone of my abilities can't adapt to the playing style of any partner. Jen and I will play as a team! Won't we Jen?'

'I didn't know you could play bridge, either, Fleece,' Jen says. 'You're going up in my estimation.'

'It's not exactly a typical topic of discussion in the bedroom,' Fleece laughs loudly (he never does it any other way of course). He carries on in a mock romantic voice. 'Picture the scene; the lights are dimmed, the candles are lit, we're in each other's arms. I say to you, 'How do you fancy seven clubs tonight, my love? A grand slam?"

Even Jen finds that amusing. Wine seems to have relaxed her significantly enough to send her into a disconcerting fit of giggles.

Fleece suddenly says, surprisingly seriously, 'I should point out that Jen is red-hot.' Then adds, leeringly, 'At bridge as well.' The serious expression has gone again - it lasted around eight seconds - and has been replaced by his loud guffaw. Jen, meanwhile, is warming up; Fleece's double entendre has her in the giggles again.

Five minutes later, a card table has been found, together with two sets of cards, one with a scene of Holyrood Palace on the reverse, the other with Edinburgh Castle. 'Present from a client,' Walnut says, almost by way of an apology.

'Where are we all sitting?' Zoe asks.

She offers to close the curtains, but Fleece wants to keep an eye on the weather outside, even although it's pitch-black outside. Meanwhile, he's been scanning the room. 'Suppose I sit here' - he picks out the seat nearest the fire, then points across the table to the opposite side - 'and you sit there, Jen.' Jen is now far too gone on the wine to know whether she's sitting on a chair or if it's Tuesday.

'I thought you didn't like the heat, Fleece,' Walnut says. 'That's what you're always telling me, at any rate.'

'Well let's see how I get on here for the moment,' Fleece replies. 'I can always move later.' As Walnut finally sits down to shuffle some cards, Fleece surprises him.

'OK, Walnut, how about making it more interesting?'

'Like how, Fleece?' Walnut knows to be suspicious.

'How about playing for a little side bet? Five pence a point, that sort of thing?'

Zoe intervenes. 'Fleece, I'm not really keen on playing for money.'

'And I don't play cards for money either, Fleece,' Jen slurs from the other side, taking another glug of her red wine.

'OK, Walnut, how about if you and me play their share, too? That'll be ten pence a point?' Walnut looks doubtful, but Fleece presses on. 'Come on, Walnut, are you a man or a mouse?' For good measure he throws in some squeaky mouse-sounds.

'I thought you didn't play money games with a solicitor,' Walnut says.

'This isn't a game,' Fleece explains. 'This is bridge. To the death.' He's trying to maintain his evil piratical grin while laughing at the same time.

Walnut studies the opposition. The opposition in question will be Fleece, who's drunk and isn't very good, and Jen, who might be very good but is so utterly inebriated that she'll struggle to keep her cards hidden. On the other hand, Walnut and Zoe play quite a bit at the Melville Club. Finally - and most importantly - Walnut sees this as an opportunity to pay Fleece back for that time last year when Fleece conned him into playing table football for five pounds a game in an amusement arcade in Leven in Fife. Walnut had to pay a special visit to the Cashline machine to settle his debts afterwards.

'OK, you're on,' he declares. Zoe looks doubtful, but she's too tired to argue. Walnut wants clarification on one or two points beforehand.

'Do you play any conventions, Fleece?' he asks, slyly.

'Conventions?'

'As in, say, Stayman, Weak No Trump, Blackwood, that sort of thing.'

Fleece looks quizzical, then suddenly brightens up. 'Of course, conventions, Walnut. Yes, we observe both the Geneva and the Hague Conventions. In the latter case, even for war criminals like you, Walnut.'

'Be serious, Fleece.'

'The Geneva Convention is a very serious matter, Walnut. As for bridge conventions, Jen and I play Psychic Slams and the Whatever-Comes-Into-My-Head Convention. Is that specific enough?'

'In the second case, fine. There's nothing in your head.' Walnut smiles; Fleece bows to acknowledge a minor point scored by his opponent. Walnut continues: 'But Psychic Slams?'

Fleece pauses for dramatic effect, then narrows his eyes, saying, 'Be afraid, Walnut, be very afraid.'

Walnut shrugs his shoulders. Jen wears a dazed-with-wine look. Zoe simply says, 'I think you should deal, Duncan.'

So the first hand is dealt. Sure enough, Jen drops half her hand onto the floor, although one card gets there via her newly refilled wine glass, so that the ten of hearts is marked for all to see for the rest of the night. Fleece looks completely disinterested; he's looking all round the room.

When it comes to his turn, he announces simply, 'Three spades.'

'Eh?' Walnut wants further clarification. 'Can I remind you of the rules of this game, Fleece? That 'three spades' call means that you and Jen - whose hand you haven't a clue about - expect to take nine of the thirteen tricks available, with spades as trumps?'

Fleece looks at Walnut as though he's something unpleasant he's discovered on the sole of his shoe.

'I think I know the rules, Walnut. Is it not now your turn to bid?'

It's a high opening bid, and neither Zoe nor Walnut can say anything; their hands are too weak. Jen, meanwhile, can say nothing either but that's merely because she is totally out of it with alcohol. Just to be sure, Fleece pushes another large glass in front of her. Five minutes later, Fleece has made the contract - just - and scored enough points to win almost three pounds already.

'Well done, Fleece,' Zoe says, quietly.

'That was impressive,' Walnut laughs. 'Great judgement, I'll give you that.'

They play another two hands, each of which Fleece plays, which means that Jen on each occasion simply sits silently as dummy. In the first of these, Fleece fails to make the contract, but it turns out that he's judged the hand well, as it transpires he's prevented Zoe and Walnut from cashing in on their own good cards. Then Fleece hits the jackpot, bidding a slam outright and making it. He and Jen are miles ahead already which means in turn that Walnut already owes Fleece in excess of twenty pounds. Meanwhile, Jen sits as very silent dummy. Not needed as a player, Fleece ensures she consumes ever more wine.

Zoe and Walnut finally play a couple of hands, and win a few points, but nothing worth talking about. Then, astonishingly, Fleece bids another out-of-nowhere slam bid, six spades, and collects seven hundred points, the equivalent of thirty-five pounds, seventy including Jen's share. Jen, meantime, is contributing as much as El Cid at the end of the film. Walnut is suspicious.

'I've never seen anything like this, Fleece. Tell me about these 'Psychic Slams'.'

'They're my speciality, Walnut,' Fleece replies. 'I have these visions. When I have a vision that I'm going to take a lot of tricks in hearts, I call a big contract in hearts. Simple as that.' He's not laughing either, although his piratical grin is there. Taking money off Walnut is a serious business.

'I don't like it, Fleece,' Walnut growls in reply.

'Lawyers never do when they lose money. Take it like a man, Walnut, take it like a man.'

Walnut studies Fleece, whose face is even redder than usual, and he's sweating profusely.

'Are you all right, Fleece? Why did you choose that seat by the fire?'

'Never better, Walnut, never better.'

Meanwhile, Zoe is studying Jen, whose eyes are all but closed. 'I wonder if Jen perhaps needs to get to bed soon.'

'I think she's all in, Fleece,' Walnut chips in. Jen says nothing; she's all but dead to the world.

Fleece looks across. 'Perhaps. But you're just trying to wriggle out of playing, Walnut, I know your game. Time for one more hand?'

'You're kidding, Fleece,' Walnut replies.

Zoe tries to intervene, 'Fleece, I really think - ' but she's interrupted by Jen as she makes her one significant contribution to the evening's cards, tipping forwards face-first across the table.

Fleece looks at her. 'Is that three no trumps you said, Jen?' He thinks it's funny, but there's serious business to be done as Zoe and Walnut help Jen up, and across the room towards the stairs and the spare bedroom.

'Em,' Fleece says.

'What?' Walnut asks, irritated.

'I make that ninety-two pounds you owe me, Walnut.'

Walnut shakes his head, seemingly in disgust at Fleece's lack of concern for his bed-mate Jen. In reality, though, both men know that Walnut - notoriously tight-fisted - is furious at having to part with money, and to Fleece of all people.

'Look on the bright side, Walnut. I see the weather outside has turned to heavy rain. All the snow will be gone in a few hours.'

With Jen safely in the room, Walnut returns to the waiting Fleece, who isn't taking his leave until he's seen the colour of Walnut's money. It's duly handed over, but Walnut still isn't sure.

'I can't work out what happened there, Fleece. You seemed to know where all the cards were. You're usually rubbish at bridge.'

'I've been practising my Psychic slams!' Fleece roars loudly. He's wallowing in victory, and in new-found wealth.

'You played really well, Fleece,' Zoe says, with rather more grace than her husband. 'Congratulations. But I think you should attend to Jen, don't you?'

'I suppose so.' Fleece gets up and waddles off in the direction of the spare room. Then he turns round, and returns to whisper something quietly in Walnut's ear. Unfortunately, Fleece's whispers carry into the next field, so Zoe can pick up everything.

'Walnut,' Fleece says, hesitantly. 'Walnut…'

'Yes, Fleece, can I get you something else?'

'You couldn't manage a couple of spare condoms, could you?'

Walnut is so shocked he can barely reply. 'Fleece, that's close to rape, the condition she's in.'

'Oh, don't worry, I'll ask first, she'll be fine.' Fleece shifts uneasily. 'Really, my friend, I'm a man of honour.'

'Really?' Walnut replies. It's more of an accusation than a question.

There's a pregnant pause, then a resigned Zoe speaks, her eyes closed throughout, 'Actually, Fleece, you'll find there's a couple in the bedside table.'

*

Zoe and Walnut eventually get to bed twenty minutes later, but it isn't to be a peaceful night's sleep. Within minutes of settling down - they're nowhere near sleep yet because Walnut is still trying to work out how they were so badly beaten at bridge. In addition there are loud peals of laughter and feminine giggles from the room down the corridor.

Suddenly there's an almighty crash, with raised voices and screams. Zoe wants Walnut to go and rescue Jen immediately, but then they both realise that the screams are Fleece's - Jen is not only alive and well, but she is laying into Fleece with all she's got. The racket continues on and off for fully half an hour, and then there's suddenly a new development as the front door slams - very violently - and a car starts up and drives off down the now snow-free driveway of Deer Lodge.

'That can't be Fleece,' Walnut points out to Zoe. 'He can't move that fast.' But he gets up and peers round the door to see what's going on, and by creeping down the hallway, he can see - through a slightly-ajar door - Fleece's back view as a rocks backwards and forwards on the bed. Under normal circumstances, Walnut would go to his friend, but Fleece has just parted him from ninety-two pounds sterling, and so he can be left to suffer till the morning. Returning to Zoe, he speculates that probably Jen woke up just as Fleece was about to do the wicked deed, and came to her senses.

The following morning, the snow has indeed all gone, and there's even a little sunshine, not entirely welcomed by Fleece who descends the stairs in dark glasses.

'Morning, everyone. Had a little much to drink last night, I'm afraid. And I'm afraid your nice spare bedroom needs cleared up a bit. A few things got broken last night. Not by me, I might add.'

Zoe and Walnut are up making a cooked breakfast. Walnut is secretly delighted to hear Fleece is feeling poorly; it's no more than he deserves.

'How's Jen?' Walnut asks. 'Was that her car…?'

'Last night? Yes, I'm afraid so. She's left me, Walnut, she's left me.' Fleece shakes his head in despair. 'She's left me.'

'She's left you, then.'

'Yes, Walnut, she's left me.'

'I think the needle's got stuck here,' Walnut says. Finally managing to move to another sentence in the conversation, he adds, 'I did try to warn you last night, Fleece.' Fleece looks bemused. 'You know, Fleece,… when you asked for the condoms…'

Fleece still looks bemused. Then he twigs. 'Oh, no, Walnut my boy, you don't understand, you don't understand at all. Jen was right up for.., well, she was right up… for it, if you know what I mean. I knew she would be. As soon as I produced those condoms, she was all over me. That wasn't the problem, I'm afraid, not at all.'

'Then what was..?' Both Zoe and Walnut are bewildered.

'Oh, it wasn't the sex. She was angry about the bridge.'

'But you won at bridge,' Zoe says. Then she adds, 'Not that Jen seemed really aware of it at times.'

'So what made her so angry?' Walnut wants to know.

'I was trying to impress her with some pre-coital sweet-talk. And I let it slip about the bridge.'

'Go on.'

'I could see all your hands in the plate-glass windows. You know, the dark outside and so on... perfect mirrors. I thought it was funny.'

'That's why you wanted the fireside seat, Fleece. Is that it?' Walnut says.

Fleece doesn't reply.

'I want my money back, Fleece. You're a cheat.'

'Aw, Walnut, come on. Don't hit a man when he's down.'

'Lie down on the floor so I can give you a good kicking, Fleece. You're no good.   You don't deserve Jen. I'm glad she's left you. I never saw what she saw in you anyway.'

'You don't understand her, Walnut.'

'Doesn't sound like you do either.'

'Yes, I do. You remember our mutual friend Captain called her a cold, stupid talentless bitch?'

Walnut smiles at the memory. 'Captain was biased. Jen was once his boss.'

'He was right, Walnut, he was right.'

Zoe looks shocked. Walnut says, 'You're just saying that because she's left you, Fleece.'

'No, she was a cold, stupid, talentless bitch right enough. But with alcohol in her, she becomes desperate for sex. I was the only man in the world desperate enough to have her. It was a marriage made in heaven - or maybe hell. She wanted me for my body, pure and simple.'

Walnut and Zoe stare at Fleece, or more particularly at Fleece's overweight body.

'It's true.' Fleece nods, 'and now she's left me.'

'Yes, we've done that bit, Fleece. So she didn't approve of your cheating?'

'No. Funny that, isn't it?'

'It will be when I get my money back,' Walnut says. Reluctantly, Fleece passes the money back to Walnut, who counts it carefully and returns it to his wallet.

Fleece turns sadly to Zoe. 'Well, I didn't use up any of your condoms, Zoe. Thanks anyway.'

Zoe studies Fleece, then wanders over to give him a hug. Walnut can't understand, though. The man's a cheat and a crook.

*

On her way back to Edinburgh at half past one in the morning, Jen is clocked at over a hundred miles per hour by a patrolling speed car and pulled over after a car chase. She is breathalysed, and with almost three times the legal limit of alcohol in her bloodstream, she is duly charged and subsequently banned from driving for two years. She is severely reprimanded at work, but retains her post on condition that she joins an Alcoholics Anonymous group.

Fleece never sets eyes on her again.

It's What We Do

C lothilde checked that the pot wasn't sticking. This dish, Henry's favourite – venison stew, served with winter kale and potatoes – had to be perfect. She'd sprung a surprise, too, with a few parsnips, a reminder of her husband's long-ago childhood. Henry had requested that they dispense with any fruit cake – he didn't like it himself and saw no reason to inflict it on anyone else.

The house was candle-lit, a throwback to days when candles were all that would have been available, although nowadays most households had sufficient battery power to see them for a further few weeks yet. Clothilde and Henry's two daughters, their partners and four grandchildren had all arrived, each sombrely dressed in black, shaking hands, exchanging supportive hugs. As Clothilde gazed bleakly from the kitchen window into the night sky, Claire and Stephanie joined her and each put an arm around her. No one spoke.

Henry was reading books to his grandchildren. Sophie, the youngest at four years old, suddenly interrupted things.

'Grandpa, is it true you're going away?'

Henry paused momentarily, the said. 'Yes'.

'Why?' The girl was simply putting into words what everyone else was thinking.

Claire tried to intervene, but Henry raised his hand.

'Because we need to bring the day back, Sophie. You know how the night has lasted for months now? Well, unless I leave, we'll live in darkness for ever, and because we need sunshine and daylight to live, that won't do. Everything will die. We'll die too.'

'So we can't live in the dark?'

'Not for long,' Henry explained. 'Nowadays we have batteries and better stores of food, so we don't have to do this as often as people used to do in the old days. But someone always has to do it eventually before everything runs out.'

Sophie took that in, then continued. 'Why you, Grandpa?'

'Because I'm the oldest. No other reason. I've lived longest.'

'Are you very brave?'

'No, Sophie. I'm not brave. It's just what we do.'

'What happens?' Once again Claire tried to speak. This time Henry just talked over her.

'I go towards the light. After that...? Well, I really don't know. All that happens is that the new day comes soon after.' Henry hadn't really prepared himself for questions from the youngsters, assuming that their parents would have been able to answer them all beforehand. Now he realised that they'd merely been primed not to ask too much at all, and Sophie was too young to understand even that.

Sophie squinted at him. 'You become a day, Grandpa? Sunshine?'

'I suppose so, yes. Although I haven't done it yet, sweet, so I can't be sure.'

This last piece of Grandpa Logic was sufficient to let Clothilde announce that the venison stew was ready, and the family sat down around the table to eat. Henry declared the stew to be 'the best ever', and thrilled with the buttered parsnips. To lighten the moment he told some of his favourite jokes, including one especially child-friendly one involving an elephant, a rabbit and a snake inside an igloo. He even sang a song, surprising everyone by keeping in tune.

Then, around nine, Henry suddenly stood up from the table. 'I think it's time, isn't it?' The others looked shocked but he went on, 'Please let's do it now. It's hard enough as it is.'

They all went outside into the night. As it was every night, the Aurora Contrastis was visible just behind the hill at the end of the path. They all walked together towards it until they reached the little wooden bridge over the stream, where Henry suggested that they stop. They could travel a little further, he said, but it would be less painful here.

Everyone hugged him, told him they loved him; he in return had special words for each one of them. Finally it was Clothilde's turn. Kissing like young lovers, they enjoyed one last, lingering embrace, but they'd agreed earlier that they would say nothing: words were inadequate. After that, it was time to watch Henry make his final journey towards the shimmering Aurora; at the last bend, he paused to look back one last time, but he didn't wave. Then he was gone.

Nothing much happened for the next ten minutes or so as the family quietly made its way back to the house. The men began to ready the children for bed while the women cleared the table – Clothilde wanted to keep busy – and began to do the washing up. Stephanie asked her mum if she had made any plans, but Clothilde said she would do nothing in a hurry. And although she'd had plenty of time to prepare for this moment, Henry's loss had inwardly paralysed her. She couldn't even weep just yet.

At the kitchen sink, the curtains remained open as Clothilde mindlessly washed glasses, cutlery, plates, pans, carefully stacking them to drain. To her left, the Aurora Contrastis continued to flicker – she couldn't see it directly but its effects on the night sky elsewhere were clear enough. She stopped washing for a moment – was it a little brighter, perhaps? Claire and Stephanie came across to look, too.

'I think we should all go outside again,' Clothilde said. 'The kids need to see this, too.'

Outside the cottage door, the nine gazed in the direction of the Contrastis, by now ablaze with colour: blues, yellows, reds, greens and oranges, ribboning rainbows weaving and waving across the sky. They watched as, over the next ten minutes or so, the colours gradually merged into a dazzling light that none of them had seen for months, a ball of fire so bright that eventually none could look directly at it.

'What is it?' asked Sophie.

Clothilde held her hand. 'That's the sun, my darling. The new day has started. It'll be here for a long time now.'

'Did Grandpa do that?'

'Yes, Sophie, Grandpa did that.'

The Shopkeeper

The day it happened, Zubair Mansoor Ali had merely been doing whatever he did day after day: opened up the till, checked the float, set his flowers and a range of vegetables outside in front of his shop. As usual, Zubair had been up since four-thirty in the morning, early even by flower-seller or greengrocer standards, and not because he enjoyed getting up in the dark. In fact, Zubair hated getting up early, but set his alarm for the same time every single day of the year so that it had become automatic and he wouldn't ever have to think how horrible it was.

The bonus of being an early-bird greengrocer was of course that he got the best of the flowers and vegetables at the market. He valued quality over profit, so that his shop's reputation had spread through Edinburgh's chattering middle classes as 'the place to go' for the best flowers, fruit and vegetables. If Zubair didn't have it, then it wasn't worth having. But he had a social conscience, too, and invariably looked for 'specials', in-season items which would be of particularly good value and yet still high quality, which he would give special prominence on the pavement and sold out completely each day by mid-afternoon. That, too, was part of Zubair's plan: encourage those looking for the bargain to come early, and to reinforce the impression that everything in his shop was fresh in each morning.

At the market, Zubair paid fair but not excessive prices for everything he bought, and he was widely respected as a man whose custom was a badge of honour, a quality mark in itself: *Zubair himself is one of my customers*. He used an experienced eye to identify those blooms which had been slightly frosted, or had been over- or under-watered; he valued ripe, flavoursome fruit and vegetables over shape, reasoning that he could sort them himself in his own shop. In addition, Zubair's wife was a skilled cook, not only of north Indian, Kashmiri and Pakistani dishes, but also of European and even American dishes, and Zubair and his family happily dispensed advice on the best way to cook peppers, okra, asparagus, leeks or whatever happened to be in plentiful supply at the time. Zubair and his wife had appeared on several television food programmes, mostly in cameo or expert roles. Once, though, a Scottish Television series called *Making The Most Of The Growing World* had showcased their knowledge of flowers as well as of fruit and vegetables. The series had been too much of a hybrid to succeed, but a book had been published to go along with the series; even now, years later, it continued to sell steadily from Zubair's own shop counter.

Zubair himself, like so many, had arrived from Pakistan in the sixties looking for a better existence than he knew would ever be available just outside Lahore. Life was hard at first. London offered the most job opportunities, but as it also had the most migrants he encountered discrimination on a level he was unprepared for, and friends advised him to go further north where he might be more welcome so long as he was prepared to do jobs no one else wanted to do – the dirty, dangerous jobs. He wasn't afraid, and soon realised that what was regarded as dirty or dangerous in Britain was just 'normal' work in Pakistan. He actually came to Scotland to answer an advert for work on Glasgow's buses, but when that fell through he finally found work in a border woollen mill in Galashiels where he stayed for eight years. Zubair worked hard in the mill, prepared to do work no-one else would take on, and was popular with his fellow workers because he was happy to stop and help them when they had difficulties themselves. But there was another thing that made Zubair popular. From the outset, he had decided that he would live like a British person, a Scot, even, and not like a Pakistani immigrant living in a foreign land. He ate Scottish food, learned how to like haggis and porridge, even drinking a little with his fellow workers. He didn't abandon Islam, but he felt Allah would understand and even approve of his desire to live at peace with his new neighbours. He said prayers in the privacy of his own home, and never discussed religion with anyone. Local people referred to him as a 'darkie' or a 'nig-nog', but Zubair simply shrugged back and said: 'I have a darker skin than you, if I call you 'big man' or 'ginger-hair' then that might also be true.'

In his twenties, Zubair played cricket for the local Galashiels club, who first assumed he was a spin bowler – he wasn't bad, actually – before they discovered that he was actually an excellent left-handed batsman. Reports of his free-flowing innings made all the local newspapers, occasionally even the nationals, but more importantly it took him across Scotland. It was actually through cricket that he met his future wife. Playing one Saturday in Edinburgh, Zubair was out unusually early and, free to wander round the boundary for much of the afternoon, he began talking to an older man called Hamid who himself had come from north India around the time of partition. He, too, was keen on cricket, and the two men struck up such a rapport that Zubair was invited up to eat at the family home a few weeks later. The older man saw Zubair as a possible husband for his daughter. For Zubair, who had begun to wonder how he might find a wife, she was heaven-sent; Kamilah, whose name meant 'perfect', was the woman of his dreams. Hamid approved of Zubair's attempts to integrate, which fitted in with his dreams for his family. He allowed Kamilah to wear jeans and tee-shirts except on special occasions, even allowed Zubair and Kamilah to date for a short while to see if they would be happy.

When eventually the couple married, Hamid – who himself had started up a small clothing business – presented

Zubair with a sizeable dowry, on condition that the young man use the money to move up to Edinburgh and open up some sort of shop himself near Hamid's home in Leith. It was the start of 'Ali's of Broughton Street', just north of the city centre. Throwing themselves into his new venture, he tried selling all sorts of food and drink – Zubair had no reservations about selling alcohol – until eventually he realised that he a natural eye for fruit, vegetables and, especially, flowers. As the decades passed, he bought up the premises next door, and later the shop next to that, allowing first Hamid's son, then his own children, to develop an interest in the business. Kamilah gave him a healthy sex life and four children – three boys and a girl – and over time all four were expected to help in the shop.

Not everything turned out as Zubair had hoped. He'd hoped his daughter Zaina would become a doctor or a lawyer, but although teachers told him she was doing well at school, her exam results weren't good enough to do better than get on a college course. (Kamilah had to persuade him to let the girl go there.) The boys had performed better, each of the two older ones going to university. Hamzah, his firstborn, became an accountant, which Zubair said meant he could 'do the books' for the shop as well. Imran studied physics at Leicester. Always quieter, Imran became more interested in Islam, and more critical of his father and mother's lax ways. He refused to work in a shop that sold alcohol at all, and tried to persuade Zubair to get rid of the off-licensed part of the business. Zubair did, by separating one of the shops from the others and passing it over to Munir, the third son, who showed no interest in school at all but was happy to work hard at anything so long as it involved making money. Munir and Imran fought venomously over the off-licence, but at least Imran had no excuse not to help in Zubair's shop now that the off-licence was separated.

And so the family's destiny became more settled into a pattern. Zubair and Kamilah grew comfortably well-off on the proceeds – too comfortable, Kamilah suggested, pointing to Zubair's growing middle. Zubair could have pointed to Kamilah's own spread, but beneath her dress it showed less and in any case he was too much of a polite British gentleman to say so. Kamilah did try to exercise in the privacy of her own house, but was determined to make sure that no-one other than Zubair knew of her vain – in both senses – attempts to make herself look better.

Of the four children, only Hamzah was married, to a young muslim woman he'd met through work. They had one very young child – not yet a year old – who was Kamilah's pride and joy; even Zubair became a little dewey-eyed when he saw his only grand-daughter. Of their children, Hamzah was the most obviously successful, measured in British terms, with an excellent salary and a professional status, and in fact his accent betrayed little of his parents' Asian background. His younger brother Imran, by contrast, had begun to distance himself a little from his family, working hard – studying, too, for he was following a part-time doctorate researching battery technology – and ever more frequently airing his personal concerns that his parents, siblings, and now even his niece were all being corrupted by an unclean western infidel society. Zubair actually wondered at one point if Imran was being radicalised, but both Hamzah and Munir assured him that Imran was all talk and simply posturing.

All of the family had experienced some degree of racism in their lives – which ethnic minorities don't? – but Zubair had always tried to teach his children that the best way to deal with abuse is to ignore it, and to remember that people in his own homeland of Pakistan could also be cruel to immigrants. He'd had a couple of problems with drunken abusive louts, but given that all shopkeepers in the area suffered that in an area so close to the city centre, he'd got off lightly. Zubair occasionally spoke of what he would do if someone ever came in to try to rob his till, take no nonsense, show them the door, that sort of stuff, but his sixty-three years of life had in truth been pretty gentle.

Which made it all the more shocking when, late one afternoon when he was beginning to think of shutting up shop for the day, five thugs with balaclavas burst into Ali's of Broughton Street and started to tip up all his produce, throw it all over the floor, and kick in the glass in his display cabinets at the counter.

As they did so, they shouted slogans Zubair had heard plenty of times before and on all previous occasions shrugged off: 'Paki scum', 'filthy nigger', 'back to your own country' and even 'terrorist'. A couple of them had knives, the rest had hammers.

Zubair, however didn't shrug it off this time. Something snapped.

Every day of his shopkeeping life, he'd kept an iron bar, a heavyweight crowbar which he'd once found on a building site and had actually occasionally been a useful repair tool in the woollen mills. Now, though, he kept it hidden for use in self-defence. Instinctively, Zubair ran round to the door so that he was between the marauding intruders and their only route of escape; they didn't realise their peril until it was too late. Fired with righteous anger that his honour and property had been so impugned, Zubair began swinging his iron bar, smashing forearms, backs, and, when the opportunity arose, their heads. The tightness of the shop meant that they couldn't take him on more than one at a time and their hammers and knives were no match for this whirling, crushing, cudgel of steel. One by one they fell, cowering and simpering on the floor, whereupon Zubair decided to go one step further to teach them each a lesson. Raising his crowbar above his head, he smashed it once more onto the heads of each in turn. Finally he stopped and called the police. He didn't even call 999, just that 101 number used for non-emergency calls.

Five police cars arrived inside two minutes, at around the same time as four ambulances. Three of the intruders – members of a known teenage gang of hooligans, some were, had been still at school – were pronounced dead at the scene. The remaining two were in a very bad way, and were only taken to Edinburgh Royal Infirmary after extensive emergency treatment from paramedics and doctors. One, the only conscious one, appeared to have a suspected broken neck, the other multiple fractures and severe head injuries. The police took a statement from Zubair then to his dismay formally arrested him in connection with the deaths of three men. Of course he didn't understand it – he insisted he was acting only in self-defence – and neither did almost anyone else in his family: Munir thought his father was quite right, should have hit them harder, Imran thought his father's arrest was an affront to Islam; and Kamilah was simply distraught. Only Hamzah understood both why his father had done it, and why he shouldn't have done it.

The community was split by the case. The boys were local, and some saw them in terms of young lives tragically cut short, while others sympathised with Zubair, a victim of racist thuggery and violent attack who simply gave back what the lads deserved. But the process of law looked bleak for Zubair from the outset. He was charged with three counts of murder – although later he was persuaded that it was in his interest to plead guilty to three counts of culpable homicide – and two more of grievous bodily harm, and was sentenced to nine years in Saughton Prison. When he emerged just over three years later on licence, Zubair was a broken man. Kamilah was taken in by Hamzah and his wife, where she lived a meek existence as a nanny for their expanding family. Imran disappeared, possibly to Pakistan, although he was rumoured to be in both Somalia and Yemen at different times. He changed his name and grew a long beard, so that even if he had returned to his family, he would barely have been recognised. The security services were aware that his knowledge of physics was being put to good use.

To his credit, Munir made a decent job of trying to get the shop up and running again, but it was just too much for him and eventually he sold the premises for a Sainsbury's Local. The business was toxic anyway. In the meantime, Kamilah developed type-two diabetes, and found it hard to cope alone with the dietary restrictions. But the biggest problem for the family was that the robbers' families had seen their balaclava-clad relations as the victims in the incident, and made it clear that revenge would follow in due course for Zubair's 'assault', especially since a group of prisoners and prison officers inside Saughton Prison had made it their business to protect Zubair himself. But in the outside world, Edinburgh simply became an unsafe place for any of the Ali family to live. In the two years that Munir ran the shop, bricks were thrown four times through the shop window, all with messages attached along the lines of 'next time we'll come for you, not the window'.

Hamzah's solution was typically practical. Taking on the role of temporary head of the family, he found a new, much higher-paid job in the City of London, and moved not only his own family but his extended one. When Zubair was eventually released, it was to the quiet suburb of Harrow, where he and Kamilah lived their remaining years in a small flat attached to Hamzah's large villa. Zaina went to Pakistan where she was found a good husband who owned a car-sales franchise in Yorkshire; Munir expanded his college education to some basic book-keeping and with Hamzah's help established a corner shop near Harrow as well.

It wasn't a long retirement. Ten months later, Zubair went to his doctor with abdominal pains; within four months he was dead, of colorectal cancer, having ignored for far too long symptoms he'd first noticed while in prison. He was embarrassed enough about his life without having to discuss further such humiliations. It's reasonable to say that Zubair Mansoor Ali, a man who did so much to be proud of in his life, died in shame, and of shame.

How sorry should we feel for Zubair? Sad as his story sounds, Zubair turned out to be fortunate, fortunate indeed in that he died before he could discover that his former son Imran had changed his name to Abdul-Haq Saajid Sayf Udeen, founder of the Spirit of Allah, and responsible for fourteen suicide bombs in Kenya, Nigeria, Morocco and the Middle East, and killing a total of over a thousand innocent people. Then Zubair would have felt more ashamed than ever, and more than ever would Zubair himself have been a true victim.

Squeak

'**Squeak' Sinclair looked** at his handiwork with considerable satisfaction. A range of test-tubes, beakers, magnifying glasses and a microscope sat on his laboratory bench surrounding a small yellow glutinous mass on a smallish square piece of glass. Delicately, he lifted it high enough to view it from below; yes, yes, as it should be. Replacing it on the table, he measured its diameter again - a perfect two point eight centimetres - and its height, seven millimetres. He tipped it slightly one way then the other, and it retained its shape without appearing entirely solid. He glanced at his watch - nine sixteen. Everyone else in the lab had gone home, of course, which was why Squeak was here in the first place, working by himself on his pet project in the research laboratory of Maddison's Dairy. A mere technician, he could only do what others told him to do in office hours, but it amused them all - most importantly, it amused Phil Walker, who headed the laboratory - to allow Squeak to do his own thing in his own time, even using the lab equipment so long as it was left in perfect condition for the next morning. Which Squeak was careful to ensure it was without fail, often giving other unused kit some tender loving care until late in the night.

They wouldn't be laughing at him any more. His pals down at the pub wouldn't be laughing. Jocksy and the Gang at the bowling club wouldn't be laughing. Those lab colleagues wouldn't be laughing. No sir, no chance, not this time, the laugh was on them.

Squeak wasn't his real name, of course. No sane parent would ever call their son 'Squeak'. But then no sane parent would ever call their son Paul Innocent Leo Eugene Sinclair, except that Squeak's parents were devout Catholics and wanted to celebrate their's son's arrival by naming him after a succession of popes ancient and modern. Most of the way through Our Sacred Mother's Primary School, Squeak succeeded in being called Paul (apart from the usual infantile 'smelly' names) but then around primary six it suddenly dawned on wee Danny Glancy that Squeak's name formed a perfect acronym for haemorrhoids. For the next three or four years Squeak's life was to be pure hell as one child after another called him scatological names that they'd found from looking up dictionaries and encyclopaedias. It wasn't really the boys who bothered him the most, although all the fights he had at school were with other boys. The girls were more mature - they always are at that age - but when they chose to stick the knife into him, they could reduce Squeak to tears; then some would confound him still further by comforting him. In turn this led to more pain when these same sisters of mercy decided that it was their turn to have a little fun at his expense. The final straw came in second year when Squeak found out that Mary McGuinness - a busty blonde who had once consoled Squeak by letting him feel her rapidly-developing breasts behind the school kitchen - had actually created a Christmas quiz in which every answer was a part of the human digestive system, and there were five bonus points for spelling 'haemorrhoids' correctly. Shortly after that Squeak began to wonder (a) if girls were really for him and (b) would he ever again get the chance to find out anyway?

In the summer holidays around the beginning of third year Squeak became ill with a mysterious illness which was widely assumed to be some form of mumps. Ordered by his mother to take to his bed, Squeak spent all day watching all sorts of old videotapes of films from the local video library, along with Jocksy Wallace, an on-and-off sort of friend whose older brother worked in the local Blockbuster. Jocksy would therefore come armed with three movies, two of which came directly from the Blockbuster top shelf and one football-related tape which could be put on shortly before Squeak's mum came home from work. There was no real incentive to get up, so when he eventually arose from his sick-bed, everyone was astounded to see that he seemed to have shot up by three inches in height. Also - and it was widely rumoured at school that the poor invalid's mumps were to blame for this misfortune - his voice resolutely refused to break. Almost immediately, he acquired a new nickname, 'Squeak', which to a poor adolescent lad's ears sounded immeasurably better than the horrors he'd endured for four full years. So Paul Sinclair decided to make the best of it and simply became 'Squeak' Sinclair instead. And there were other benefits. One February after school, Mary McGuinness and Donna Shaw asked if was really true that Squeak had no testicles (an entirely reasonable question in the circumstances). Squeak negotiated a trade-off where all three went back to his (as usual) empty house where all three then removed their clothes for mutual study. So in the end it all worked out rather well.

In fact, the close study of these two human bodies triggered a lifelong interest in science, and biology in particular. It immediately became his favourite subject at school, closely followed by chemistry, although an intelligent English teacher briefly managed to seduce him to literature with science fiction - Bradbury, Asimov, even Mary Shelley's *Frankenstein*. Squeak was especially fascinated by artificial and alien life. Mrs Owen, his Higher Biology teacher, realised quite early on that Squeak was no Einstein - a bit lazier than Einstein, too - but played little games with him at her 'Biology Homework Club' on Tuesdays and Thursdays after school. If Squeak did all his homework for her on time, she would do some other little extra biology experiments with him, dissecting a sheep's eye, watch a pregnant gerbil give birth, studying a spider making short work of some aphids. Occasionally Squeak's classmates would tease him, suggesting that he 'fancied' Mrs Owen, more particularly that he fancied her 'decent-sized tits', but they were wrong. Mrs Owen - a woman in her early thirties, no more - was indeed far more attractive than a teacher had any right to be, but Squeak didn't fancy her, he loved her, or more accurately he loved what she taught him. When Squeak got a B pass in his Higher Biology that summer, she rewarded his sixth year with a class visit to the Roslin Institute where Dolly the Sheep had first been cloned from Something Else the Sheep. It was there that he first asked the question that was to set the agenda for the rest of his life.

'Miss?'

'Yes, Squeak?' Even his teachers - the ones he respected at least - called him Squeak.

'Why does an egg become a chicken?'

Mrs Owen chuckled. 'Is this the start of an old joke, Squeak, or have you just got the punchline wrong?'

Now it was Squeak's turn to chuckle.

'No, I mean it. How come something that looks runny and yellow turns into something that has wings?' Seeing her blank look, he went on. 'I mean, why doesn't it just stay yellow and runny?' then, pointing across to a sheep, 'or why doesn't it turn into Dolly the Sheep there?'

'Easy bit first, Squeak. That's not Dolly the Sheep.'

'Answer the hard part.'

'I don't know,' Mrs Owen replied. 'Be thankful I'm not religious or I'd have said God did it.' This was why she adored teaching as a job - you never knew what question you'd be asked next.

'Yellow egg yolk becomes chicken with wings. God got those bits of the jigsaw a bit mixed up, eh?'

'In defence of God - ' she began.

'You're not going to defend God are you now, Miss? Not after all these years?'

'In defence of God, the chicken eventually manages to come up with a few more runny egg yolks.'

'Some trick,' Squeak said, and left it at that.

Somehow or other, Squeak Sinclair's limited school qualifications found him a place at Edinburgh's Napier University on a Biological Sciences degree. It wasn't an unqualified success - there was a lot of stuff about disease he couldn't be bothered with - but after four years he just about emerged with a piece of paper that suggested he knew something about biology. Not that it made much difference; his first job was in a call centre for Tesco Bank. By the time he managed to start even getting interviews for science-related jobs, his qualification was already eight months cold, but eventually he landed a technician job in Maddison Dairy's research laboratory. And far from taking part in cutting-edge science, Squeak's rôle in developing long-life bio yoghurt amounted to ensuring that all equipment was clean, that materials and chemicals were on hand every morning, and that plentiful supplies of tea and coffee were on hand for all the staff.

Still, it paid the bills. And despite a high-pitched voice and premature baldness that, even at twenty-six years old, made Squeak look like a white-coated bank manager, he had enough interpersonal skills to become a popular member of the team. Women in particular wanted to care for him. They brought him cakes and scones, suggested ideas to help his image, and of course asked him about his love life - by which they really meant his non-existent sex life. At the age of twenty-three, Squeak eventually lost his virginity shortly after leaving the lab Christmas Party with Doreen MacDonald, a forty-two-year-old divorcee who absolutely insisted on teaching him all she knew - which turned out to be a fair amount, as it happened. And not content with that gift, Doreen then let it be known around the lab that Squeak was a sensational lover, which she then discreetly tried to ensure would be true during a series of clandestine training sessions with him in her Dalry flat.

One Sunday afternoon, while Squeak lay exhausted beside Doreen, she asked him what he most wanted out of life. In the circumstances, others might have suggested something more romantic, but the first answer that popped into his head was the truth: he wanted to develop something special, specifically, he wanted to develop the perfect easy-cook egg. He'd love to have the freedom of the lab to be able to try. Doreen was still interested in sex, though, and she made the mistake of offering to use her influence with 'Dr Phil' - usually known as 'PhD', of course - if Squeak could manage to make her have three climaxes in the space of fifteen minutes. She set her iPhone alarm to count down the time, and lay back to see what would happen. What happened was that Doreen was actually midway through round five as 'Marimba' sounded, and accordingly Squeak demanded his full prize. What was more, he made it clear that if Doreen didn't deliver on her side of the bargain, he would spread the word all round the lab about the sort of woman she was. Round about that point, Doreen MacDonald realised that Squeak was not a man to be messed with; the sessions stopped.

However, Doreen came up with the goods. She was able to 'use her influence' with Phil because she happened to be his Personal Assistant; also because she was prepared to use exactly the same charms on Dr Phil Walker as she'd used on Squeak. And him a married man, too, with three children.

As a result of this erotic blackmail chain, Phil Walker felt obliged to call Squeak in for a quiet chat about his research ambitions. It was agreed that so long as any research was done out of hours, that Squeak made sure his work didn't suffer, and that everything was left 'squeaky-clean' afterwards (Phil really did use those words), he could have the run of the lab in the evenings. In turn, Squeak explained what his aim was: to create the easy-cook egg.

'Em, are eggs not quite easy to cook already, Squeak?' Phil wondered.

'Clearly you don't do much cooking, Phil.'

'Martha does most of the cooking in our house. I can do cook-chill in a microwave, though.'

'When did you last boil an egg?' Squeak asked.

Phil considered this for a moment. 'A while ago, right enough. I did egg and toast soldiers for our youngest a year or so ago. Does that count?'

'That counts. What was the egg like?'

'Now that you mention, hard as a rock. Wee Mark launched a complaints procedure. Screamed like fuck.'

'And after all the work you put into boiling the water in a pan, pricking the egg so it wouldn't burst, timing it, and then burning your fingers on the bloody thing as you manoeuvred it into an egg cup.'

Phil smiled. 'Next time I'll use oven gloves.'

'Don't bother. You'll drop the egg and end up cleaning the floor and fielding a starving child all at the same time,' Squeak said. 'Don't you think it would be good if someone developed the easy-cook egg?'

'Just for a boiled egg? Get a grip, Squeak.'

'Not just a boiled egg - fried eggs, too, omelettes, and the prince of eggs - the poached egg.'

'Ah,' Phil said, 'I'm a sucker for a good poached egg. Sadly, Martha hasn't quite mastered the art yet.'

Squeak laughed. 'I hope you haven't made the mistake of telling her that.'

'Don't be silly. She'd just tell me to make my own poached eggs.'

Squeak sat back smugly. 'Which is where I come in. Poached eggs so simple that even you can make them.'

'Even me?' Phil said, screwing his eyes into slits to look at Squeak. 'Even me? Cheeky bugger.'

'And while we're at it,' Squeak said, 'do you know anyone who actually likes the egg white in an egg more than egg yolk? We could lose the egg white.'

Phil shook his head. 'What am I agreeing to here? I'm allowing one of my technicians to try to develop an egg with no white, one that pretty well cooks itself perfectly in a number of styles, in my dairy lab?'

'That's about the size of it,' Squeak said quietly. As he held Phil's gaze, he knew that Doreen's dalliance with the head of research was working its powers.

'Well, I suppose so,' Phil said.

That was it, a done deal. And Squeak, determined to make the most of it, launched himself into an out-of-hours programme that bordered on the obsessive. Five nights a week, and often all day Saturday or Sunday as well, he set about his task. From the outset, he decided that there were two separate problems to overcome: the 'egg' itself, and the means of cooking it. Working in an 'industrial' dairy environment, he realised that his 'egg' might actually only be distantly related to the the things found packaged in grey cardboard boxes in supermarkets; more specifically, his egg was likely to work best if it were dried and reconstituted immediately prior to the cooking. Having made the decision to dispense with any sort of egg white, he then discovered that he needed to create some sort of artificial amniotic membranes to retain everything, and he could do this best by drying out a tiny amount of super-whipped whites into thin hollow egg-shaped containers. Later, this would offer a further advantage - he could add more of the egg white for 'easy-cook' fried and poached eggs.

Then it was just down to establishing the right quantities of everything. It turned out that there was a fair amount of latitude here, but Squeak was a perfectionist and he wanted to develop the perfect egg. In addition, he decided that the addition of salt and even a little white pepper made his mixes stand out over conventional eggs. And he experimented with other flavours, too: cheese and onion, paprika, and his personal favourite, jalapeño chilli. (He could see this last being of limited appeal to three-year-olds, however.) And it was his conscious decision to add monosodium glutamate to his eggs to make them more addictive.

Such was Squeak's progress that he was soon able to turn his mind to the other part of the project, the cooking system. Luckily, he had an idea for this, too. Recalling those widgets that make a can of beer or a pre-made gin and tonic suddenly go very cold, he sought a widget that gave off heat instead, and eventually managed to create something with materials that, in larger quantities, would create a bomb that Al-Quaida would be proud of. (Squeak actually had a visit from the Anti-Terrorism Squad one day when they picked up what he'd been ordering online. It was probably the one awkward moment in the entire three-year project, but Phil Walker was able to reassure the two policemen that Squeak was harmless.)

It took longer to create the actual widget, and by the time he'd added it to the rest of the container, the 'egg' was now just short of twice the size of a large hen's egg. Squeak felt it needed testing on a wider public to see if it worked, so one evening he marched down to Tanfield Bowl Club with a range of these new 'egg' containers - their contents remained top secret - to see if they stood up to the test of being handled by Jocksy Dougan, Bert Ronson and the others. Jocksy, now transformed into a grossly overweight beer-swilling chain-smoker, destroyed the first one straight away by picking it up to roughly and crushing it in his hand.

Seeing the disappointment on Squeak's face, Jocksy spread his arms wide and simply said, 'Aw, come on, Squeak,' - actually, he pronounced it 'cam oh-an' - 'if it canny stand up tae up ma gentle mitts, it's nae fuckin' use whaat-sae-ever.' He pronounced the last word in three distinct portions.

Bert Ronson was a thin, bearded Mancunian who thought he had a good sense of humour but actually had none.

'Perhaps you were a bit brutal, Jocksy. This is just a prototype, isn't it, Squeak?'

Squeak had a bag of forty of them, but kept quiet about them for the moment.

'No, Bert, Jocksy's right. That's why I wanted to test them out. They need to work for everyone.'

'Even a clumsy bugger like Jocksy,' Janet Wood called from behind the bar. 'Are ye goin' tae ask him tae sit oan wan, tae?'

Jocksy glowered. Bert thought a smile should be safe, although in fact he couldn't understand a word of Jocksy's accent when he was in full flow after four pints of Belhaven Best. 'Have you got any others, Squeak?'

Squeak smiled smugly. 'One or two,' he replied. 'Do you want to try one?'

'What do they do?' Bert asked, curiosity stirred.

'Oh… different things.' Squeak reached into the large John Lewis plastic carrier bag he'd brought with him and passed a few out to a rapidly growing audience. 'You fill the wee container with whatever you want,' he explained, 'then tap the egg thingy hard on the counter. They're colour-coded. Some of the eggs heat what you put in it, some boil in water, some make the contents go very cold.'

'Can I try it out?' Bert asked.

'That's why I brought them along. You're guinea pigs.'

Bert asked Janet for some water, unscrewed the lid of a cup with a yellow label, and filled it. 'I just hit the base on the bar counter here, Squeak? Yes?'

'That's it.'

Bert hesitated, then tried it. There was a clear pop, then a fizzing sound inside the egg, then Bert quickly laid the egg on the counter.

'Hey, that's hot,' he said, surprised but impressed.

'That one's supposed to boil its contents,' Squeak explained. 'Others do different things.

Janet took one with a blue label, filled it with water and smacked the base hard against the bar. 'Oh that's cold!' she said. 'Very good, Squeak, I'm impressed.'

Big Gordy Robertson - as tall as Squeak but with a girth to match - tried one with a green label, which heated more slowly than the yellow one Bert had tried. 'The green one's got two compartments, I see, Squeak,' he said. 'Any reason for that?'

'They might all end up like that, Big Gordy. You can put different things in the different compartments and they all mix up when the egg pops.'

'Do I get a shot?' Jocksy asked, which was met with a resounding chorus mix of 'After the last time?' and 'Dinna let that clumsy bugger near them, Squeak.'

But Jocksy wouldn't be denied. He spotted a red-labelled one in the John Lewis bag and held it up. 'I want tae dae this yin,' he announced, unscrewing it. And before Squeak could stop him, he'd persuaded Janet to fill it with Irn Bru from the draught tap behind the bar and resumed his customary seat on the stool at the corner of the bar.

'Jocksy, don't fill it with a fizzy...' Squeak called out, but it was too late. Jocksy had hammered the egg against the counter. At first nothing happened. Then suddenly there was a rumbling noise as the egg exploded, spraying hot Irn Bru all over the bar, the tartan carpet, and over Jocksy's face.

Jocksy reacted entirely predictably. 'Yah… yah… yah fuckin' bastard, Squeak! Yah fuckin', fuckin' bastard!'

'I tried to warn you, Jocksy.'

'Yer a fuckin' menace, Squeak. Ye shouldny be allowed!'

Fortunately, Jocksy wore thick glasses and so nothing got into his eye, but his face was scalded in a couple of places. Janet came round and mopped him, and her tender ministrations seemed to calm him down.

'You would insist on the Irn Bru, Jocksy,' she reminded him quietly. 'I did warn you. Squeak tried to as well.'

'The red-labelled one is extra-powerful, Jocksy,' Squeak explained.

'What are you going to do with these things, anyway, Squeak?' Bert asked. 'I'm curious.'

'Cook with them,' Squeak replied. 'Cook eggs with them, to be precise.' And everyone laughed at him - well, everyone except Jocksy, who looked likelier to kill him instead.

It was Big Gordy who said it. 'I don't think Jocksy quite gets the yolk, Squeak!' he yelled, and he was right - everyone got the yolk except Jocksy. Squeak got the yolk all right but just smiled; he was having a Eureka moment. Now his invention had a brand-name.

Squeak had work outside the lab, to do, too. Maddison's Dairy employed a part-time patents expert, a serious but friendly whizz-kid from near Wolverhampton, called

Simon Denton, and Squeak realised that he needed Simon's advice. Fortunately, Simon was fond of the odd pub-crawl, especially at someone else's expense, and one Thursday night Squeak met him for a pizza in Caffe Torino followed by a joint stagger along Rose Street. Plying Simon with his third pint of the night in Milne's Bar, Squeak finally came clean.

'Simon, I need some advice.'

Simon was already a little the worse for wear. 'Shure, Shqueak, what... what cannI do for you?'

'I want you to help me patent something.'

Simon rocked back in his seat, which fortunately was fixed to the wall.

'Patent shomething?'

'Isn't that your job?'

'Shpose so.'

'Well? Can you patent something for me?' Squeak found it irritating when these English wimps couldn't hold their beer as well as him.

'Shpose so... Patent what?' Simon was about to wait for an answer, then suddenly he said, 'I've got it! This your egg project, isn't it? Don't tell me you've actually made something?' Simon found the very thought quite sobering. 'I suppose I can help you, yes. What's it called?'

So almost a year to the day after the exploding Irn Bru egg incident, and just seven weeks after discovering the perfect round artificial egg, Squeak created the prototype Yolky-

Doky, the world's first self-boiling egg. It wasn't hard to interest large processed food manufacturers; once they saw the prototypes working, they couldn't get enough of them, and a bidding war to buy the patents ensued. Squeak negotiated a five-figure sum from Terroir Foods International for the self-boiling egg, but it turned out he had a business acumen to match his expertise in food chemistry. He held back many of his secretly-patented variations and further inventions until Terroir had started making significant profits - it only took eighteen months, in fact - then slowly he started to offer a trickle of other possibilities. First came the Fried Yolky-Doky, then a few months later the long-awaited Poachy-Doky, with its stunning possibilities within the catering industry. Terroir - terrified that they'd lose control of the market - were prepared to pay telephone numbers for these two.

With the money he received for Boiled Egg Yolky-Doky and Fried Yolky-Doky, Squeak took out a lease on a small piece of lab space of his own and hired a couple of staff. Surprisingly, he himself carried on working in Maddison's Dairy for a while - first full time, then three days a week - because being a cautious type he wasn't sure he wanted to cut his ties once and for all until he could be sure that Yolky-Doky would deliver genuine security. He needn't have worried. Once Terroir's Chief Executive Maxwell Groves saw his first Poachy-Doky in action, he ordered an immediate worldwide advertising campaign to be launched.

Breakfasts would never be the same again, the campaign insisted. Children now went to school well-fed on a cooked breakfast of boiled, fried or - the healthy option - poached egg. Their parents headed for the gym either having cooked one themselves, or they had egg and cappuccino afterwards in the cafeteria, both dispensed from a machine. Pensioners stocked up on an easy supply of ready-to cook warm food. That winter, the lunch of fashion was a Fried Yolky-Doky roll. A ridiculously successful TV advertising campaign featured Squeak himself, proudly demonstrating Yolky-Dokys of various sorts, while in the background nineteen-fifties-style singing sisters trotted out one of those irritating jingles that simply refuse to leave your head.

Squeak, meantime was still busy. The following spring he finally left Maddison's Dairy and retreated into his own new lab to experiment with different flavours. Not all of them worked - salt and vinegar Yolky-Doky was a disaster - but cheese, cheese and chilli, and a strange anchovy version all worked really well. These were top secret, so his test panel were brought into the shiny new Sinclair Sciences lab in Sighthill. Picture the scene one evening...

'Good of you to come, everyone,' Squeak said.

'Nae bother, big man, nae bother. Anything for ma old pal Squeak,' Jocksy answered. 'Where za booze?'

Squeak stood before a 'focus group' of fifteen of Tanfield Bowling Club's worthiest members, who had been invited to come, along with partners. In addition the Tanfield junior team had been asked along to lower the average of those present by twenty-five years.

'You all know what tonight's meeting is all about. I need your feedback on some new flavours for Yolky-Doky.'

Big Gordy rolled back in his seat; twenty stones of pure blubber rotated. 'Flavours, Squeak? You don't think think this is getting a bit silly now?'

'Not at all, Big Gordy. In industry you have to keep moving forward to stand still.'

Bert Ronson nodded agreement. 'It's like a treadmill, Gordy. I've got one at home, I should know.'

Aware that any discussion between these half-wits would distract everyone, Squeak nipped it in the bud immediately. 'We're testing eggs here, everyone, not treadmills,' he said firmly, to approving nods from all. In the kingdom of the bowling club, Squeak was now a man of substance, a hard-nosed businessman not to be tangled with. 'We have six flavours here,' he announced, 'cheese, cheese and chilli, smoked salmon, super-anchovy, smoked pancetta - '

'Smoked pancetta?' Jocksy yelled. 'What's wrong with old fashioned 'smoky bacon'?'

'You said it yourself, Jocksy, it's old-fashioned. Anyway - smoked pancetta and Marmite.'

A grumble came from one of the juniors at the back: 'I so hate Marmite.'

'And what on earth is 'super-anchovy'?' another voice asked.

Squeak ploughed on. 'Super-anchovy is a mix of anchovies and mackerel. The mackerel makes it cheaper. Anyway, we're not telling you what flavour's what - they're just numbered A to F - '

'They're letters.'

'- lettered A to F, and we'd like you to rate each, tell us what you think they all taste of, and any other comments - too salty, too sweet, that sort of thing. Good things, too.'

So the thirty-odd present spent the next hour discussing different flavours of Yolky-Doky. Squeak was astounded to discover that the taste-buds of the assembled group were so poorly honed that less than a quarter detected any bacon flavour in the pancetta version, and almost everyone thought the super-anchovy not only tasted better than smoked salmon, but actually *was* the smoked salmon. It was an important commercial discovery - the anchovy/mackerel mix cost less than a third of smoked salmon to make. Meanwhile everyone hated the Marmite flavour, even the four Marmite fanatics present, which suited Squeak fine, because he'd been concerned about the cost of licensing the name anyway.

It was also an important commercial discovery for Squeak personally. Armed with a whole new set of flavours to offer Terroir, he only agreed to sell the new ones for a forty-percent share of the entire firm. Using the money he'd kept in reserve from his initial Terroir windfall, he quietly acquired more shares until he owned more than two-thirds.

*

Within weeks cheese, cheese and chilli and super-anchovy were all on the market, to which 'salt and vinegar' was added at the insistence of his brand new marketing department. The entire team (one) was 'redeployed' to production within a month. (One of Squeak's strengths as an employer was that he tried not to sack people, although in this case the poor fellow was so ashamed that he resigned shortly afterwards and went to work at a council recycling centre.) The vinegar blip apart, Yolky-Doky was going from strength to strength. Squeak started to be interviewed on chat shows, first on Daytime TV, then in a strange business-style quiz game where he was the 'studio expert'. Appearances on the cover of magazines began: first the colour supplements, then the Big Issue, then eventually Business Insider, Fortune, and even Time, which picked him out as its 'Entrepreneur of the Year'. The New Year Honours List brought an MBE for 'services to industry'. And all before the age of thirty.

Now in total control of Terroir, he renamed it simply 'Yolky-Doky Foods', dissolved its marketing department and embarked on a marketing plan of his own. Surprising many insiders in the food manufacturing and retail sector, he started to create his own advertisements, first in newspapers and magazines, but then graduating through radio to television and cinema adverts. His experimental radio work was a revelation. Squeak learned that the first principle of advertising is to drive the listener mad with a jingle that simple won't leave the mind - which meant it probably had to be mindless, irritating, or both. Basing his ideas on jingles he'd heard for a vicious fifties American brand of cigarette, he wrote a little song which simply repeated

Yolky-doky, yolky-doky, every single day,
Yolky-Doky, Yolky-Doky, A-OK!

Irritating, empty, pointless, American-style nonsense - Squeak knew it was perfect, and if repeated often enough would eventually enter the national psyche ('Hitler tried the same trick and almost conquered the world,' he would joke). He found a girl-band that imitated the sound of the Andrews Sisters of the 1950s. Later, the girl-band covered the song themselves, with different words. Of course, Squeak's secret was as ever his careful market research: the bowling club. Indeed, Bert Ronson probably deserves some credit for encouraging Squeak to stay true to his 'one jingle only' strategy, because even he wasn't sure that the public could stomach it. But Bert was right, and the jingle's place in national culture was finally sealed when minor royals - Prince Martin of Sheffield and his bride to be - bizarrely chose an organ arrangement of it for their anthem as they left Coventry Cathedral. The Queen was not amused, but the Duke of Edinburgh was seen tapping a walking stick to it.

*

Then it happened. One night over a bottle of red wine while listening to Mike Oldfield's *Tubular Bells*, Phil Walker finally told his wife Martha about his 'peccadillos' with Doreen MacDonald. Martha shook her head in despair.

'I've been waiting years for you to confess, Phil.'

'You've known all along?'

'There are some things it's pretty easy to spot. She wore cheap perfume - and that's how I know it was a very short-term affair - I suddenly stopped smelling the stuff on your clothes. What did she get out of it?'

'Something strange,' Phil said. He explained that Squeak appeared to have some hold over her.

Martha's jaw dropped. 'That big guy with the squeaky voice who went from your lab to start up that Yolky-Doky thing? What did she see in…' She hesitated, then added, 'But then she saw something in you, didn't she?' But Martha wasn't stupid. Forgive him, and Phil would be like putty in her hands, now and for evermore. Picking up the remainder of the bottle of wine, she led Phil straight to bed, and - just at the key moment - made two demands. First, find an excuse to sack Doreen MacDonald; second, point out to Maddison's that Yolky-Doky had actually been developed in their laboratories by one of their own staff.

A week later, Squeak received a letter from a firm of London solicitors claiming that because Yolky-Doky had been developed on their premises - albeit at night and with the agreement of Phil Walker - all patents rightfully belonged to Maddison's Dairy. What was more, Yolky-Doky's own solicitors reckoned that there was a good chance that Maddison's case could be very strong, and advised him that he - or was it Yolky-Doky, they seemed interchangeable? - should settle. This brought the world of high finance into the dark corridors of the bowling club.

'Aye, Squeak, yer in the the brown sticky stuff this time. Ah telt ye's!' - Jocksy, of course.

'Now, now, Jocksy,' Bert said, his quiet smiling countenance just the same as ever, 'there's no need for that.'

'Dinnae yes speak tae me like that, Ronson.' Calling Bert 'Ronson' was a sure indicator of Jocksy's growing irritation; even Squeak sometimes coped better with Jocksy's moronic utterances than he did when Bert started to patronise everyone. Nothing a good punch in the nose couldn't deal with, however. Bert got the message.

With the stage to himself, Jocksy pulled himself together and decided to let Squeak have it with both barrels.

'Ah read it in the Sun,' he said. 'I might not have spotted it but it wuz oan the page right ower frae that photo o'the bird wi' the big tits. D'yae ken the lassie ah mean, Squeak?'

Squeak swallowed. 'No, Jocksy, I haven't seen the page three girl today. I'll just have to take your word for it.'

'Oh - ah can dae better than yon, Squeak!' Jocksy cried, pulling a rolled-up Sun from his hip pocket to brandish in Squeak's face. 'Look, there she is! A stoater!' he cried, laying the paper down on the Bowls Club pool table for all to see.

Big Gordy, wee Tam the ex-singer from Falkirk, Sparky - actually Mike Flynn the electrician - and Jocksy himself all carefully studied the page three girl's attributes. Even Janet came round from behind the bar to have a look.

'Impressive,' she declared. 'No silicone in sight. But mind you, wait till she's in her forties. They'll be down at her knees,' she informed the assembled crowd. Then she added, 'But I thought it was Squeak's business you were supposed to be showing us, Jocksy,' she added with a wink at Squeak himself, who couldn't have been less interested.

'Aye, aye, aye,' Jocksy said, pulling himself together. Shaking the paper dramatically, he held it up and, in his best dramatic voice, began to read out loud:

Yolky-Doky Founder On Brink Of Exit

Leading Scottish entrepreneur Paul Sinclair stood on the brink of ruin last night as his giant Yolky-Doky food empire neared collapse. Faced with a massive lawsuit from former employers Maddison's Dairy for breach of patent rights, the legendary Sighthill 'Eggmeister' is expected to settle by handing over all ownership rights of Yolky-Doky to Maddisons in a deal rumoured to be worth over £45 million -

---

'Is that right, Squeak?'
'£45 million?'

'Really?'

'All of which I'm about to lose, of course,' Squeak pointed out.

'You might have shared some of it with yer friends, Squeak,' Jocksy said.

Squeak looked around slowly and pointedly.

'Did you contribute to our big clubhouse renovation earlier this year?' Bert asked. 'That 'anonymous benefactor' the secretary talked about?'

'I paid for it.'

A stunned - and slightly shamed - silence followed until Sparky eventually said, 'Squeak, are you saying you're about to lose forty-five million pounds? That's as in four, five, million?'

Squeak nodded, shrugged his shoulders.

'Sweet Jesus,' Big Gordy said. Even Bert Ronson stopped smiling for a moment.

Jocksy produced an ancient-looking handkerchief from his pocket and dabbed his eyes. 'I'm so sorry, Squeak, I'm so sorry,' he muttered, stretching his arm - just - around Squeak's shoulders for good measure.

For the rest of the evening Squeak was treated like a king. He bought no drink, everyone in the bowling club came up to shake his hand or embrace him, and a stranger might have thought that he had stumbled upon the booze-up after a funeral. Squeak dismissed all with responses such as 'these things happen' or 'it was nice while it lasted'.

*

Within three weeks Squeak had lost Yolky-Doky for ever; it was Maddison's. Not that Maddison's found it quite such plain sailing from then on. Yolky-Doky, it transpired, was locked into long contracts with a little firm called Firm Flavours to supply most of the popular flavours - all patented, of course; a publicity contract with a firm called NVision; and of course the copyright on all the jingles belonged to Squeak himself. It wasn't quite clear who owned Firm Flavours and NVision, but the name 'P. Sinclair' appeared on the board of each. Each of the contracts gave very favourable terms to the supplier. For instance, it turned out that every single time one of Squeak's jingles was used either on television or radio, he would be paid five hundred pounds, and NVision insisted to Maddison's Dairies that 'only the best jingles' would do for such a key product as Yolky-Doky. The public expected class advertising for a class product.

The shadowy ownership of Firm Flavours and NVision kept the rumour-mills going, but in fact Maddison's took the view that it was better not to cause trouble by being greedy. Yolky-Doky was a nice little earner and even if more than half of the profits seemed to disappear on advertising and other deductions, Maddison's weren't complaining.

For Squeak, things couldn't have worked out better. As far as most in the Bowling Club was concerned, he'd lost all of his hard-earned money, and he wasn't about to set the record straight. He could safely meet his friends and not be the centre of attention or be expected to contribute large sums of money just because he was rich. As a cover story, Squeak set up a little company that wrote advertising jingles to order, which earned just enough money to make everyone think that was all he had to live on. He even allowed Jocksy to make one up for a brand of nail gun - perfect for Jocksy's personality - and paid him for it. No-one ever found out about the three million pounds that he still made each year - apart from Her Majesty's Revenue and Customs, of course. By paying his taxes on time, even deliberately overpaying them sometimes, he kept his earnings under the radar. Stacking the boards of Firm Flavours and NVision with his friends from the bowling club - and paying them a nice salary to go with it - gave them all a huge incentive to keep quiet as well; Squeak had made it clear that 'gossiping' about business, including earnings and who owned what, was a sackable offence. Fifty thousand a year for each of them saw to that.

Five years later, a Shanghai-based firm called Sunshine Foods came up with an alternative to Yolky-Doky, cheaper and ideally suited to the burger-chain market. With lower labour costs, and by pitching their adverts at a new young sports-following market, Sunshine Foods quickly made inroads into the global fast-egg market. The financial pages of the newspapers weren't slow to predict difficulties for Maddison's, who were perceived to have been a little complacent and slow to develop, and these predictions turned out to be all too true. What they had done to Squeak they themselves suffered as Sunshine Foods made a successful hostile bid for Maddison's, incidentally creating a political storm over the passing of Scotland's largest dairy into foreign ownership.

But as ever these things are never as simple as they look; Sunshine Foods were also locked into a long contract with Squeak's Firm Flavours and NVision. Squeak persuaded the Chinese to allow their new product simply to be called 'Sunshine', as in 'Golden Sunshine' (the basic), 'Chilli Sunshine', 'Soya Sunshine', 'Bacon Sunshine' and so on. Squeak's jingle - he paid for the royalties to Frankie Vaughan's *Give Me The Moonlight* and adapted it accordingly - for the new product was simple and cleverly pitched so that any number of groups of football supporters could adapt it to their needs. Virtually every televised football match became a running advert for Golden Sunshine, and needless to say Squeak arranged to have real Golden Sunshine adverts at half-time and full-time. Squeak saw all the angles, he pulled all the strings.

Did it make him happy? It's hard to say. Squeak never married, although he had plenty of female company and never seemed to spend a night alone if he didn't care to. He ended up with three houses in different parts of Scotland, but he was always most at home with Bert, Jocksy, Big Gordie and the others down at the bowling club every Monday night. At least down there he was just Squeak, or at least he was until the day before his forty-third birthday, when he suffered a massive stroke at the club just as he was about to send up his final bowl of the fifth end. His funeral was a small affair, just the folk from the bowling club, a couple of cousins, and a humanist celebrant all gathered at Warriston Crematorium.

He may have had a small funeral, but he left a large estate - sixty-one million pounds, to be shared among his old friends - and he even included a smallish bequest for Phil and Martha Walker. And his will contained one special request: that a new pavilion be built for the bowling club, to be called the Paul Sinclair Memorial Pavilion. Quietly, he'd changed his name by deed poll to dispose of the 'Innocent Leo Eugene'. And certainly not 'Squeak'.

Yolky-Doky Jingle

The Beginning of Something Beautiful

The IRA always used to say that the British needed to be lucky all the time to stop bombs going off; they, the IRA, only needed to get lucky once. I know how they feel.

You see, time is on my side. I'm here inside you from the very outset, constantly popping up here and there, being knocked back, then regrouping to target you somewhere else. Most people don't like to think about me but that's just a matter of sticking your head in the sand. I'm here all right, I'm not going away. I'm with you in your every movement. I'm coming for you.

I'm not one of your new kids on the block. I've been around for a long time, probably since the Big Bang or whatever put us all on Earth. They named a constellation after me, even half of the tropics, proving that some people can be in more than one place at the same time. I have what you might call experience, an understanding of the human body far greater than any anatomy lecturer. Of course, I understand that I'm up against some pretty smart battle-scarred heroes, soldiers who take me on at the front line. To them, it's a matter of life and death; they're absolutely correct there, too. But when they knock me down, it's my solemn duty to pick myself up, dust myself down, and start all over again. Same place, or perhaps somewhere else, it doesn't really matter. Last week I tried an assault on the brain, the week before it was the thyroid. Both times I lost, had to retreat, maybe even take a little rest before setting off for somewhere else.

Like the seasoned traveller that I am, I have a number of different identities and travel on a range of passports. Many of my names end in '-oma', gentle, sweet titles that rhyme with 'Roma', Oklahoma, and – my personal favourite – aroma. Your immigration experts tell you to watch out for me in my many different disguises, as though I were some sort of terrorist. I feel quite insulted by that; I'm an entirely natural, living entity, all I want to do is to live my own life, growing the way I need to. And I'm totally one hundred percent organic, even if I'm not all that vegetarian.

I admit you're getting better at providing your troops with intelligence, forewarning yourself of my imminent attack. Once upon a time people like me could just about slip under the radar and take up complete occupation before anyone had noticed, but nowadays there's any number of tests you can do, taking blood and urine samples, lumps out of you and swabs from the most intimate parts of your body. You even test your shit, for crying out loud. The one thing on my side there is that half of you are too scared or embarrassed to get yourselves checked out so I get in there anyway. As usual it's the poor who are most likely to take the hit, either because they're too busy and stressed to take to take expert advice, or because they're just not well-enough educated. Perhaps it's some sort of natural selection, but you can make your own mind up on that subject. I'm just here to do my job.

I'm seen as an enemy. People who meet me talk defiantly about 'promising to beat me', as if they're going to take a big stick to me, or perhaps they're feeling a bit as though they're three goals down to Arsenal already. The spirit of Winston Churchill is invoked. I don't seem to have many friends, only a few relatives, and life as me can feel just a little lonely. But I don't care. I've got used to the hostility, the looks of horror, the anguish at the mention of my name, so often whispered or mentioned only by my initial, equating me with some sort of Dark Lord like Voldemort in the Harry Potter books or Sauron from *Lord Of The Rings*. It's all a lot of nonsense, because I'm real, I don't go away in a happy ending at the finish of the book.

The most important way in which my relationship with you has changed in recent years has been in the weapons you use against me. Some of these are pretty nasty, actually. You hack me out of your body, you try to kill me with poisons and – worst of all – you microwave me. (At least I think you microwave me, that's what it feels like anyway when you feed us both into that tube or whatever and everyone disappears into another room. It's always a bit scary when they take cover like that.) But there's a downside for you, too, because if it hurts me to be attacked then it hurts you, too, and after the smoke has blown away from the battlefield, if there's any of me left then you're even more vulnerable than you were before. You buy some time at least, though, and fair enough, if you get the gamble right, all of me dies and all of you doesn't. While we're on the subject I'd admit that I'm a bit concerned about this new secret weapon you have, some sort of genetic modification of your cells and mine which not only kills me but also cures you. That's not fair and I need to remember to put in a formal written complaint about it.

Did you feel that? I didn't think so. I almost got hold of an interesting bit there. A sexual attack is always promising because you're likely to be too embarrassed to go and see about it, drop your underpants and let someone other than your nearest and dearest look at your most private parts. But something in you fought back at me there, so you won another round.

The other big change in our relationship has been your lifestyle. Let's take a few examples. Finding out that cigarettes could let me into your lungs was clever, and my work became a lot harder after that. Asbestos? That was great for me – still is, of course, in some places – so when one of you noticed that even a little asbestos and a little of me could make sweet music together, that was a bit of a pain, but I consoled myself that there are always lots of places in the third world where miners are forced to work unprotected. Some interesting minerals can be very helpful to me as well.

Some of you in your well-off, developed west try your best to fend me off with healthy eating, placing endless faith in super-foods like açai berries, broccoli and olive oil; or running endless half-marathons either on the streets or, for those with money, in the gym. You end up in agony with arthritis or, if you're lucky, dying of a heart attack, but I'm not sure that too much of anything doesn't just play straight into my hands. But in any case, though, I'm a little ahead of you. No sooner do you ban one thing that invites me to call than you go and invent something else which is just as tempting. Everyone worries about electricity pylons, mobile phones or nuclear power stations, but they overlook omnipresent exhaust pollution, particularly diesel fumes from public transport. I can really catch you out there while you ride your nice healthy bicycles to and from work, too. And don't think it's any safer in the countryside. That nice clean country air is just full of weedkiller and chemical fertilisers, as well as all sorts of promising substances dumped by helpful fly-tippers.

And of course, nothing quite beats a foreign holiday, does it? A little sun makes you all feel so much better, and you show off your nice olive tan to the opposite sex when you return. Once you couldn't afford trips abroad, but nowadays every Tom, Dannielle and Harry fries his or her skin a couple of weeks each year then hides it under their office garb again where no-one can see the damage done, where I've managed to get a foothold, and from where I can make real inroads into the rest of you. I still can't believe that even although you know about sun-beds, so many of you will insist on going to them anyway simply to make yourselves look more Mediterranean than you really are. It's altogether very thoughtful of you, very considerate, to give me such a sporting chance.

Sometimes I get a foothold but not strongly enough to make a difference. I can make some men's lives miserable when they go to the toilet – or can't, as the case may be – but I can't always see it through to a proper conclusion. When that happens it's a kind of stalemate, so I suppose you'd count that as another point to you. As you might guess, I'm more successful in some forms than in others, but that's only to be expected, and my best work is usually in places where you don't realise I'm there until it's too late. All the same, it's surprising how often I'm not discovered at all, that you die of something else perhaps, maybe an accident, or even that it's so slow a process that no-one even bothers to look to look to find me. When that happens, I feel a bit neglected, but que sera, sera.

That was another one. Did you feel that? Pay attention, now, you won that round again but one day it'll be my turn.

Despite my best efforts, I can tell you still don't like me. Being me, I can feel that shiver down your spine, I can feel that sweat on your palms developing, down your back, even in the soles of your feet. It's that 'cold sweat' people talk about, because you're certainly not warm, running about, trying to cool down; that sweat is the sweat of fear. At this very moment you're almost certainly saying you don't want to listen to any more of my 'sinister talk inside your head' but I'm really just another set of living cells, just like you, or for that matter herring gulls, rats or maggots, performing my important function in maintaining the balance of life on earth. People need to die sometime, after all, and it's down to me and a few others to make sure they do, to clean things up a little bit. Actually, I probably need to step on the gas a bit there, there's far too many of you by a long shot. I do feel I need to reeducate you a little, to make you see me in a different light, to see why you should not only not fear me, you should positively welcome me as your friend, your ally in life.

Benjamin Franklin once said that the only certainties in life were death and taxes. I don't work for the tax department, but I wish you could accept that death is inevitable, and, to quote another favourite phrase of yours, in the midst of life there is death. They go together, like love and marriage, horse and carriage, yin and yang, and it's the essential precariousness of life and closeness of death that makes your lives feel so rich, exciting and fulfilling, so that you rejoice in dangerous sports like skiing, driving fast cars, and playing hard contact sports. Death – or at least the idea of death – sets your pulse racing. I accept that I can't quite compete with the Formula One Ferrari deaths such as aeroplane crashes, terrorist bombs, battlefield bullets or falling off a mountain, but the idea that you've 'looked me in the eye' and 'faced me down' makes you feel pretty good, doesn't it? You can wear me like a campaign medal, admit it. There are ribbons and bows of all sorts of colours, wristbands, balloons, and lapel badges and flowers; you take pictures of yourself supporting charities that raise money to fight me, and you post any amount of stuff on social media sites saying you're 'standing shoulder with your friends' or whatever (not that it'll make the slightest difference, of course).

But I want you to think for a moment what would happen if I didn't exist. Just imagine. More of you would live, sure, to go on to develop unpleasant conditions such as multiple sclerosis, motor neurone disease or muscular dystrophy; or develop type-2 diabetes and all its complications; go blind, deaf, develop painful conditions, become incontinent, doubly so, probably, or have a series of heart and chest problems making it harder and harder for you to breathe, or have a stroke and have that awful 'locked-in syndrome' where you know what's going on but are totally paralysed. I mentioned Alzheimer's, but there are actually any number of long-term problems where you end up in some miserable care home, draining away the money you worked so hard for all your life and intended to leave to your lovely children, who perhaps come to visit you and perhaps don't. But do you really want to live long enough to see your own children die? Do you really want to live for ever?

No? I didn't think so.

So what can I offer you? I can offer you a managed death. I can offer you time to settle your affairs, to gather your loved ones around you and tell them how much you love them, how you've always loved them all your life but never quite got round to saying before. I can offer you the chance to discuss with one of your experts whether you want pain relief or extended life, and to make your own choices. And, best of all, perhaps, I can offer you the chance to die in a place of your own choosing, one of those nice hospice things with people who always seem to know what you want before you ask, who look after your children and grandchildren as if they were their own. I can offer you a brief glimpse of heaven on earth, knowing that the things you care about are going to be fine after you no longer have to care about them.

That doesn't sound so bad does it?

Are you ready yet? Because I've got some news for you.

Paradise Lost

Elizabeth Charlotte Grainger looked out from the upper-floor drawing room window of her large Edinburgh Southside villa and sighed in despair. The council bin men had been round again and, as usual, had failed to return her wheelie bin to its proper place near the three-car garage. Of course, Max the gardener would put it back, or perhaps Mrs Dunne if she was still on the premises. It was so irritating. True, the bin men left the wheelie bins of every other resident in the street on the pavement, but she and husband Donald paid rather a lot of tax to the Council and she expected their employees to know their place. Briefly, she considered going downstairs and moving the offending object herself, but then thought better of it doing the servants' jobs for them would set a bad precedent. Donald, meanwhile, was on the golf course and intended to stay for lunch, so there was no prospect of the wheelie-bin situation being rectified that way either.

Charlotte – for she was indeed the famous 'E. Charlotte Grainger' – was doubly annoyed because she was in full swing writing her latest piece for the *Scotsman*. Twice a week, she penned a 500-word column reviewing the latest books to hit the shelves. It was headed *Writing from the Heart*, and invariably signed off with her initials 'ECG', but everyone knew that the critic was actually E. Charlotte herself.

Charlotte had achieved a little success with each of her own three novels. The big break had really been the first one, *On the Dark Side of Paradise*, a disturbing novel about a couple who go on holiday to a Caribbean island to celebrate their silver wedding, only for a series of revelations to tear their marriage apart. The novel was all right, no better than that, but Charlotte had persuaded Donald to ask a few favours at the golf club. That in turn had produced a publishing contract, then a place on a couple of short lists for debut authors. Even then, the book hadn't sold that many copies, but the media attention had brought Charlotte a contract to write two more novels, together with (more lucrative) journalism opportunities.

Donald, in fact, had been very busy that day. A semi-retired corporate lawyer, he was a non-executive director or part-time chairman of seven different companies, one of which was a small local publisher, the other one of the biggest in the world. Charlotte's first contract had been sealed on the par-5 fifth green at the expense of generously-conceded four-foot putt. It suited Donald to keep

Charlotte busy as it allowed him more time at the golf club. A few years younger than him in her early sixties, she was ageing well. She could afford to take care of her body – she was slimmer now than she had been as a teenager – to dress, to wear her hair attractively, and to spend time on her make-up, all thanks to Donald's considerable allowance. Trained as a chiropodist, she'd been more than willing to heed his suggestion all those years ago that it might be better if she became a full-time mother to their four children. With these children now scattered to the four winds, Charlotte had time to write, something that gave her genuine satisfaction and even a small income for doing it. And Donald seemed pleased to support her, 'my wife is a successful writer, nominated for the Dewar First Novel Prize, would you believe?' sounding rather more suitable at the golf club than 'my wife cuts people's toenails.' It was odds-on that he would be appointed Club Captain next year, and the year after that the course was due to host the Open Golf Championship, when he, as Captain, would be in the public eye. So a lot was at stake.

If you're not familiar with the publishing business, you might not be aware that hardly any author makes money by writing fiction. The odd superstar can sell books by the million, sell the film rights and so on, but those really are rare beasts. For the most part, authors simply hope to make a small living and then supplement their income as journalists, critics, or even as teachers, lawyers, or office workers. Terry Pratchett wrote nineteen novels before giving up his job at the Electricity Board. Charlotte was no superstar, but her review work brought in a good deal more cash than the royalties from her books.

Charlotte's 'ECG' reviews, though, were avidly followed by her fans. Everyone knew that her background was from the Edinburgh middle-class establishment, and she was both a social and literary snob. Her reviews particularly had it in for cheap pulp fiction that she classed as 'toilet paper' but yet sold large numbers of copies. She denounced these books and their authors as formulaic, predating on target readers who had an average of well over eighty: Charlotte dismissed such books as 'incontinence pad-lit'.

As 'ECG', Charlotte was never short of new material to wade into. In an attempt to modernise, Hendry & Wylde, the market leaders in easy-to-read women's fiction, had spiced up their novels a little, much to the dismay of their older core readers. That had created a gap in the market, and the vacuum had been filled by a new group of writers known as the 'Sabbath Set'. They were more than happy to meet the continuing demand for lightweight, unthreatening and – above all – sex-free prose.

The queen of this new 'Sabbath Set' was Elizabeth Buckley. Buckley had already produced 83 novellas at the astonishing rate of one per month; indeed, there was even a rumour that 'Elizabeth Buckley' that she wasn't one person at all, but was in fact a group of writers who combined to write under the same name. It had been Charlotte herself, though, who in her ECG column had debunked that theory by pointing out the many consistencies in style in all 83: the use of specific words, the use of commas and semi-colons, sentence length, dialogue style and so on. This learned study had only enhanced Charlotte's status as a critic with a keen eye for detail.

Not everyone in the group had succeeded in remaining anonymous. Jessica Searle, Lily Bannister and Amelia Beaumont were all known to be real people, albeit that Beaumont chose to write under a pen-name rather than her real name, Asha Amelia Kaur Singh. But whoever Elizabeth Buckley or any of her group really were, everyone agreed that the stigma of writing 'incontinence pad-lit' – usually shortened to 'pad-lit' – was detrimental to a writer's aspirations to be taken seriously as a writer. It might be profitable, but what should it profit a woman to inherit the earth yet lose her soul? At Society of Literary Writers meetings, respectable writers whispered gossip to each other behind cupped their hands. 'Pad-lit writers' were pointed out, shunned figures of shame. And these poor souls knew it. But the trouble was that no one knew who the chief villain, Elizabeth Buckley, really was. All that was known was that she was somewhere in their midst. 'Buckley' sent her work through an agency that she'd set up herself using an offshore account based in Jersey, but on one occasion had been careless and left a Society of Literary Writers logo in her signature at the foot.

Only a couple of days previously, Charlotte's Tuesday 'ECG' column for the Scotsman had posed the possibility that Buckley was actually a man. Her logic was simple: nobody could work out which woman was the real Elizabeth Buckley, ergo Elizabeth Buckley had to be male. Charlotte had even hinted that one of the well-known Edinburgh establishment authors might be the culprit – one, a retired lawyer, wrote comedy fiction and crime, so why might he not also be Elizabeth Buckley? Or alternatively he might be that Edinburgh crime writer who wrote hard-boiled police thrillers. The lawyer and the crime writer had been amused at the thought and said nothing, reckoning that there was no such thing as bad publicity, but within hours a warning quietly filtered back to Donald at the golf club that Charlotte might eventually have to retract her suggestion in a future article. Two other Edinburgh-based female superstar writers added their names to the 'little note' as well.

But Charlotte knew what she was doing. Just ninety minutes after watching the bin men misplace the garden rubbish wheelie bin, she found herself now at the Annual Prizegiving Lunch of the Society of Literary Writers in the Balmoral Hotel at the east end of Princes Street. The stir created by her article would ensure that Charlotte herself would be the centre of attention.

This year there was a new development. For the first time, self-published authors had been invited and there was even an award for 'Best Self-Published Book of the Year.' It was a controversial award: many authors, privately including Charlotte, felt that self-publishers weren't 'proper writers' and had no place in the hall. But unless they were pad-litters (sadly, many of them were, though) at least most of the mainstream writers spoke to them politely.

Charlotte would normally have ignored the self-published writers herself, but today she had she had been asked to announce the winner of the inaugural Best Self-Published Book of the Year award. She'd enjoy holding everyone's attention as she opened the envelope, keeping everyone in suspense for a moment, then calling out the name written on the card inside. The media would be there, of course, so she should make the most of her moment in the limelight. And it might drum up a few more sales for Charlotte's own books, too.

First of all, though, everyone was expected to mingle in the hotel foyer, the classic champagne-and-canapés time. For Charlotte this was a good time to put a face to each of the five short-listed writers for the 'Best Self-Published' award, wishing them luck both today and in their future careers. All but one of the five were women, and she was relieved to learn that there were no pad-litters amongst them. They wrote a range of genres: science fiction, historical romantic drama and crime; the man wrote poetry, and one woman had produced a non-fiction book about child bereavement. Charlotte tried to sound interested even although she wasn't, although she found the crime writer a little unsettling – her gaze was very penetrating, almost as if she was trying to reach inside Charlotte's mind.

Then everyone moved through to the vast dining room for lunch. As a minor celebrity, Charlotte merited a place beside several other well-known authors and a couple of literary critics. One of the writers was a comedian and she found his need to show off a little irritating. Generally, though, she was able to enjoy some quiet chat and three very nice courses. The Balmoral could deliver on the food front, she decided. But from time to time she caught a glimpse of the self-publishing crime writer whom she'd picked out earlier: unsettlingly, the writer seemed to be studying Charlotte, sometimes with a frown, before looking away whenever Charlotte caught sight of her. The woman made Charlotte feel slightly uncomfortable anyway, almost as if they'd met at one of these meetings before; but given that it was the first time self-published authors had been recognised, it seemed unlikely. More probably, she simply *looked* like someone famous. Racking her memory, she wondered if the woman might be called Claire Something, perhaps Davies or Davidson. However, she spoke with quite a broad Edinburgh accent, and Charlotte concluded there was no way, no way at all, that this woman moved in her own circles.

At the end of the meal, the Chair of the Society stood up and gave the annual speech. Jokes were expected but rarely were they any good, and this year's Chair had the added annoying habit of waiting for the audience to laugh – even if no laughs were forthcoming. So it was with some relief that the Awards Ceremony formally began as the rather more efficient Secretary began to read out the prizes, followed by the nominees for each.

There were many technical awards – for editing, cover design, best typesetting, best marketing performance, best billboard poster, even best Advance Information sheet. Then, at last, came the literary prizes. Short stories, poetry, graphic novel and eventually, third last…

'And now, a new award, the Best Self-Published Book of the Year. And to present it we have the renowned author and critic, E Charlotte Grainger. Charlotte won the best debut novel award herself just four years ago for her *On the Dark Side of Paradise*, but of course she's just as well known to you all for her acerbic wit in her *Scotsman* column.' The Secretary turned to usher Charlotte up to the microphone, handing her the envelope that contained the winner as she did so. 'ECG, will you do the honours?'

Charlotte allowed the applause for her own appearance to drift on as long was decent, allowed herself a brief 'thank you' and a broad smile, then continued.

'The winner of the Best Self-Published Book of the Year is…' – Charlotte opened the envelope with as much drama as she could muster – '…is… Claire Dawson for *Lost in the Mists of Time!*'

There was a brief whoop of joy from somewhere in the audience, then suddenly the woman who had spent her time looking at Charlotte was approaching the dais. She stepped up, took the envelope, and turned to face the audience to say a few words.

'This is so unexpected! Thank you!' she said. 'And what a joy to receive the award from the legendary E Charlotte Grainger! We haven't seen each other for so long, and here she is presenting me with my first major prize.'

Charlotte made the mistake of looking mystified.

'You don't remember me, Betty?' She turned back to the audience to explain. 'I need to explain, everyone. Betty and I were at Broughton Primary School together, same class and everything. Back then she was Betty Buckle, I was Claire Cant. We used to be pals, remember? You don't remember me? You used to say you'd rather be called Buckley and I just wanted to be anything but Cant. The others in the class used to call us Cannae Buckle.'

Speechless, Charlotte was too shocked to be mortified. Yet.

'Remember Miss Simpson? The old boot used to insist on calling you Elizabeth Buckle. She even made you re-write your name when you wrote it as Betty in your jotter at the end of your stories. And she gave you the belt that time, too. That was awful.'

'That was for...' – Charlotte stopped, but it was too late.

'That was when you tried to get your own back by calling yourself 'Elizabeth Buckley'. She took you out to the front of the class and gave you two of the belt. I never saw anyone else ever get it primary school. I talked all the time. I deserved it far more than you. It wasn't fair.'

By now, the entire room was buzzing. Could it really be true? Could ECG herself really be the mysterious 'Elizabeth Buckley', the missing pad-lit writer?

In other circumstances Charlotte might have managed to deny it, but Claire Cant's sudden reappearance in her life had now engulfed her in a tsunami of embarrassment and she was desperately aware that her face was a deep, deep crimson colour. Her life was crumbling all around her: she'd have to give up her 'ECG' *Scotsman* column for a start, and her new contract to write two new novels would be cancelled as well, for sure.

Charlotte was too humiliated even to cry.

She returned to her seat at the table, but her next-door neighbours pointedly looked away from her. She heard words spoken in a low hush: 'hypocrite'; 'cheap'; 'shocking'; 'despicable woman'; and even 'harlot'.

That evening, the Grainger household received two telephone calls. The first, for Charlotte from the Chair of the Society of Literary Writers, suggested that Charlotte's resignation from the Society might be appropriate.

The second call was for Donald, from the Golf Club Captain. Something had come up, he explained to Donald, which meant that it would be better if someone who was also a Royal & Ancient member were to be the next Captain of the Golf Club, and therefore Captain for the Open year. The Captain was extremely apologetic, especially as the chances of Donald ever being made Captain now were highly improbable. Donald was politeness personified during the call, of course: these things are always civilised.

But once he came off the phone, Donald wandered through to the sitting room where Charlotte was sitting staring blankly at the wall and for the first time that day thought to ask her something.

'Charlotte, my dear, how was your lunch? Did anything happen?'

Celtic
Conundrum

In the short time she'd been on George Street, Kelly
had already been kicked twice and spat upon once. She
didn't deserve that. Sure, she didn't expect everyone to
understand or even be interested, far less put some money
in the little box perched on the pavement directly in front
of her crossed legs. Kelly was new, she was starting that day.
She thought she was braced for whatever would be thrown
at her: after all, she was a veteran of the wars in Iraq and
Afghanistan. But, as she had to admit to herself, no Al
Qaeda soldier ever spat on her.

Every fifteen minutes or so things got quiet enough,
even on a cold winter's Saturday morning, to allow her
thoughts to get the better of her. How she'd been in the
army, good job, promotion looming, when suddenly her
life had been turned upside down. How she'd been on leave,
off-piste skiing in the Alps with some friends, when she'd

hit a submerged tree root and gone flying. How she'd cracked her spine, caused permanent damage to one of her eyes, broken each of her legs as well as a number of ribs, and generally given her vital organs a massive jolt.

Waking up in hospital, Kelly's first thought had been that her position in the army was compromised. The Army was the only real home she'd ever known; born to a drug addict mother and a dealer father, she'd spent her life in care from the age of seven. In fact the Army had been very good to her, insisted that she needn't worry, that her health came first and she wouldn't be abandoned. After she was transferred back to a hospital near her home in Musselburgh, her commanding officer had even made the effort to stop off to see her while on his way back from his own Scottish golfing holiday.

The Army had given her paid leave during her recovery, and when eventually several months later she'd felt fit enough to return in some capacity, it had found her desk work in Edinburgh. But it didn't take Kelly long to realise that she would never be fully fit again and that her days on the front line, or even anywhere near it, were over. It wasn't the job Kelly had signed up to do. She began to get depressed: she felt dependent and a burden on her colleagues; she began drinking heavily. She became resentful, patronised, and started to imagine colleagues' slights in her own mind that were either non-existent or unintended. In short, she became difficult, and it became clear that even a desk job wouldn't suit Kelly and she wanted out. In truth, the decision that she and the Army part company was, in football manager terms, 'by mutual consent'.

And there was a problem. Kelly's injuries were sustained while on leave, not on active service. She discovered that her entitlement to an Army pension was actually limited to the point of being almost non-existent. She applied for a few jobs. She worked for a while as a supermarket checkout operator but had to give up because the constant sitting was too uncomfortable. Her Army work had been in the catering corps, but working as a chef in a couple of restaurants proved that constant standing was difficult, too. She was difficult in the kitchen as well. More used to giving orders than taking them, especially from – as she saw – inferior cooks, she could be argumentative. Nor did her continued drinking help, although whether her drinking caused the work issues or whether it was the other way around was always open to doubt.

In the end she took on a delivery van job for a parcel courier firm. Despite not being well paid, Kelly worked hard for a few weeks and managed to make enough to survive in her rented flat. But her drinking never went away, and one morning she was pulled over by the police after taking too much of a chance on a red light. She failed the breathalyser, and that was that. Out of a job, unemployable, and a criminal record into the bargain.

Ineligible for benefits and unable to pay the rent, Kelly found herself homeless. Desperate, she tried busking in

George Street; Kelly had whiled away many boring hours on duty learning to play the harmonica, and her colleagues had reckoned – with typical Scottish reserve – she 'wasn't too bad'. Anything was better than working the streets, although on cold winter's nights even Kelly was tempted was sometimes tempted by the promise of a warm bed. And if people were generous, she could earn just about enough for a night in a hostel anyway.

Kelly became well-known on the corner of George Street and Hanover Street both for her virtuosity and for her choice of music. Much of it seemed familiar, but passers-by could always expect the unexpected. What they didn't know was that Kelly liked to write some of her own music, and several of the tunes that they heard so frequently were in fact self-penned. Kelly didn't realise folk noticed, though, she was just trying to make enough small change to survive.

So she was hardly going to notice yet another passer-by stop to watch her that Saturday morning. She was playing one of her favourite tunes, a haunting air she'd thought up one night when there was no one around. She didn't read music, nor could she write it down. The passer-by had his mobile phone out: probably a photo for Instagram or something. There might have been a time when she'd have complained, but she'd long ago learned that the less she drew attention to herself, the less likely it would be that she'd end in trouble with the police. But the observer had her attention looking from the corner of her eye. Was he some sort of journalist? Was he a pimp? Life had taught her to be suspicious, and she was relieved to see him move on after a few minutes.

*

Billy Jordan fancied himself as a folk singer. A regular at The Dribble Inn, 'Edinburgh's Foremost Folk Bar', he turned up with his guitar each Tuesday, Thursday and Sunday in the hope of being allowed to play something on one of the open mike spots that the owner Ian offered on each of those nights. All sorts could be found at these events: other wannabes like himself; virtuoso instrumentalists; there was even a slightly unusual boy boy band called the C-U Jimiz. Billy reckoned he was the pick of the bunch, and certainly he thought he was better than the Tuesday and Thursday 'resident' singer, Danny Something. Danny, he reckoned, just played covers of other people's songs, accompanied by three-chord guitar. But the real buzz of excitement came when a famous face appeared for a pint in The Dribblers: that was the moment. The McConnachies, a bearded guitar-bashing folk trio with sixteen albums to their names, were the most regular visitors. A solo performer of traditional Gaelic songs called Isla McLeod turned up quite a bit, too; less well-known, she commanded more respect than the ultra-commercial McConnachies amongst the self-styled cognoscenti of The Dribbler Inn.

Billy Jordan's lucky night came one Thursday a few weeks after his encounter with Kelly of George Street.

Danny, the regular singer whose surname Billy could never remember, had just vacated the stage and invited singers from the floor to perform. No luminary special guests were present, so Billy was keen to perform, but not desperate. A little practice would do no harm anyway. Billy had a new song, with an excellent tune and stirring, patriotic words that he reckoned would get him noticed by Ian and– if he was very lucky – get him one of the prized weekly nights at The Dribblers. Billy's new song had fairly old-fashioned lyrics; indeed the entire song was quite old-fashioned and wouldn't have been out of place in the repertoire of a music-hall tenor such as Josef Locke or John McCormack. It probably wasn't the sort of song best suited to the denim-clad:

> *If the flowers should never open, if the birds should*
> > *never sing*
> *If tomorrow brought a winter without a hint of spring*
> *If the skies should cloud forever and ne'er again be blue*
> *I'd still be full of sunshine, so long as I have you.*

The other verses were just as bad, and then because Billy still felt his listeners hadn't suffered enough, he repeated verse one.

But as I said, Billy was lucky that night. Billy was lucky because the entire Kilkenny Rugby Club, currently on tour against Scottish counterparts and touring Scottish pubs but not necessarily in that order, had just at that moment descended on The Dribblers. Already on the their fifth pub of the night, Billy's 'song' was completely drowned out by a chorus of Irish-accented requests for 'pints of best'. And when Billy's song came to an end, the Irish rugby players turned and – in a show of exceptional politeness – applauded and cheered loudly. Billy mistook this racket for approval.

Thus encouraged, Billy sang his song on each of the next three weeks. On the first occasion it was the only song he was allowed to sing, because The McConnachies were in and everyone insisted on 'having their turn' at showing off while they had they chance. On the second Thursday, The Dribble Inn was empty because there was a football match on the television; even Ian himself wasn't there. One week later, though, Billy grabbed the microphone at the interval and played his song once more. At the end of his brief slot, Ian invited him across to the bar for a drink.

'Did you write that new song yourself, Billy?' Ian asked him

Billy nodded as he took a swig from his free pint. Ian had never offered him anything for free before.

Ian clapped his hand firmly on Billy's shoulder. 'It's crap, son. Don't sing it again, do you hear? Or I'll throw you out before you finish it.'

Billy got the message. He never sang the song again and his songwriting career was over as quickly as it had begun. Beside him at the bar, a dark-haired man with a dark jacket and neatly cultivated designer stubble smiled consolingly.

Billy was mortified that the stranger had overheard the entire conversation; the man looked faintly familiar but at that moment all Billy wanted to do was to throw the beer down and run.

*

Jake Lennox rubbed his chin and smiled to himself: once again his 'generic musician' appearance had stood him in good stead. More often than not he could stand in a crowded room and not be recognised, and that was just the way Lennox liked it.

A classically-trained pianist, he'd branched out into studying obscure wind instruments while attending the Glasgow Conservatoire, discovering particular potential in an electronic set of bagpipes he'd had made specially to fit him. His own band had already made three groundbreaking albums, each different from the other, and he wasn't afraid to interpret traditional material in extraordinary ways. To supplement his income, Lennox also gave expensive lessons in electronic pipes. However, as he became better off and more successful commercially, he also gave free lessons in bagpipes – plus sets of electronic bagpipes – to school pupils in deprived areas. It was a clever move, as Lennox became the darling of the Scottish cultural media, and also of the Scottish Government. That in turn brought... better gigs, and better-paid appearances.

And here he was, having a quiet pint of beer in The Dribblers, and he couldn't believe his luck. A magpie by nature, Lennox based much of his original material on themes picked up elsewhere, and here was one delivered straight into his hands. Ian was right, the words were dreadful, but get rid of those, Lennox thought, and there's a half-decent piece to work on.

By the time he'd made it home Lennox could see a format. Inspired by the famous Dave Brubeck album *Time Out*, where each track is in a complex rhythm, he reckoned he could take the simple theme he'd heard that evening, turn it into a minor key, and develop it through many different time signatures into a significant piece. Desperate not to let go of the muse, he worked all night and by the morning had fallen asleep across the kitchen table over a complete work of art. Wakened by his wife Safia, the excited composer nevertheless was alert enough to insist on playing it to her before she left. (The long-suffering Safia only pretended to be impressed: she'd heard Jake in this mood before and he was making her late for work.)

But he was right. Hastening into his local recording studios, he talked the engineers into making a little space for him that very day while laid down the basic melodies and rhythms, then he took the recording home to turn into something a little bit special. And when he played the result to Angular Records, they decided there and then to make *Celtic Conundrum*, as Lennox had titled it, the lead track of his next album.

The new Lennox album proved a smash hit on both sides of the Atlantic, and proved to be a significant breakthrough in the North American market. When his band headlined at Glastonbury, Cropready, T in the Park, Reading and similar festivals in the States, his act centred around the new album and, in particular, the title track. It was played extensively on radio stations around the world, and the track *Celtic Conundrum* itself was downloaded half a million times from streaming services in its first year. Even Safia began to take notice. As a television producer, she'd used her position in the past to gain airtime for her husband, but now Safia Patel was in demand as the woman best placed to ask the great Jake Lennox to guest on shows. He didn't let her down. And suddenly, they were very, very wealthy indeed.

You must be wondering: did Billy Jordan recognise his tune? Of course he did. But he overplayed his hand. He wrote a stiff letter to Jake Lennox accusing the great man of plagiarism and demanding a share of the royalties. Lennox paid no attention; he could afford to let his lawyers sort it out. And sort it out they did. A week later, Billy received a letter from Duncan McIntyre, senior partner of the law firm Marsden McKinlay McIntyre Bell. The letter denied everything, and instead accused Billy of defamation in return. Billy was eventually advised to settle for a five-figure out-of-court settlement and an undertaking to stop playing his guitar for good.

*

Two years later, Kelly could still be found on that same George Street corner. In the intervening twenty-four months she'd been seriously assaulted three times, including twice sexually, not including the sly kicks and spitting she had to endure as part of her daily routine. She'd managed to stay out of trouble with the police, who'd got to know her well and quite liked her. She still didn't have a job, although she'd twice been sent for job interviews by the Department of Work and Pensions local office. As usual, Kelly's problems were her lack of a fixed address, her past record of depression and the huge hole in her CV: what employer was going to prefer Kelly over, say, a young school leaver?

But her years hadn't been wasted. Never other than competent, Kelly had become an outstandingly good harmonica player. Mostly she played covers, but there was one tune – for a reason she couldn't quite fathom – of which she felt particularly fond. It was a cut-down version of *Celtic Conundrum*, and whenever she played it, the takings in her upturned hat soared.

Celtic Conundrum

(from the short story of the same name, by Gordon Lawrie)

Jake Lennox

The Second Best Parking Attendant in the City

I f_rst noticed him from the window of my top-floor flat. It was just after 7.30 in the morning and he was at the opposite corner of the street; a pile of dead leaves had been blown in underneath a hedge and he was scuffing them away with his shoe. My car was parked hard against the hedge in question, where I could keep an eye on it, clearly displaying the permit required to park in the residents' bay. (That's not entirely true. I prefer to display my parking permit somewhere that makes life as awkward as possible.) He'd abandoned his little L-plated scooter on a double yellow line as if he were above the law – which was theoretically impossible because he actually *was* the law.

I was going out to the shops to buy a paper and some rolls anyway. I hadn't intended to use my car, but I thought I should go and find out what he was up to. It took me a minute or two to fetch a jacket and make my way downstairs. When I arrived, I was more than a little put out to find a parking ticket attached to my window and that an alien from outer space was taking a photograph of my car from all angles, with the recently-added adornment fully visible.

'Eh… what's this?' I asked him, a blend of incredulity and anger in my voice. Close up, he looked much the same as he did from a distance: like Darth Vader in the Star Wars movie. He was dressed head-to-toe in black leathers, save for a black motorcycle helmet and a high-visibility yellow tabard bearing the dreaded words 'Parking Attendant' on his back. He appeared not to be carrying any light sabres, but right at that moment I couldn't have cared less anyway. The blood-red parking ticket was provoking me like a muleta to a bull.

As he turned round to look at me, I realised that the Parking Attendant had actually pushed his visor up, allowing me a little glimpse of the monster within. I could see that he was Asian, wore glasses, and had a round, chubby face. He was quite tall, not far short of my height, and he wore an air of permanent bewilderment. For some reason he saw no reason to reply to my initial question, so I repeated it.

'I asked you… what's this?' I summoned up as much menace as I could.

'Is this your car, sir?' I took note: 'sir'. Very polite for one who's gone over to the dark side.

'You answer my question first,' I said. 'I was watching you upstairs, kicking the leaves away to see if that car was on a yellow line.'

The alien became quite animated, without losing the bewildered look.

'I did not kick any leaves away, sir. I do not do such things.'

This was not the correct answer. I'd seen him do it with my own eyes.

'I was watching you from a distance. Please don't lie,' I said.

'I am not a liar,' he insisted. 'I do not like being called a liar because I do not lie. I am a good Parking Attendant.'

'OK,' I said, 'it's your word against mine. So tell me – what's wrong with the way this car is parked?'

'Is this your car, sir?'

I'd heard this question before and saw little point in prolonging the point. 'Yes. Are you going to answer my question?'

'Come with me, sir.' His expression didn't change at all: still one of bewilderment.' He invited me to come with him to study the rear of the car.

'Your car is parked on a double yellow line, sir.'

I could barely believe what I was looking at. A double yellow line had indeed been painted, and my car was the first one legally parked next to it. Or so I had assumed. However, in their rush to finish, the workmen painting the double yellow line had dropped two further blobs of yellow paint nearby, and my nearside rear wheel was just touching one of the blobs.

Very patiently, I pointed out that the yellow blobs and the double yellow line were not connected.

'That's not the point, sir. You're not allowed to park on double yellow lines in this zone, Parking Zone N7. It's in contravention of section 28 of the Road Traffic Offences – '

'They're two blobs of yellow paint. They're not yellow lines.'

'Why else would the road be painted yellow, sir?'

'It was an accident!' I said, my voice raised slightly. 'It's a careless paint spillage!'

'I'd rather you didn't get angry, sir,' he said.

He had a point. It was early in the morning and getting cross would get nowhere with this moron. So I changed my line of attack, and producing my mobile phone, I started taking photographs of my car, the swept-away leaves, Darth Vader, and his scooter, which was still parked on the double yellow lines. Two car spaces along, conveniently, was a nice spot where he could quite legally have parked his scooter. I photographed that, too.

'What are you doing, sir?'

I walked up to him and took a photo of him, close-up, and the number on his uniform: E1515.

'I'm taking a record of your number and all of the circumstances so that I can complain about you and your conduct,' I announced grandly, with a smug, sinister grin. 'You have behaved in an unprofessional manner, you have attempted to tamper the evidence by moving the leaves – '

'I told you, I did not move any leaves – '

'Well, E1515, I think my photographs will show otherwise. What do you think your superior officers will do when I make my complaint, backed up by so much evidence? You've let them down, haven't you?'

'No, sir, I have been doing my job. I haven't moved the leaves at all.'

'Are you certain, E1515?' I was warming to my task now, and switched my phone to video mode. I always have a little trouble taking videos, but I managed to set it running.

He hesitated. 'I did not move the leaves, sir.'

I pointed the phone at him. 'Think carefully, E1515. Are you sure you didn't move the leaves. Would you swear to it?'

I could see a little trickle of sweat forming on his brow and for the first time I began to feel like the bully I was being.

'I did not move any leaves, sir.'

'So why didn't you book me for having no Resident's Parking Permit?' I said. I could see suspicion creep across his otherwise default bewildered gaze.

'I checked your Permit already, sir. Your permit is in order, sir.'

'Show me,' I said. He squeezed round between car and hedge. I grinned wickedly. E1515 had been forced to move some leaves. He'd fallen into my trap! Not only that, but I now had video of him on my phone's camera, first denying that he'd moved the leaves, then being forced to move them later.

'I think I've made my point, E1515,' I said, quietly. 'You lied. I have it all here on camera. All you were interested in was picking up another ticket towards your target. You said you hadn't moved the leaves when you must have. You've let your city down, you're a substandard traffic warden. I'm going to report you, E1515.'

Now there was genuine panic in his eyes

'Please sir, please do not report me. I did not lie, sir, I promise you,' he said – I waved the phone at him by way of reply – 'and I am not a bad Parking Attendant, sir. In fact I am the second best Parking Attendant in the entire city.'

That stopped me. 'Really?'

'Yes. I even book members of my own family.'

You must be popular, I thought to myself.

'Is that a good thing?' I asked him, without thinking.

Without hesitation, he replied, 'I think so, sir. I have a job to do, and I do it honestly, to the best of my ability. I am proud to be the Second Best Parking Attendant in the entire city. One day I hope to be the Best Parking Attendant in the entire city.'

'And yet you cleared away leaves at the back of my car to reveal two yellow blobs of paint. Is that honest?'

'I promise you, sir, I did not clear any leaves away around your car.'

I had certainly seen Darth Vader/E1515 shovel away leaves at the back of my car with his foot, and there was undoubtedly a ticket on my car front windscreen as a result of two spilled blobs of paint on the road. And yet... as he flatly denied everything, for the first time I began to doubt the evidence of my own eyes. He clearly believed he'd never moved so much as a single leaf. His sheer persistence was making me doubt myself.

And all this at around a quarter to eight in the morning. I shook my head in despair.

'You know, E1515, I don't know how you can sleep at night. Your job makes other people miserable and angry. The reason you came here so early today was precisely because we live near your headquarters and we're the first area you come to. You have targets to meet, and we're soft targets. We're the soft targets for your targets. How many tickets do you have to issue each day, E1515? Tell me that?'

'I do not have any specific targets, sir. My job is – '

'Your job is to collect as many as possible,' I said. 'That way the Council makes lots of money and you get to keep your job.'

'Sir,' Darth Vader said, 'if I might take issue with you, I do not make people's lives' miserable. They make other people's lives miserable by parking inconsiderately, by parking against the law, by parking in dangerous places. If they refuse to be considerate, it is my job to try to persuade them to improve.'

'At £100.00 per lesson.'

'It's only £50.00 if they pay within fourteen days, sir.'

'That's thoughtful.'

'Would you rather I ignored these thoughtless and dangerous drivers, sir? Would you rather a child was knocked over and killed because someone parked in a dangerous position?'

'I hardly think anyone's going to die because I've parked my car on top of two stray yellow blobs that Jackson Pollock might be proud of.'

'Jackson Pollock, sir?'

'Never mind. Tell me, E1515, don't you ever wish you had a different job?'

'All the time, sir, all the time.'

'What would you like to be instead of being the Second Best Parking Attendant in the city, E1515?'

'I've told you already, sir. I'd like to be the Best Parking Attendant in the city, sir. I love my job, sir, I think it is valuable and important. My family has shops all over the city, sir, but I want to be a part of your great society. I didn't come over here from Bangladesh to recreate it here in Britain. I came to be part of what I believe will be a better future. I will sit my motorcycle test soon, and if I pass I will get to stay on this scooter. Perhaps I might buy one for my personal use, too. I like the freedom. I will be the first member of my family to have his own scooter.'

'The first member of your family to have a scooter, eh?' I said, my voice dripping with sarcasm. But at the same time I began to see the guy in a different light. He was only doing his job after all. Just not very well. I was about to address him as 'E1515' again when I suddenly thought to ask him something.

'I'm calling you E1515 here. What's your real name?'

He'd have worn a bewildered expression on his face but for the fact that he looked bewildered all the time anyway. 'My name is Ali, sir.'

'My name is, Tim, Ali. Let's shake hands and start again.' He took my hand, suspiciously. I took a deep breath and said, 'OK, I'm going to try to get off this parking fine.'

'It is your right to appeal, sir.'

'Would you like me to appeal, Ali?'

'It's not important to me, sir.'

'What about your targets, Ali, aren't they important to you?'

'No, sir If I give a car a ticket and the driver successfully appeals later, it still counts as my ticket.'

'How would you suggest that I get off paying the fine, Ali? Do you have any ideas?'

Ali/Darth Vader/E1515 thought for a long time. Then he went to the back of the car and, using his shoes, scuffed some leaves over the offending yellow lines so that they were hidden.

'I'd suggest you take a photograph of those leaves, sir. Then you can say that the wind must have been blowing them backwards and forwards. At the time you parked, the yellow lines were invisible, whereas at the time I gave you a ticket, the yellow lines were visible.'

'Yellow blobs.'

'Yellow lines,' he insisted. 'I'm trying to be helpful, sir.'

I couldn't help but smile: he *was* trying to be helpful. I thanked him, we shook hands again, and I wished him a nice day.

Six weeks later I received standard letter 28B from the local council informing me that my appeal had been successful and that on this occasion my parking ticket had been cancelled. However, the letter insisted that the ticket had been correctly issued – despite claiming that my offence was 'parking in a (non-existent) bus stop' – and that I should not expect to be so leniently treated in future.

A few weeks after that, I heard that Ali had failed his motorcycle test and had been compelled to return to a foot patrol in another part of the city. I didn't see him again.

Waxwings

Waxwings are beautiful birds. They're around the same size as a starling, perhaps slightly smaller, and if you're lucky enough to see one up close in good light you'll see brightly coloured streaks of red, yellow and black at various points around its head, at the tip of its wings, and in its tail. They look completely out of place in Scotland, in fact, more like exotic African birds. Unfortunately, waxwings are rarely seen in good light in Britain because they turn up in the winter when the light is poor. Then, birdwatchers depend on its other obvious characteristic - a crest on the back of its head.

Waxwings are actually pretty rare visitors to Britain; their real home is in Scandinavia. But if the breeding season is good, and there is a shortage of berries in Norway and Sweden, these beautiful birds hop across the North Sea to see what they can pick up easily over here. I suppose it's a bit like those Londoners who pop across on the Eurostar to stock up on cheap French wine. This mass migration is known as an 'irruption' in the trade, a word which sounds made-up but is probably real. For birdwatchers, the coming of waxwings is certainly very real, an event rather like a solar eclipse, and they flock to catch a glimpse. (Technically, of course, the waxwings do the flocking.)

Geoff and Sheila Arrowsmith are keen birdwatchers. Sheila has been a birdwatcher all her life, but Geoff is a late convert, something he's taken up with gusto since his retirement from his job as an art teacher. He sees it as an interest he can share with Sheila. 'Goodness me,' he's forever saying, 'if you can't beat 'em, join 'em, that's what they say, isn't it?' Incidentally, Geoff simply finds it impossible to say a sentence without the words 'goodness' and 'me' in it.

It's been a wonderful winter for waxwings, but thus far neither Geoff nor Sheila has seen so much as one.

Sheila always spots birds first, she has better eyesight, she simply has more talent, and she can also use her twenty-year-old binoculars faster than anything Geoff can manage. Like everything else he does in life, Geoff has thrown himself into birdwatching, spending considerable sums on 'the best kit' as he puts it, although of course there's a 'goodness me' in there, too. His binoculars are top-of-the-range, image-stabilising Canon affairs which cost plenty and weigh quite a bit, too, but his real birdwatching pride and joy is his zoom telescope, complete with tripod and weatherproof case, which set him back over a thousand pounds. Sheila freely admits that Geoff has more money than sense. She should know; she worked in the Bank of Scotland all of her life and she's seen enough spendthrifts to recognise one sharing her bedroom each night. Despite all of Geoff's 'kit', almost every bird they see is spotted by Sheila first, who then spends the next five minutes trying to point it out to Geoff, who sometimes picks it out, although more often the thing just flies off somewhere else.

But at least the two of them are level on the waxwing score. Picture the scene: it's a beautiful, cold, January Saturday, and Sheila is busily pruning back some holly and other bushes, while at the same time chatting with Martin, her immediate neighbour to the south who is doing some tidying up of his own. She likes Martin, an ordinary sort of chap in his forties who doesn't try to impress her, but listens to Sheila as if she were a wise old owl. Today, the wise old owl has been talking about waxwings. If you listen carefully, you can just about catch what she's saying.

'They're really lovely birds, Martin. And they have this habit of popping up where you least expect them,' she says.

'I suppose you need binoculars,' he responds. 'We've got an old pair in the house somewhere. I should really look them out.'

'No, no, not with waxwings. You should be able to spot the crest even in the poor light. To tell the truth, Martin, binoculars are just a bit of a nuisance, sometimes. Just keep your eyes peeled. Applies to a lot of birdwatching.' Sheila is a 'birdwatcher', not a 'birder'. She doesn't like the new term, regards it as pretentious.

'I'll keep it in mind. And now that I know what to look for, perhaps I'll spot a waxwing, too.'

'If you spot one, you'll probably see lots. They flock together. Let me know if you do see any, though, I'd not want to miss them.'

They chat on other topics for a while, then they agree that it's too good a day to waste the chance to do some gardening, and they spend the next half hour in silence. Not that there's complete silence, though, because from Sheila's upper floor, Geoff can be heard practising his electric guitar. Geoff practises his guitar twice a day, scales and arpeggios first thing in the morning - and for Geoff and Sheila, outrageously early risers, that means around five-thirty - and melodies after lunch. Because it's well past two, the street echoes to the sounds of *Johnny B Goode*, *Samba Pa Ti*, *Hocus Pocus*, and a host of other guitar standards. Geoff likes to have the window open for the fresh air as he plays, but fortunately he's not too bad a player, goodness me, he's quite good these days, in fact.

Suddenly, the music stops, and within seconds he's down in the garden talking with Sheila and Martin. Goodness me, he's rather excited, and he's waving his mobile phone at her.

'Sheila, Sheila, goodness me, Sheila, they're in the car park at Asda! Goodness me!'

Martin smiles quietly. Asda is a large supermarket just over a mile away. 'Goodness me, Geoff, *what* are in the car park in Asda?' Sheila says nothing - she just smiles benevolently - because she knows that Geoff is like a runaway train in this mood. There's no stopping him from going on no matter what.

'Waxwings!' Geoff yells, 'Goodness me, Sheila, waxwings"

Sheila can put two and two together and come up with the right answer.

'Is this your mobile phone 'app', darling?'

"NearbyBirds', dear – goodness me, yes, 'NearbyBirds'. It's such a good app, you know, it tells you on your mobile whenever there's a sighting of exciting birds in the local area. Goodness me, yes.'

Sheila knows all about NearbyBirds, as ever since Geoff purchased it for his phone he's talked about nothing else. But she knows it gets her husband excited to tell her about it, so she simply smiles benevolently and lets him do so yet again.

'Goodness me, why don't we go and look for them right now?' (By now you should have worked out who says that.)

Sheila's slightly taken aback. 'What about your guitar practice, dear?' Privately, she was enjoying her quiet afternoon in the garden, not to mention her chat with Martin. In any case, quite a lot of the shrubs still need to be pruned back for the winter. However, Geoff's got the bit between his teeth.

'My guitar practice can wait, I'm sure. Goodness me, we must see the waxwings while we have the chance, mustn't we?' Then he stops and realises that Sheila's not so keen. 'Oh goodness me I'm sorry, dear, I wasn't thinking of you at all. Of course you'd rather stay here. Goodness me that was rather thoughtless of me, wasn't it?'

Sheila smiles at Geoff, and Geoff realises that once again his affectionate wife is perfectly happy to accommodate his enthusiasm for birdwatching.

'You could never be thoughtless, darling. Just the opposite, in fact, you're the most considerate man I know. Let's go and see what's in Asda's car park.'

And so, just five minutes later, they're setting off in Sheila's Micra, which perhaps doesn't seem very exciting by comparison with Geoff's sports car, but she's persuaded him that (a) the Micra is a lot quieter and (b) it carries all Geoff's bird-spotting equipment much more readily. Geoff goes with two pairs of binoculars, one a general-view pair, the other a pair with more magnification; his telescope, complete with tripod; and last but not least a digital single-lens reflex camera with which he hopes to capture the moment. As for Sheila herself, well… she takes nothing. She reckons her eyesight will do well enough.

The day is both cold and icy so that Geoff – always the most careful of drivers at any time, and he's volunteered to drive, goodness me – takes almost twice as long as expected to get to the Asda car park. At least Sheila's wrapped him up warmly, as Geoff himself tends to underdress for winter birdwatching then shivers almost uncontrollably – although Geoff himself would never complain. Goodness me, he never actually complains about anything.

Geoff doesn't even complain when they get out of the car and there's not a waxwing to be seen, not so much as one, goodness me. Plenty of starlings, yes, even the odd sparrow, and Sheila spots a long-tailed tit in the trees above her, pointing it out to Geoff, who unfortunately is quite unable to follow the direction of her hand and therefore consequently sees nothing. Sheila, of course, has benefited from knowing that long-tailed tits not only have a long tail, they have a distinctive 'tse-tse-tse-tse' call which they twitter all the time, and this sound alerted her to look to see where they were.

But in any case Geoff is in 'waxwing mode' and if a golden eagle flew past right now he'd barely bat an eyelid. He wanders over to an elderly couple and asks if they've seen any waxwings around; they in turn simply look at him as if he's asked which planet he's just landed on.

Sheila suggests that while they're in the Asda's car park, they might as well stock up on a few provisions, which as ever turns out to be ten days' worth of shopping, so twenty minutes elapse before they merge with a trolley-full. The reception for Geoff's mobile isn't too great inside Asda, though, so that it's as they leave that a strange noise suddenly erupts from Geoff's left-hand trouser pocket.

Sheila doesn't need to ask: it's the alert from 'NearbyBirds', a nightingale call, a bird which coincidentally neither have ever seen or heard in real life. (Nightingales are not to be found in Asda's car park in Edinburgh, not even in a 'good year'.)

'Goodness me, Sheila,' says Geoff, 'there are waxwings at the Royal Mail sorting office at Sighthill!'

Sheila sighs. Sighthill is on the south-west edge of the city, just about as far from where they are now as they could be. But she loves her husband, he's a kind and decent man, and this is a small sacrifice to make for him. She takes the wheel, primarily because she knows Geoff's mind is completely focused on one thing, and it isn't driving. It takes longer than she'd hoped to get the sorting office – which happens to be closed, but that's not the point.

They arrive and get out – the gates being locked, they're on foot from here on. Geoff prowls round the perimeter fence, hoping to find some sort of entrance, and he's lucky: there's a hole on the far side where some kids have been playing. Because the trees overhang the car park so much, you really need to be inside looking up to get a clear view of what's in the trees. Geoff looks backwards and forwards along the trees, hoping to catch a glimpse of something that might be a waxwing, but eventually – fully fifteen minutes later – all he catches a glimpse of is Sheila's resigned expression.

'I don't think you're going to be lucky,' Sheila says, stating the obvious.

Geoff turns round towards her and says, 'Goodness me, you're right as usual, my love. You're right as usual.' He has a slightly bewildered look at the best of times. He frequently frowns and smiles at the same time, confusing not only anyone looking at him, but sometimes confusing Geoff himself. But Sheila knows the signs: his shoulders are down.

'How about heading for home, my love?' she says. 'We could have a nice cup of Nescafé and a Penguin biscuit.'

'A Penguin biscuit, Sheila? Goodness me, there's a good idea.'

But it's not going to be that straightforward. They set off for home, but of course now that Geoff isn't driving, he's free to study his mobile phone and its NearbyBirds app, and it transpires that he's missed an alert while he's been patrolling around Sighthill.

'Waxwings!' he yells. It must be serious – that's all he says.

Sheila slams on the brakes and looks all around. There are trees over by a nearby tram line. 'Where?'

'In Princes Street Gardens, Sheila! Over 200 reported just eight minutes ago. Goodness me – that's an awful lot, isn't it? They're surely still there, too.'

Sheila sighs. 'You'd like me to head for Princes Street Gardens?'

Geoff doesn't say a word. He just smiles and frowns, frowns and smiles, then smiles and frowns again. The Gardens are right in the centre of the city, underneath the Castle, and there's nowhere anywhere near that they can park.

Sheila loves Geoff dearly. She loves his childish enthusiasm for everything – particularly his childish enthusiasm for birdwatching, taken up purely to please her. How can she turn him down?

It takes just over fifteen minutes to reach the gardens, twenty-five more to find a parking place, and a further ten to reach the gardens on foot, laden with all of Geoff's kit. As they make their way down Lothian Road, Geoff gets a few strange looks from shoppers making the most of the January Sales, but he's not bothered: he's on a mission. Sheila keeps him company, but following slightly behind she catches a brief sight of something that might or might not be the outline of a couple of waxwings. She won't tell Geoff about that, though.

Needless to say, there are no waxwings left by the time Geoff finds his way into the Gardens. They're due to close in half an hour anyway, and – frowning and smiling in equal measure – he eventually admits defeat.

'Goodness me,' he says, 'I think the waxwings have beaten us today, Sheila, haven't they?'

'Penguin, Geoff, darling?'

'Penguin, Sheila! Goodness me, that'll be one bird I'll get today, won't it?' He chuckles at his little joke as they get into the car, muttering, 'goodness me, goodness me' repeatedly.

As they drive home, there's yet another nightingale call on Geoff's mobile phone.

'Goodness me, Sheila! Waxwings at Longniddry! Can we – ?'

Sheila sighs yet again. Longniddry is a dozen miles down the east coast. 'Geoff, it'll be dark by the time – '

'Oh, goodness me, how thoughtless of me, Sheila. Of course it's too far.'

'Think of your Penguin and cup of coffee, dear,' Sheila says.

'Goodness me, yes, what a good idea.'

It takes only ten minutes to get home. Remarkably, Martin is still pottering around, pruning, weeding, generally tidying up. He's been making the most of the beautiful, crisp winter's afternoon. As Geoff and Sheila get out of the Micra, he greets them with a cheery smile.

'Hello, Martin,' Sheila says as she gets out of the car. 'Have you been busy?'

'I've been at it all afternoon,' he says. 'It's just been too good a chance to miss. I managed to clear a whole area of the front garden across there.' He waves in the general direction of an area that looks as if it's been flattened by a steamroller.

'Very impressive,' says Sheila. She summons Geoff across to admire Martin's work.

'Goodness me, Martin. Goodness me!' Well, what else was he ever going to say?

'Thanks,' says Martin. 'Did you see your waxwings?'

Sheila explains that they've been away for over two hours, had a nice tour of the city, but seen not so much as a single waxwing. She doesn't mention the two she probably saw in Lothian Road. Geoff simply frown-smiles.

'Oddly enough,' Martin says, 'I had a little visitation here.' He points to a tree in the front corner of his garden, a tree that actually overhangs Geoff and Sheila's, too. 'Remind me,' Martin says, 'the birds you're talking about have that crest, don't they?'

'Yes,' says Sheila, rather deliberately.

'I thought they might just be starlings to start with, or some sort of finch, or tits, even sparrows – I mean, I really don't know much about birds. But they were really close, and the light was great – well of course it's been such a lovely afternoon.'

'Yes,' says Sheila. She's resigned herself already to what's coming.

Martin carries on. 'Anyway, they're quite tame, aren't they? They weren't really bothered by me being here at all, so long as I stayed reasonably still. They were as near to me as I am to you now, I'd say, certainly the ones on the lower branches. They had these red and yellow bits. You could see it quite clearly. Quite colourful, really. I'm not that interested in birds, really, but I have to say that these were nice to look at.'

Sheila and Geoff are simply listening now. Eventually, Sheila manages to say, 'That's great, Martin. Were there a few of them? Sometimes they come in flocks.'

'That's another thing,' Martin said, 'there were scores of them. There must have been almost a hundred on that one tree alone – they seemed to be everywhere. Made a lot of noise, too.' Then he added, 'You probably wish you'd stayed at home now.'

'Yes,' says Sheila, quietly. 'Yes, I think we probably missed something. Lucky you, though, Martin.' She turns to Geoff and says, 'Wasn't Martin lucky? Wasn't that wonderful?'

Geoff, who has been totally speechless until now, starts to mouth something.

'G——'

But the sound just won't come out.

Agent Orange

In truth, I didn't really know what to expect.

The only picture I'd ever seen of Fiona was a small black and white passport-sized thing on her website, the same photograph she used on her Twitter page and on a social networking site for business people. I had a vision of her as tall, thin, elegant, perhaps a stereotypical artist, all based on nothing but my own extrapolation of a head and shoulders shot into a sophisticated, modern young woman. The Fiona of my imagination had poise, confidence, and power over people.

I can't really say I was nervous. I'd corresponded with a couple of literary agents before but I'd never actually met any, and certainly none who had ever made the effort to make the train journey through to Edinburgh all the way from Glasgow just to meet me. If, at last, someone was going to accept my novel, then I was excited rather than intimidated at the prospect; and Fiona's emails and text messages – once we'd exchanged mobile phone numbers – were friendly enough. We'd even dropped into the habit of closing our messages with a 'X'. I'd sent her the manuscript of my novel, and she'd said she'd like to come through and discuss it with me. I'd suggested meeting for coffee near the station, and it all sounded more than promising, but I was aware that you can never tell with these things.

We'd arranged to meet at a quarter-past eleven in the morning in Haymarket station, which was the last stop the Glasgow to Edinburgh Scotrail Express was destined to make before it reached the end of its journey at Waverley. Haymarket had recently been redeveloped. I'd not been inside since, so I was somewhat thrown when I discovered that only passengers are allowed anywhere near the trains or the platforms. Fiona had texted me to say she was on the half-past ten from Glasgow Queen Street, but the trains run through Haymarket below ground level and are hidden from the street-level entrance. I had no idea what was coming or going other than from the far-too-loud-yet-barely-audible announcements echoing through the concourse. I had imagined trying to pick her out in the crowd, perhaps wearing some sort of identification such as a white carnation; instead I was condemned to a soulless 'Meeting Point' tucked away in the corner of the foyer.

I took out my mobile phone and started to send her a text to explain where I would be. It was all a bit of a struggle, since at my age I need to take my glasses off, which in turn meant that in the cold weather I had to remove my hat as well. I was still fumbling with the screen when I was aware that I wasn't alone, and a female figure was beside me, smiling, but looking slightly quizzical.

'Tom?'

'Fiona?'

We shook hands a little awkwardly.

'I'm sorry – your train arrived slightly earlier than I'd expected. I wasn't expecting you yet for a few more minutes,' I said, then realising how that might sound, 'Oh, I'm sorry, of course I'm delighted you could come. I'm being so rude. Was your journey okay?'

'You're not being rude at all,' she said. 'I just told you the time it arrives at Waverley, forgetting I was getting off the stop before. My journey was fine, thank you.'

I didn't want to stare, but it was as well she'd approached me rather than the other way around; I'd never have recognised her. She was probably not much more than five foot three – almost a foot shorter than me – and with a curved, rather than a slim, figure. She wore a bright orange crocheted hat and a long scarf to match. She carried a satchel over her left shoulder. And she had a wide, friendly, welcoming smile. She wasn't so much stunningly beautiful, just that her personality was immediately attractive.

'You're wearing glasses,' I said to her. They made her look better, softer, actually.

'So are you. You weren't wearing them when I first saw you in the station, though. It made it easier to spot you.'

I had forgotten. 'I wear contact lenses when I'm being vain – glasses are my default position, I'm afraid. For photographs I just take the damned things off and hide them.'

She laughed. 'Looks like we're two of a kind,' she said. 'It's a sign of age, I suppose,' she added, and although I might have been almost twice her age I allowed her little confidence to linger between us.

By now we were outside the station and as we made our way across the maze of roads and tramlines towards the city centre, I suggested we take coffee across the road in CoffeeLovers, a former bank building with rustic interiors and bare wooden floorboards.

'Good idea,' she said. 'I like CoffeeLovers – so much nicer coffee than in Starbreaks. We have them in Glasgow, too.' I hadn't realised that CoffeeLovers existed outside Edinburgh, and felt slightly deflated. But we found a seat by a window, and she allowed me to buy her a small americano and share a chocolate orange tiffin. She removed her coat and laid it, together with her orange hat and scarf, on a nearby chair. As we sat, we made small talk, exploring a little of each other's personal back story. She'd been a journalist, and still did some freelance work, particularly book reviews, but the offer to go into partnership with an old school friend in her literary agency had been too good to refuse. Her husband, who was some sort of IT expert in the Clydesdale Bank, was very supportive. I told her I'd been a civil servant but the office had been relocated and rather than pay the cost of moving me, I'd been offered an early retirement package. We both mentioned families a couple of times. It felt like we were drawing lines in the sand: this is very nice but I'm not available. She arranged most of her meetings during the school day while her only daughter was at school. I, of course, have grandchildren these days. But there was some sort of chemistry there between us all the same, even if it was simply a genuine friendship. At one point I was reminded of another scene which took place not so far from a railway station, in *Brief Encounter*, without a hint of an affair, of course. I tried to remember the music. Not that much happened in *Brief Encounter* either.

We drifted on to other topics, common interests, books, music, movies we both liked. Her tastes in film were quite close to mine, and she was amused that I'd seen *The Graduate* at least fourteen times. A surprising number of albums appeared on both of our iPods. We talked about some of the places we'd been on holiday. I liked New York, she preferred Boston; I liked Venice, she Rome. She crocheted, and had made the orange hat and scarf herself; I couldn't match that. But we agreed on more than we differed. It was Rachmaninoff, *Second Piano Concerto*.

Briefly, I was reminded what it felt like to be nineteen again, discovering a new woman in my life, her likes and passions; and, if I'm honest, flattered by being in the company of an attractive woman many years younger than me.

Eventually, however, she reached into her satchel; I knew what was coming.

'This is very nice, but we need to discuss your manuscript,' she said. I remained silent, so she continued, spreading out the first few pages of my precious work on the table for no apparent reason. 'It's good, Tom. It shows promise...'

Some sentences seem for ever destined to finish with the unspoken word 'but'. I let her speak, but I had very little to say anyway. I took a sip from my glass of water in an attempt to hide any disappointment in my face.

'I like the way you paint your characters, and the plot line is excellent. I even like your writing style a lot. You have talent, really.'

'But you don't like my novel,' I said, finally helping her out.

She took a long, deep breath, then let it all go very slowly. 'It's not for me, Tom. I'm not sure if the problem is your novel, actually, more likely it's me. Perhaps I wasn't in the right frame of mind when I read it but...'

She must have seen the look of dismay on my face, because she reached across the table and gently squeezed my hand.

'Tom, you must keep trying. Don't give up. Work on your novel here a little bit more. Try writing something else.'

I looked down at the table. 'I can't deny I was half-hoping... I rather thought that because you were prepared to meet me in Edinburgh... come all the way through just to have a cup of coffee with me here... that meant you liked what I'd written.'

Fiona looked away, a little shocked. 'Oh dear,' she said. 'I'm sorry, I should have explained. I was making the journey through to Edinburgh anyway. I have a client to visit here – we're meeting for lunch – so I thought I'd kill two birds with one stone.' She looked back at me and squeezed my hand again. 'I'm terribly sorry, Tom. I can see you're so disappointed. You obviously thought I was making a special visit to see you.'

Now it was my turn to look at the table again. I'd picked up on her description of her other writer as a 'client'. I was just another piece of business. 'No, it's my fault, really,' I said. 'I read more into it all than I should have. And one thing I've learned about being a writer is that you need to get used to being kicked about.'

She looked a little hurt. 'Oh no, I didn't mean to kick you, Tom. Please – you must believe that. Please don't say that.' Then suddenly, she was upbeat again, pushing my novel towards me. 'Look, take your manuscript back. I mean it, work on it, polish it up.'

I didn't have the heart to tell her I'd been 'polishing it up' for four years.

She looked at her watch and stood up. 'Listen,' she said, 'I must be going. I've got lunch with that client in the West End at one o'clock. I must be rushing.' She grabbed her smartphone and starting texting. 'I'll just let him know I might be a little late.' Then she put her coat back on, her orange hat, then wound her orange scarf around her neck a few times before closing her satchel and hitching it up onto her shoulder.

'I'm sorry I must be rushing off, Tom,' she said. 'I feel a bit ungrateful, allowing you to buy me coffee and then disappointing you so.'

'It's OK,' I said. 'It's been nice meeting you. I've enjoyed it.'

She looked into my eyes and smiled – the big wide smile looked different somehow, now. 'Except for the knock-back,' she said.

I smiled back, trying to put on a brave face. 'Except for the knock-back.'

She gazed at me for a moment, then she reached up and gently kissed me on the cheek, tenderly rather than in any way sensuously, but an act of genuine intimacy nonetheless.

'I've got to go, really I have,' she said. 'Keep at it. Rework that manuscript. Write some other stuff. And above all, let's keep in touch.' Then she turned and hurried out of the door.

It goes without saying that our paths never crossed again.

The Audition

'**N**ext!'

A rather odd-looking man got up from his chair and made his way over to the desk. He'd been sitting in the waiting room of Magnetic Records for over two hours and now that his turn had come, he was stiff and bent half-double. He wore a long brown coat and a wig not unlike those worn by judges in British courts. He might or might not have been carrying a pomander, but either way he carried a strong perfume.

'Full name,' the woman behind the counter yelled, even though the man was only a foot or two away from her.

'Johann Sebastian Bach.'

'Could you spell that please?' The visitor patiently spelled out his full name and she wrote it down on a fresh form. On went the receptionist. 'Well, Jo–Hann,' she said in a deep Tennessee accent. 'What do you play? Do you sing? Lead guitar? Bass guitar? We could do with a nice bass

– ever since the man that played with Johnny-Lee Williams and the Oklahoma boys passed away. 'Lil unfortunate, that, but shoulda pointed the gun in the other direction, wouldn't ya say?'

She looked at the strange man, expecting a reply, but he was too bemused to speak and she began to take pity on him.

'Why now, Mr Batch, my name's Mary-Lee. Why don't you just take your time and tell me all about it?'

The stranger took a deep breath, then began. 'Three weeks ago I sent a couple of demo tapes in to your studio here, and yesterday I received a letter from your company, Magnetic Records, asking me to come in for an audition.'

Bach waved the letter at her; Mary-Lee glanced at it and handed it back. 'Why bless me, Jo-Hann, ain't that just the thing? You must be so excited! Is this you-ah first aw-dition?'

'I've done auditions before, but this is the first I've done in Nashville,' Bach replied.

Mary-Lee stood for a moment, arms akimbo, then wiggled her hips and said, 'Well, Jo-Hann, Ah-ma just so pleased for you. But I gotta do mah job and just take a little bitty detail first, is that all rightee?' Bach nodded, so she continued. 'So, Jo-Hann, well ah need an address.'

So off they went, while Bach supplied a temporary address – a hotel in downtown Nashville – a mobile phone number and an email address, jsbach@brandenburg.com, his next of kin and some details of his education.

Then Mary-Lee moved on to the next part of the form.

'Well, now Jo-Hann. Just what do you do?' She smiled broadly and expectantly.

'Well, I sent a demo tape of some music I thought you might be interested in. Partitas, inventions, preludes and fugues, that sort of thing.'

'Are they in-stru-ments, Jo-Hann?'

'No, no, I played them on my clavichord,' he explained.

'Clavichord? What's that – some sort of mouth music?'

'It's a keyboard. Like a harpsichord, I suppose.'

Mary-Lee suddenly became excited. 'You play keyboards? Well bless me, Jo-Hann, this I must hear. Have you brought it with you, this keyboard?'

'The letter from Mr Weinberg said I wouldn't require it today.'

Mary-Lee sat back, content. 'Well then, Jo-Hann, if Mr Weinberg says you won't need your in-stru-ment, then you won't need it. Here in Nashville, Mr Weinberg decides what's goin' down, ya know?'

Bach didn't, but said nothing.

Mary-Lee pointed over to a glass door on the other side of the corridor. 'Why don't you go and sit you-ah self down in the waiting room, Jo-Hann? Mr Weinberg will be out to see you in just a little bitty minute.'

Bach simply nodded and did as requested.

It was to be a full forty-five minutes before Bach was attended to. The waiting room was full of other hopefuls of all shapes and sizes, some carrying guitars or sheet music, and one or two were quietly rehearsing their acts in corners of the room. Bach had all but given up hope of his turn ever coming round, and was on to the fifth cookery magazine on the waiting-room table, when suddenly the door burst open and two men looked part-way into the room, the way doctors do when your turn has come to be seen.

'Which of you is Jo-Hann Seb-as-tian Bach?' the smaller man asked. He wore a conservative grey suit, while his younger and taller colleague wore a brown suit. Bach raised his hand slightly sheepishly. He was beginning to wonder if this recording contract was a good idea after all.

The smaller man extended his hand. 'Well my, Jo-Hann – can we call you Jo-Hann? – we're real sorry to keep you waiting. Pressure of work, of course. Say, I'm Sam Weinberg and this gentleman is Max Golding, one of our rising stars at Magnetic.' Bach shook hands with each in turn. 'Say Jo–Hann, you just call us Max and Sam. Let's keep it all informal.'

Bach nodded. 'You said I should come for an audition… Sam. In your letter. Did you get my demo tapes?'

'Tapes? Demo tapes? Oh we probably won't need those,' Weinberg said. 'Tell me what you do.'

'I write music. I sent you some examples, a lot in fact. Did you like them?'

'Oh we ain't got time to listen to all the tapes we get sent in. Why don't you just tell Max and me what you do?'

Bach sighed, realising that once again he was going to have to tell them everything. 'I play organ, harpsichord, clavichord – '

'What's that?' scowled the taller Golding guy.

'It's a type of keyboard,' Bach explained.

Weinberg suddenly sounded ecstatic. 'Ah, so you play keyboards, Jo-Hann! Excellent! We can always use a keyboard player.' Then he dropped his voice and added, conspiratorially, 'You any good, Jo-Hann?'

Bach cleared his throat. 'I'm considered quite good in my home town of Leipzig.'

'As in Leipzig, North Dakota? Well, my, Jo-Hann, ain't that just the thing?' Before Bach could correct him, he was off again. 'So you're a frontiersman, Mr Bach?'

'Leipzig is in Germany,' Bach said, patiently.

Weinberg scowled. 'You ain't one of them Nazis are you? I got issues with Nazis.'

'I'm not a Nazi, Mr Weinberg,' Bach replied. 'To be honest, I'm not quite sure what a Nazi is, but I've heard they aren't very nice.'

'They sure ain't, Mr Back,' Weinberg growled, mis-pronouncing his name yet again.

Golding tried to lighten the mood. 'What are you going to play for us, Mr Bach?'

'I was going to play my Theme and Variations in G.'

'Theme and Variations?'

'Yes, I play a simple tune and then variations of it.'

'You can make that last for a three-minute single?' Golding said disbelievingly.

'Well over half an hour,' Bach replied.

Golding and Weinberg looked across at each other.

'Look Mr Bach,' Golding said, 'I don't wanna offend you but could we keep it to our standard length of three minutes? Can you leave out a couple of verses?'

'Naturally. I can tailor the piece however you wish.'

'Now you're talking my language, Mr Bach,' Weinberg chipped in. 'And if it's good, we could release the long version as an album – say, but we haven't heard you play yet. Where's your keyboard, Jo-Hann?'

'I didn't bring one, remember? I was rather hoping I could borrow one of yours.'

'One of our 'whats'? We don't have no clavichord here.'

'I can play it for you on an organ or even on that piano over there,' Bach said, pointing to the upright in the middle of the floor. 'It sounds different on each instrument of course.'

Weinberg stroked his chin.

'OK, Jo-Hann. Let's go to the party!' and ushered Bach to the piano while he himself and Golding took a chair.

Bach began to play, play such a beautiful melody that the notes soared to the ceiling and resonated all around the room. The theme – in two parts – was slow but tuneful, each glorious phrase quietly in turn simultaneously exploring the most inaccessible corners of the studio, and of the listener's soul. Only the most hardened individual could not be moved by its sweetness.

Unfortunately, two such individuals were seated before Bach.

'Say Jo-Hann,' Weinberg said, 'care to speed it up a bit?'

At that moment, Bach moved on to the first of the variations, which was much quicker.

'Hey, that's more like it!' Weinberg called, then after a moment said, 'But not too fast. That needs rhythm and bass, Jo-Hann.'

Bach stopped playing. 'Rhythm and bass? For a keyboard piece?'

'Sure, and a brass section, too. Jazz it up a bit.'

Golding suddenly sat up. 'How about making a hip-hop version, Johann? Could you try that for us? Or could we line you up to accompany Dolly Parton?'

Bach shook his head. 'I don't think this is working, gentlemen,' and with that he stood up at the piano and turned for the door.

'Hey, Jo-Hann, don't go!' Weinberg cried out. 'Don't be downhearted, please. We might be able to adapt your music somehow, after all this is Nashville! Anyway, what's this song of yours called? Does it have a name?'

'Not yet,' Bach replied. 'Any suggestions? I don't care, really. You could call it the 'Weinberg and Golding Variations' for all I care.'

'Nice try, Jo-Hann,' Weinberg replied, smiling, 'but we should keep our names out of it, I think.'

Bach sensed an opportunity. 'Or combine your names in some way? How about 'The Wining Variations'?'

The two laughed uproariously. 'Now that is real funny, Jo-Hann. I almost like that,' said Weinberg. 'Just not quite funny enough. Perhaps you'll come up with another title some day.'

'OK, gentlemen, I think that means we're done. Thank you for listening.'

'Unless you have anything else to let us hear?'

'Most of it's in the same style,' Bach said. Returning to the piano, he said, 'How about this? Like the other tune, it's in the key of G,' and with that he played a few lines.

'Sounds not too bad, Jo-Hann. Does it have words?'

Bach shook his head. 'Not at the moment. Nobody listens to the words anyway, they're often in foreign languages. For all I care you could just make it up as you went along.'

'Show us,' Golding suggested.

Bach played the new tune and sang along with it, using the first words that came into his head – stuff about 'fandangos', 'middles', 'cartwheels on the floor' and so on – just to fill the space. When he couldn't think of anything else, Bach simply sang 'a whiter shade of pale'. Golding and Weinberg listened politely to the end.

'Well,' said Weinberg. 'That was some song, Jo-Hann. But you'll understand that it'll never catch on. Who'd buy a three-minute single about 'fandangos', for goodness sake?

I'm not sure even our own lyricists could ever come with anything for your melodies, Jo-Hann.'

Bach sighed. 'You're probably right,' he said. He stood up, this time for good, and made his way across to the studio exit, wondering at the same time how he could ever persuade recording studios to take his music. Perhaps one day.

But in the meantime he faced yet another day of auditions tomorrow, somewhere else, in yet another studio.

Bach's *Goldberg Variations* were published in 1741 and have gone on to become one of the great pieces in keyboard repertoire. His *Air On A G String* – actually in the key of D – was probably written earlier, around 1720, and was later to form the core of the 1967 Procul Harum No 1 hit *A Whiter Shade Of Pale*.

Magda

Try **and picture** the scene: it's winter. Edinburgh is renowned for being cold and windy, and that's just its residents. The prevailing wind is from the south-west, as it is almost everywhere in the island, a wind that brings raw, wet Atlantic storms, often at gale-force speed. Two or three times each winter, though, the wind swings round to the east and biting winds drive in from the North Sea for days on end. The weather might be dry, even sunny, but it's bitterly cold, sweeping across from Scandinavia and the Russian Steppes to chill the warmest heart. Edinburgh is right in the firing line of these meteorological villains.

At least Edinburgh doesn't normally experience much snow; that's mainly reserved for the hills and the ski resorts north of the Central Belt. But March 2018 wasn't part of a normal winter: like the rest of Britain, the entire country had inches – in many places, several feet – of snow.

Edinburgh ground to a halt. Actually, its city leaders ordered it to grind to a halt, sending schools, non-emergency hospital patients, and non-essential workers home to cower in the shelter of their own homes until the snow disappeared and it was safe to come out.

One might debate whether my job fell into the category of 'essential worker' or not. Since taking slightly early retirement from my job as a teacher, I'd been supplementing my income by doling out americanos, cappuccinos, macchiatos, lattes and flat whites in the West End Costa Cafe shop. The great and the good of Edinburgh West End society certainly depended on and appreciated my high-class barista skills. I'd even won 'Costa Barista of the Month' the previous November.

Now, though, I'd been sent home, and there was nothing for it but to turn my collar up, although that wasn't a lot of use, really. What I really needed was my cap, a navy blue item with a short peak that had been given to me by a very good friend who insisted on calling me 'Captain'. I didn't really mind, and to be honest the cap does look a bit like the sort of thing old guys on barges wear. But I minded having accidentally left it at home because I'm old enough to be more than a little thin on top and I could feel some more pretty nasty stuff starting to descend on me.

At least I didn't have far to go, because I still lived in Eton Terrace, no more than five minutes' walk across the Dean Bridge from the cafe. I'm not sure if what I could manage in my early sixties constitutes 'running', but I broke into a breathless sort of fast jog as I crossed the Dean Bridge itself, every bit as exposed as the Himalayas. Irritated, I was held up, first by a bunch of youths coming in the opposite direction who seemed to think my antics were amusing; then by someone in front of me who was plugged into earphones and neither knew nor cared about my presence directly behind her. Eventually, I found the shelter of my little haven on the north-east side of the bridge, and in no time after that I was inside my flat, settled in for the rest of the evening, and with a cup of coffee in my hand. Instant, of course.

So I was therefore not in the best of moods when the doorbell rang not five minutes later. I hadn't a clue who it might be – I mean, it could have been a serial killer. But you open the door anyway, don't you?

Whatever I was expecting, it wasn't the young woman in her thirties who was standing in my doorway. I'd met her before, in a past life, and she wasn't a serial killer but she might have been a serial one or two other things instead. She was dressed casually, in denim jeans and a thick woollen jumper, over which she'd draped a rather worn-looking black jacket. Given the six inches of snow even in the city centre streets, her trainers looked a little inadequate.

The last time I'd seen her, she was wearing one item of clothing, just one, a black leather one-piece thing which zipped all the way down the front from the neckline to the crotch. And she was wearing glasses, quite needlessly as she had perfect vision, but the frames were a fashion item, incredibly expensive Crespo frames valued at over a thousand pounds a pair. The spectacles were the only survivors of our last meeting.

'Magda,' I said.

'Kuptin,' she replied. 'I um homeluss. And they vunt to depurt me.'

'But Magda,' I said, although the words were no sooner from my mouth than I knew the answer that was coming, 'why do they want to depurt – deport – you?'

She looked at me as if I were an alien being. 'Brrexitt, Kuptin. Do you nuffer read the news?'

Magda was a Polish acquaintance who had once performed an enormous favour for me. She'd come over some years previously looking to earn enough money to support her ageing parents. But then she'd fallen out with them over something petty, leaving Magda neither wishing to go back to Poland, nor particularly needing to find a settled job. To keep body and soul together, she'd picked up a job as a 'dancer' in a Falkirk night club without quite realising that the 'dancing' involved a few other things as well. Not that Magda minded, so long as she got something out of it, too, be it money or pleasure. And she could look after herself: more than once, rough or over-zealous clients found themselves staring at a knife pointing directly at their eyes from a distance of less than an inch.

Then Magda had met Tam Cantlay. Tam had been a very, very minor pop star around 1970, but he'd been exploited mercilessly by his recording company on account of his diminutive size: just 4'7' in his stocking soles. By the time their paths crossed, Tam was much older, but Magda had instantly felt sorry for Tam, in whom she saw a decent, gentle soul. He had felt more than a little sorry for her, too.

And he didn't let her down either. He teamed her up with a Falkirk boy band called the C-U Jimiz for an adventure that brought them all a little fame and even a little fortune: promoting a little rock band called The Flying Saucers. That was where I came in: I happened to be The Flying Saucers' front man and songwriter.

'So… what happened after The Flying Saucers?' I asked her. By now, she was sitting on my sofa, warming up beside my hot, but completely fake, wood-burning stove.

'Nothing. I vent back to vot I hudd been doing before I met you. Dancing and sux.' Magda's life always seemed to involve an awful lot of sex, some of it remunerated, some not. 'But now ve huff Brrrexitt,' she added.

Magda had lived in Britain for quite a few years and had a perfectly good grasp of the nouns and verbs that make up the English language, but her accent was resolutely eastern European. It became worse when she got angry.

'What reasons are they giving for trying to deport you, Magda? Do you know?'

'They say I do not belong here because I am not Brrrittissh. You Brrrittish treat voreigners so buddly.'

'I didn't vote for Brexit, Magda.'

'It's vot they ull say, Kuptin. They are all snecks here.' I'd almost forgotten: Magda regarded all people she distrusted – and that was most of them – as reptiles.

'Up here in Scotland, we voted strongly to stay in the European Union,' I corrected her. 'Here in Edinburgh more than anywhere else.'

'No, some of you are not snecks, purrhupps. You are feesh. Your MPs in London are snecks.'

It took me a few moments to work out that Magda was referring to Alex Salmond and Nicola Sturgeon, Scotland's two most recent First Ministers. It hadn't previously occurred to me that Magda might be so observant. Yes, I had to accept that we Scots were drawn towards maritime species for leadership: the captain of the most successful rugby team in modern times had been called David Sole, while I myself had always loved Captain Haddock in the Tintin books. He might not have been Scottish, though.

'Very clever, Magda,' I said, utterly condescendingly. 'But you can't stay here.'

She looked at me blankly. 'Vy nutt? Huff you no other rooms?'

'No… it's just that…'

'Vot?' Not angry, simply persistent.

'Well… there's Jane in the flat upstairs.'

Even through her glasses, Magda managed to look bemused: Jane was my ex-wife. Our marriage had gone up in flames some years previously and the fact that she had ended up as my next-door neighbour was a long story that I knew Magda could never understand.

'Do you have suxx with her, Kuptin?' Magda's principal life currency was still sex, despite her circumstances, it seemed. Briefly, I wondered how she managed to earn any money at all, then put the thought quickly out of my mind.

'Magda,' I said, 'I'm afraid that's none of your business.'

'Thut means yuss. Good. Everyone needs suxx.'

'Do they?' I said, stumbling around. 'I mean, it's none of your business.'

'So you and she do nutt huff suxx?'

'Magda, what Jane and I do together is our business.'

'So you do something together, Kuptin? There, that wasn't so hurrd.' She managed a smug, triumphant smile.

I was about to say more, then realised I was digging myself slightly deeper into my hole. I decided to outstare her, a titanic contest that lasted fully three minutes before she – to my surprise and delight – blinked and looked away.

'You huff turned into a bully, Kuptin. I do nutt like you any more. You are a sneck.'

'No I'm not, Magda. I simply want to stop you being deported. Do you want my help or not?'

She looked away, hurt. It took me a few seconds before I realised that her eyes had become a little moist, a sight I'd never seen before. It was a moment that required great strength of character on my part: I must not show weakness. There was no chance of that. Gently, I reached across, took her in my arms and hugged her. To be honest I was a little surprised that she allowed me to do so.

Eventually Magda pulled away, stood up, grabbed a paper tissue from the box on the kitchen worktop and dabbed her eyes.

'They say I um Polish, Kuptin. I um not Brrittish. That seems to be enough to throw me out of the country.'

'I've heard that's how it works, Magda.' I could offer no consolation.

'I am nutt needed. I am vurthless,' she sniffed.

'You're not worthless, Magda. Nobody's worthless, and you're certainly not.'

'Thunk you, Kuptin. You are kind. But your country's snecks say I do not belong here. I need to be of exceptional value, and they say I am not.'

Then she sat down, took a deep breath and looked around my room to find something else to talk about. Her eyes fell on my guitar, which was propped up in the corner.

'Are you still singing and playing your guitar, Kuptin?' she asked.

'After a fashion.'

'Are you still writing songs?'

'After a fashion.'

'Are they still pish?' This was a new departure. Magda had never previously indicated that she thought my songs were either good or bad. I was a little hurt.

'I didn't know you didn't like my songs, Magda. Why don't you like them?'

'The words are push, Kuptin.' She said it to rhyme with 'crush' or 'mush'.

Now I found myself moving on from 'hurt' to 'stung'.

'You were happy enough to dance to to them.'

'I was getting paid to dunce to them. I liked getting paid.'

'Are you always this unpleasant, Magda?'

She looked mystified. 'But Kuptin, I um nutt being unpleasant. I um being truthful. Do you vont me to tell lies?'

I wasn't quite sure how to respond. Eventually I said, 'I'd like you to be a little kinder to me, Magda. Those songs I write are the best I can manage.' Then I added, a little petulantly, 'Anyway, you can only speak for the ones you've heard me sing. Perhaps some of my other songs would meet your approval?'

'You have written other songs?'

'For other people, yes.'

In truth I had written just one song that anyone else had shown the slightest interest in singing. The avant-garde folk musician Jake Lennox was best known for singing a mixture of his own original pieces and Scottish traditional music accompanied by a selection of electric bagpipes, accordions, penny whistles and harps. Lennox and I shared the same solicitor, Duncan 'Walnut' MacIntyre. Lennox was a notorious snob about the sources of his material. For a bit of fun, Walnut had pushed my song his way without saying who had written it, challenging him to say why it wasn't good enough for him to include in his shows.

Lennox had taken the bait, but decided that it would actually complement the rest of his act better if he sang it unaccompanied. Over the past few months the song had caught the public imagination, all the more so because Lennox was having to admit that the identity of its composer was as much of a mystery to him as it was to anyone else. However he went on to reassure audiences that someone was receiving royalties. (In fact the royalties were all going into an account that Walnut had set up especially for my song. I had asked him if I was going to see any of it, all he would say was 'All in good time, all in good time.')

Being a little less off the wall than some of his own work, Lennox found that my song was the one that everyone wanted to hear. He was asked to appear on at rugby internationals, at political party conferences, even on that year's Hogmanay broadcasts. Biggest of all, though, he was asked to finish with it at folk and rock festivals, including Glastonbury.

'So, Kuptin,' I am allowed to hear this song you huff written?'

'You might have heard it already.'

'Can I dance to it?'

'No,' I had to admit.

'In which case I vill huff pedd it no attention.' Then she added, 'But you may sing it for me anyway.'

'It's a difficult song to sing. It's hard to get the breathing right. In fact, one reason I let Walnut tease Lennox with my song is because I really can't sing it myself. I'm in my sixties now and these things are getting harder.'

'Are you saying you don't vont me to hear it?'

'No. I'm just saying I might not be very good.'

'I know that already, Kuptin.' Seeing my hurt, she added, 'Do you vont me to lie? Anyway, I'd like you to sing this song for me. Then I vill tell you if it is pish.'

So I sang my song, or at least gave it my best shot. Titled *The Shores of Caledonia*, it was very different from the rock and pop stuff I'd written previously. I thought of it as my anti-Brexit song, my answer to the racists and xenophobes who had joined forces with those who, perhaps for quite genuine reasons, had voted in 2016 for Britain to leave the European Union. Scotland had voted strongly to stay in, my home city of Edinburgh even more so. I was furious that I felt so powerless to do anything, and I felt furious that migrants – people like Magda – should be made to feel so unwelcome. The Brexit referendum didn't speak for me. *The Shores of Caledonia* was my way of saying that incomers were still welcome in Scotland.

I'd no way of accompanying the song – it didn't work on a guitar – so, like Lennox, I just sang it unaccompanied. When I reached the end, I waited for some sort of reaction from Magda. None was forthcoming, not a flicker.

'Well,' I said, eventually, 'what do you think?'

'Pish.'

'Is that your verdict on the song or on the singer?'

'Both, Kuptin. Your singing is pish. You used to be better than that. But the song is utter pish. I um nutt velcome, you know that verry well. So your song is utter pish. I vould curry on pretunding you huffn't written it.'

I sat back and smiled wryly. I was getting used to her directness. 'So that's a thumbs down, then?'

'It's pish, Kuptin. Vot more can I say?'

'You could pretend you like it. You're asking for my help.'

'Are you going to put me back out in the snow, Kuptin?'

'Of course not. You could die out there. You can stay here tonight in the spare room.' Then I added, 'Just tonight.'

'Thank you, Kuptin. You urr a good man.'

I had the sense that, for Magda, it was mission accomplished. She had somewhere to stay for the night, and tomorrow was another day. And perhaps she had a point about *The Shores of Caledonia*.

The following morning brought glorious sunshine, but fresh heavy snow had fallen during the night and in my basement flat I almost felt snowed in. With no sign of Magda, I made myself a little treat: a breakfast of orange juice, a bacon sandwich and some coffee. Just as I was helping draining my coffee mug, Magda appeared wearing a tee shirt that was short enough to have me looking away in some embarrassment, especially when she sat down on a chair at the far end of the table.

'Sleep well, Magda?' I asked, keeping my eyes firmly fixed on yet another shirt catalogue that I'd thrown aside earlier.

'Yes, thank you.' She said nothing, which somehow made me glance up. Even more of her was visible. She added, 'This is your house, Kuptin. You can look at whatever you like. Do you find me unattractive?'

'Magda, I'm twice your age.'

'But do you find me attractive?' Then she added, 'Suxxy?'

'Of course I find you attractive, Magda. But you're a attractive young woman, a guest in my house, and I want you to feel you can trust me.' I ignored the sexy bit. To change the subject, I suggested she make herself some breakfast while I had a shower. Magda nodded, but asked if she could use my washing machine to let her wash her clothes.

That gave me the chance to escape to the relative safety of the shower, although it had been a long tome since I'd last had to lock the bathroom door. Showers are loud, especially mine, and I'd never been able to hear anything going on outside. Later, I was to discover I'd missed the phone ringing.

When I emerged from the shower almost thirty minutes later, Magda had turned into my ex-wife Jane.

'Hello,' I said. 'How are things with you?'

Jane explained that she'd called to see if I was in, received no reply, so just let herself in anyway. We shared routine pleasantries, which gave me the chance to explain that Magda had dropped by the previous evening, although I didn't have the time to explain that she'd spent the night in my spare room.

For all that our marriage had gone up in flames, I still liked having Jane close by. She could be dangerous to fall out with, prone to throwing things, but we still shared a great deal. Most of all, we shared two children and two grandchildren, and we saw more of them if we lived near to each other and managed to co-exist in each other's company. We each tried to be friends as well as neighbours, and we even had keys to each other's flats. But our relationship was fragile, and she could be easily upset.

So the last thing I needed at that point was for a completely naked Magda to stroll into the kitchen. Actually, not completely naked: she was still wearing her Crespo glasses.

Understandably, it took everyone a moment to take everything in. Magda always looked quizzical behind her glasses anyway. I wanted to explain everything but couldn't work out where to start. Jane was putting two and two together and coming up with entirely the wrong figure.

'Brian,' she said in low voice filled with fury, 'how could you? How could you?'

I didn't get the chance to explain. She turned back around towards the front door, opened it, stepped out, then slammed it shut behind her with a force that caused every pane of glass in my house to shake.

Magda looked at the front door.

'She has nutt changed, Kuptin. Why do you allow her into your house?'

I shook my head.

'Magda, why are you standing there without a stitch of clothing on?'

'My clothes are in the vosh. Are you getting forgetful in your old age, Kuptin?'

'But why aren't you wearing something in the meantime?

'Because – it – is – all – in – the – vosh, Kuptin. I verr my clothes then vosh them. Is that nutt vot you do?' As ever, her logic was impeccable.

'Can I lend you something to wear in the meantime, Magda? A shirt? A pair of shorts?'

'I think I might be the wrong size for your shorts, Kuptin. Your shirts might be like a dress on me. Do you find me ugly? Would you like me to wear a dress?'

'I most certainly don't find you ugly, Magda. But I think I'd prefer you to wear some clothes while Jane's around, please. That's if she ever speaks to me again.'

'Do you care about this woman, Kuptin?'

For once, I didn't have to think.

'Yes, Magda, I care about Jane. She's the mother of my children, we've been through a lot together and she also happens to be a close neighbour. I like to think we're still friends. So I'm not happy that she's not happy. Can't you at least wear that tee-shirt I gave you last night?'

'You urr a strange munn, Kuptin. The tee-short is in the vosh, too. I thought you'd be huppy.' She turned around and stretched out on the sofa, which didn't help the situation at all. Looking up, she added, 'This is your house, Kuptin. I really don't mind if you look at me. Actually, I'd be insulted if you didn't.'

Instead of looking at her, I tried to think what to do to appease Jane. There was little point in going up to see her to explain: she'd started to hoover the flat, which created a tremendous racket on her bare floorboards. I knew from long experience that it was unwise, even dangerous, to interrupt one of her temper-tantrum vacuum cleaning sessions. Today, she was clearly using her industrial-strength model, a yellow and black beast which she knew drove me mad in my flat below.

Magda, curiously, seemed unconcerned. 'If your wife's house is that dirty, perhaps she should clean it more often.'

'I'll let you tell her that,' I yelled over the top of the mayhem.

Jane kept it up for around twenty minutes or so, when by chance the washing machine cycle and her hoovering came to an end almost at exactly the same time. In my confusion, I hadn't noticed that Magda had actually hand-washed a pair of black knickers and a matching bra and had been drying them over a radiator. It was a major relief to see her at least pulling on some underwear. Not that it covered very much.

I realised that I needed to speak to Walnut about Magda's situation, so I phoned his office. I had to remind myself that in the world of Edinburgh solicitors, he had a different identity.

'I'll see if Mr MacIntyre's available, sir. Who shall I say is calling?'

Seconds later, Walnut's dulcet Edinburgh tones were singing down the telephone. 'Good morning, Brian, old boy! To what do I owe the pleasure? Your song's coining in the royalties, I must say.' No wonder he was pleased with himself: he was collecting twenty percent.

'Do you know Magda's here?' I said, dismissing all niceties.

'Ah well… I suppose that was my idea,' he confessed. 'I thought you might be able to help her. After all…' Walnut's voice tailed off. He knew that I was due Magda a favour. In fact he'd been involved in that episode in my life, too, which was why he was apparently prepared to be her solicitor for nothing. Mind you, I suspected that Walnut, being a lawyer, would simply make sure that his other clients would share the burden instead.

'What am I supposed to do with her?' I said, exasperated. 'Magda can't stay here. She needs a home of her own, and she needs work, or the authorities will kick her out.'

'Even with a home and a job, the authorities might still kick her out. She needs to convince them that she's a special case.'

'Isn't it enough that Magda's a one-off?' I asked, although I knew I was was simply being hopeful. Magda was a good dancer, but then so were plenty of other young men and women.

Sure enough, Walnut ignored me. 'If she doesn't qualify by being British, Magda can only stay here in the 'exceptional circumstances' category. She needs a home, a job, and she needs to offer something special to our society. I could probably employ her in the office here, but I could employ anyone, really. You could supply the home – '

'She'd still be homeless,' I pointed out.

'I was about to point out, before you interrupted me,...' – Walnut paused for effect – '...that staying with you only stops her from dying of hypothermia. She needs somewhere permanent. And her job needs to use her unique skills. I thought you might know more than most of us about those.' I heard a chuckle at the other end of the phone line as a few sordid thoughts passed through Walnut's brain. He had a sleazy side to him.

Now it was my turn to ignore him. 'I think that's going to be the difficult part, Walnut.' I knew he hated anyone using his nickname. 'We need to make Magda into something special in everyone's eyes, not just ours. It seems to me that it's your job to create a case for her. Isn't that what lawyers do?'

'Well personally, I can't see what we can do to help her,' Walnut snapped. 'The girl's her own worst enemy sometimes.'

There was little point in falling out with him. And he was right, Magda was a loose cannon who didn't always seem to appreciate how much was being done for her. But those six inches of snow outside meant I was stuck with her at least in the short term. And when I apologised to Walnut, he returned the apology, so that our conversation was civil for its final few minutes before he rang off.

It was only when I returned the telephone to its charging point in the kitchen that I realised that I'd no idea where Magda was. I called out her name, but there was no reply and she seemed to be hiding in my flat somewhere. I was just starting to become concerned when the front door opened and the young woman in question swept through, closely followed by Jane and a blast of arctic air. Jane had thrown a coat on; incredibly, Magda was still only wearing her underwear.

'Can someone please explain what's going on here?' I said, before I turned specifically to Magda and said, 'Please tell me you haven't been out in the cold dressed like that.'

'Of curse, Kuptin. The rest of my clothes are not yet dry. It is verry cold out there, though.'

'I'll bet.' I looked at Jane. 'Can you tell me what's happened here? Please.'

Jane chuckled. 'Where do I start, Brian? Magda came up, dressed like that... and tried to insist that your

relationship with her was non-sexual. At first I didn't really
believe her, but then I realised that she must be desperate to
convince me if she had stepped outside in her underwear
only. And when she offered to sleep with me – '

'What?'

'I offered to huff sux with her, Kuptin. For all I knew,
she might have preferred women to men. I prefer men, but
I'd have had sux with her to make her happy. Although I'd
have done it for you, Kuptin, not Jane. You are a good man.
You do not try to use me. And although I've slept in your
bed a couple of times, you've always left me alone. That is
verry strange, but quite nice, actually.'

'So I've come down to apologise, Brian,' Jane added. 'I
should have known you better than that. And of course I
have a key to your front door which meant I could make
sure that Magda didn't have to stand on the doorstep in the
snow for any longer than necessary.'

I shrugged my shoulders. 'It's OK, Jane, Magda confuses
me rather a lot.'

Magda was looking backwards and forwards between
Jane and me as we spoke. 'I um confused, too, Kuptin. You
divorced this woman – she is surely your enemy?'

'No, Magda, it's not as simple as that. We do try to stay
friends.'

'Well, Kuptin, your marriage is as strange as your song.'

'What song?' Jane said. 'Have you written a new song?'

I was about to get cross with Magda for letting the cat
out of the bag. But then I had a brainwave.

*

'You can't be serious,' Walnut said down the phone. 'You'll never pull it off. No one would ever believe it.'

'Not at all,' I said. 'It's perfect. It solves all the problems.'

'Apart from costing you a lot of money?'

'Is it really a lot?'

There was a pause at the end of the phone. 'Shed loads, Captain. Shed loads. The fact that Jake Lennox himself doesn't know who wrote it has caught the music world's imagination. I keep getting calls from the media about the damn thing.'

'But of course you can answer that it would be a breach of client confidentiality to say who wrote the song.'

'That's exactly what I do say, Captain. All they know is that the person who wrote it can't really sing it properly, but it's very personal. But all that does is heighten interest and increase your royalties.'

'What does Lennox himself say?'

'He's thrilled with how things are going. This album of his, Celtic Correspondence, has gone platinum. He's in the States just now playing to sell-out stadium audiences. So long as the pennies are rolling in, Mr Lennox is happy.'

'Sounds like he'd make an excellent lawyer.'

'He probably would,' Walnut said, ignoring the jibe. 'Meanwhile, does the woman in question know of this hare-brained scheme of yours?'

'Not yet. I thought I should run it past you first to see if it's possible.'

'It's entirely possible, Captain. But it's also madness.'

'Do you think it'll work?' I asked him.

Walnut said nothing for a while. Then I heard a faint, strange noise from the other end of the line, which gradually grew louder and louder until I realised that Walnut was laughing – no, guffawing.

'Are you all right, Walnut?' I said, alarmed. 'Speak to me!'

'I'm – sorry – Captain – it's – just – so – funny,' Walnut said, gradually bringing himself under control.

'But will it work?' I asked again, patiently.

'That's what's so funny,' he said, still struggling to get the words out. 'It just might, if she's up for it.'

Later that day I invited Jane down to my flat for a cup of coffee with Magda and me. Magda was fully clothed, there had been no more snow that day, and a thaw was forecast at last. Hopefully, things were looking up all round. Jane and Magda were even sitting on the same sofa, directly across from me. Jane had bought a packet of those little chocolate-covered ginger biscuits as a peace offering, and we tucked in contentedly for a few minutes before Jane asked what I wanted to discuss.

I produced a single sheet of A4 sheet music from a ring binder.

'Magda's heard this already, Jane, but I'd like you to hear it, too. She doesn't think it's very good and I don't really have the ability to sing it very well any more. If I ever did,' I added hastily. 'But these days I'm older and this song really tests my sixty-year-old lungs.'

'You're actually sixty-two,' Jane remanded me.

I started to sing *The Shores of Caledonia*, unaccompanied. As I did so, Jane said, 'But that's....'

'Vy urr you singing this song, Kuptin? It is pish. I told you that before. I do not like this song.'

I ignored them both and carried on until I reached the end.

'Well I like that song, Brian, and I strongly agree with its sentiments. I'm not sure you're really up to singing it, mind you – you sounded as though you were struggling a little.'

'Guilty as charged. I admit I can't sing it very well.'

'Hang on,' Jane said. 'That's what Jake Lennox says about the song when he sings it. Are you trying to tell us that you know who wrote that song, Brian?' Jane said. 'Or are you trying to tell us that you wrote it yourself? It's a client of Walnut's, I know that, but it's very different from your other stuff. It never really occurred to me.'

'Not me. I didn't write it,' I lied, passing the sheet music across to the pair of them.

Jane looked at it, spotted the name in the corner, then looked at Magda, who looked even more bewildered than usual. Jane covered her mouth to conceal her own laughter – this song of mine seemed to be a source of great mirth – then leant across and whispered something in Magda's ear.

"Words and music by Magda Czezlawska?' No, Kuptin, this is pish. Utter pish. It is a pish song and if you wrote it you should be ashamed to be trying to blame me. You are a sneck, just like all the other snecks. Vurse, actually. You urr a sneck sneck.' She spat the last few words as though she herself were a hissing snake.

'You don't like it?'

'No, Kuptin. I do nutt vish to be associated with this pish. I am nutt velcum in this country so this song is pish.'

'I think I get the message, Magda. Do you know what royalties are?'

'Is that your king and queen?'

'Not quite. Royalties are what songwriters get paid every time someone plays, or records their song. It's not a lot. I get four pence every time one of my songs gets played.'

'Four pence isn't much.'

'Some songs get played quite a lot. There's over £80,000 sitting in an account waiting to be collected for *The Shores of Caledonia.* '

'£80,000?!' Jane and Magda said in unison.

'And counting. There's a lot more coming, I'm told. That money would be yours, Magda. What's more, how could any government kick you out now? The reason you can't sing the song is because your accent isn't Scottish enough yet, but you're trying as best you can. Meantime, you've just written an iconic song about how we Scots see the world.'

'You're not exactly selling your song short here, are you, Brian?' Jane said with more than a touch of sarcasm in her voice. "Iconic?"

'A song only as good as its spin,' I suggested. 'Even you have to admit it's a great story.'

Jane chuckled. 'I suppose it might work…' She turned to Magda, who still seemed to be taking everything in. 'What do you think, Magda?'

Magda looked at each of us. 'Did you say £80,000?'

'No, Magda, much more,' I reassured her.

She sighed, then cocked her head to one side in thought, another gesture I'd never seen before.

'And they vill nutt deport me?'

'Walnut says that there's no way the author of that song could ever be deported, Magda. The song's become a second Scottish national anthem. And unlike *The Flower of Scotland*, it's not got that anti-English theme. So everyone likes it.'

'I think I huff written a verry good song, Kuptin.'

Jane looked at me carefully. 'It's a generous gesture, Brian. An awful lot of money. You're sure about this?' But she knew the answer in advance.

'Definitely. I'm comfortably enough off, what with my work pension and the income from my other songs. There's no need to be greedy. Only you, me, Magda herself and Walnut reed ever know. And I'll get a lot of pleasure out of seeing the song being used for good.'

Magda tuned in at last.

'Vot pleasure did you have in mind, Kuptin? Of course I vill have sux with you. That vill be my pleasure. Vot else would you like? You are being verry kind to me.'

I reached across and cupped Magda's cheek in my hand.

'Magda, the pleasure I get will be that you owe me nothing at all.'

'Not even sex?' I noticed that her Polish accent was all but gone for a moment. Tears were running down her cheeks. Something else new. Today was witnessing a lot of Magda 'firsts'.

'Especially not sex,' I said. 'You need to believe that men – mostly – just aren't like that.' Jane passed me a tissue and I dried Magda's eyes a little. 'Go and phone Walnut, Magda. After all, he's your lawyer. Tell him you're ready to go public with your story.'

'And claim the money?'

'Definitely. Claim the money. But get Walnut to advise you about what you need to spend your money on – getting a house, a job and so on. Don't waste it, you're going to need every penny, believe me. Anyway, go and make that phone call.'

She disappeared into the spare room, leaving me alone with Jane.

'Are you sure you're doing the right thing, Brian?'

'It's too late to go back on it now. But of course it's the right thing.'

'A man of principle then. I always did like men of principle. And you resisted the offer of sex.'

I looked at her. 'She's young enough to be our daughter, Jane. Not that these things seem to matter to Magda.'

She laughed. She glanced at the window. It was a beautiful sunny day, but the snow was still deep. She drew me closer to her, surprisingly close considering that she and I had once been through such a bitter divorce.

'We'll need to find Magda a house to live in,' I said. She needs a proper place of her own, quickly, at least until the authorities give her formal permission to stay. She can't live with me.'

'I need to be honest with myself, Brian.' I wondered what was coming next. 'I'm relieved that you and Magda never…' Her voice tailed off.

I looked at her and smiled. 'Are you saying that you were a little… jealous?'

She shrugged her shoulders. Her admission was a surprise. She looked away, embarrassed, before she turned back and broke the silence.

'I can think of one place Magda could stay. You might not like it.'

I looked at her, genuinely baffled.

'She could stay here in your flat,' she said. 'You could rent it to her and move out yourself.'

I burst out laughing. 'Thank you very much!' I said. 'So you make me homeless so that Magda doesn't have to be.'

'I said you might not like the suggestion. But you wouldn't be homeless. You could move upstairs in with me until Magda finds somewhere permanent. After all, we've done it before.'

'Are you serious?' To be honest, I wasn't sure what Jane was offering.

'It would save on my heating bill,' she said. I still wasn't sure. 'And it would just be until Magda gets herself sorted.'

'OK... when would this arrangement start?'

'As soon as possible, I'd suggest. Now?'

'Now? Right now?'

'Why not? Grab some clothes and a toothbrush. Bring your guitar if you want. But I think you should leave a note for Magda.'

Hurriedly grabbing a Post-It, I scribbled something to leave alongside a spare key on the kitchen worktop. Jane glanced at what was written over my shoulder..

'Well, Brian, that's pretty explicit,' she grinned. 'Perhaps you have the wrong idea?'

'That's for Magda's benefit. She'll approve of what's written there,' I said. 'And she'll leave us in peace for a bit. What actually happens upstairs is our private business, don't you think?'

'Indeed, Brian. It's our private business. Come on, let's go,' she said, and we let ourselves quietly out of the front door.

The Shores of Caledonia

Words and music by Gordon Lawrie

Freely ♩ = 120

Come all ye ci - ti - zens a - cross the land and lis - ten here by me, Come ye friends and neigh-bours doc - tors, nurs - es, en - gin - eers, join - ers, plum - bers, too, All ye car - ers for the all from the oc - ean to the sea, Come all ye wand - er - ers from far and near who - ev - er you may nanny do what - ev - er you can do, Come in and share your cul - ture, share your skills, and if your spir - it's

sa, Join me here on the shores of Cal - e - don - ia. 2.Come all ye true we'll find a place for all of you in Cal - e - don - ia. So reach a - cross, take my hand, Come and join me where I stand, Come and help to make us strong in this land where I be - long and if you stay we'll take you in with op - en arms and op - en doors. You're wel - come here on the shores of Cal - e - don - ia.

Verse 3 They came from Trinidad and Pakistan, Poland, France and Spain,
Our English cousins crossed the border and decided to remain,
Just like the Irish, who so long ago, gave this land their name
To the land the Romans knew as Caledonia.

(Chorus)

Verse 4 So no matter where you come from, what you do, or what you came here for
We'll build our bridges strong and solid like our ancestors before
And in the evening as the day goes down, we'll share a glass or four
In the sunset on the shores of Caledonia.

(Chorus, twice)

The Last Bus

J ack and Margaret waited patiently for the last bus back into Edinburgh in the shelter outside Gullane's branch of the Bank of Scotland. Not that there was much need for 'shelter' as such; even at half-past-ten at night, the summer sky still afforded plenty of light and a surprising amount of warmth after a simply glorious late June day. The couple had been down to visit Margaret's sister Annie and her husband Bob, spending most of the afternoon in Bob and Annie's back garden enjoying a barbecue.

'Gorgeous evening,' Margaret said to Jack, as they gazed west across the Gullane golf courses. She was right; everything above the horizon was some shade of blue, ranging from a royal blue to the deepest indigo.

The main attraction of the shelter was that it had a small bench on which they could perch until the number 124 made its appearance. They'd decided to use the bus so that they could have a drink or two with their meal.

Margaret looked at her husband. 'You feeling OK?' It was just a casual enquiry.

'Yes, yes, I'm just finding it a bit chilly, that's all.'

'Really?' she said, 'I'm finding it's still quite warm.'

'I was outside most of the time with Bob. You know what he's like with that gas barbecue of his,' he smiled, shaking his head. 'And I was expected to keep him company.'

'You should have been wearing your hat.'

'I know, I forgot it though. Could have used a pair of sunglasses, too.'

'That expensive pair you spent almost forty pounds on are still lying on the hall table, I think.' She might have been reprimanding Jack, but he chose to let it go, changing the subject instead.

'It's great that we've got our bus passes,' he said. 'We can do this for nothing.' Like all Scots over sixty, Jack and Margaret had permits to allow them free travel on all buses. Both aged seventy-six, they'd made good use of them over the years.

Margaret smiled. 'It's great at times like this, isn't it?' Neither of them spoke for a while, then she added, 'It's been a lovely day.' It was a statement of fact rather than a subject for debate.

'Mmm,' Jack said.

'Sure you're OK?'

'Yeah, yeah,' he said.

They were early for the bus, of course, that was Margaret's way. She was forever worried about being late for this or that, Jack was always going on at her for fussing. As far as he was concerned, they'd left Annie and Bob's about ten minutes too early, and he'd had to throw down a beautiful glass of Port Charlotte Islay whisky just a little quicker than he'd have liked. But Jack knew the day had been a nice one overall and he wasn't about to spoil it now. Anyway, because they'd been early they'd also been the first to arrive for the last bus - as Margaret had pointed out, that had given them the pick of the seating in the bus shelter - but now, slowly, others began to arrive.

There were quite a few of them, and they were of all ages, which surprised both Jack and Margaret straight away. Couples, single young men and single young women, a woman who might have been Polish, a tallish bearded man with a rucksack, and a man with a huge beer-gut all began to appear at the bus stop. A couple came into the shelter to study the timetable, as if they wanted to reassure themselves that the bus really was about to come. Margaret, an inveterate timetable- and map-reader could understand that, she'd pored over the figures herself when they'd first arrived. Jack and she were the oldest, though.

Suddenly there was a murmur from the others waiting: the last bus had been spotted at the far end of Gullane Main Street. Two more young people arrived, a teenage boy and a teenage girl, unconnected, and then just as the bus approached one final woman appeared, running towards the bus from the direction of the golf clubhouse: a member of the clubhouse staff, perhaps a barmaid, still in some sort of black uniform, at the end of her shift. Sweating a little, too, by the looks of things.

As the bus approached, everyone started to move forward and Jack and Margaret found themselves just one of a crowd, but they needn't have worried, the throng seemed aware of priorities and they all waited back to allow the older couple to get onto the bus first. Jack checked the bus number as the two of them got on, showed their passes, then took a seat together halfway back on the single-decker.

The bus driver seemed to know most of the other passengers, acknowledging them as they got on, often by name. He made a special point of talking to the barmaid.

'I'd have waited for you, Tina, you know that. I've told you before,' he said, as the bus set off. It was said as a sort of reprimand. The driver was a chunky, stubbly-bearded sort of man aged around forty, who wore glasses and whose hair was receding a little.

'I know, I know,' Tina replied. 'You're good that way, Dean.' The bus had set off without waiting for Tina to take her seat, and they talked quietly for a short while until she made her way up the bus, past Jack and Margaret.

Margaret said, 'This is the right bus, isn't it, Jack? I never checked.'

Jack sighed. 'This is the right bus, Margaret, I checked it. It had a big sign in the front which said 'The Last Bus'.'

Margaret laughed. 'It's supposed to say 124, Jack.'

Jack gave a little grin. 'I'm sure it said 'The Last Bus', my dear. Shall I get off and check again?'

Margaret didn't reply; instead she gave him a playful slap on the thigh. They sat in silence for a bit, looking out of the window. From inside the bus, the blue skies seemed a lot darker, almost pitch-black.

Suddenly, Dean the Driver shouted out, 'Who's going to sing a song?' Barely waiting for a reply, he yelled out, 'Come on, who's going to sing a song? It's the last bus, it's the party bus!' and without waiting for any further encouragement instantly set off with

The wheels on the bus go round and round,
Round and round,
Round and round,
The wheels on the bus go round and round,
All day long.

Remarkably, the passengers started to join in, which Dean the Driver took as his cue to up the ante a little. Driving along the winding roads at Longniddry, he peeped the horn of the bus in time to *The horn of the bus goes beep, beep, beep* followed by setting of the windscreen wipers - on a completely dry night - to accompany *The wipers on the bus go swish, swish, swish*, and so on. Then some of the passengers filled in: cows mooed, sheep baahed, pigs oinked, horses neighed and so on until eventually they seemed to run out of ideas. Then Dean moved on to Tom

Paxton's *Goin' To The Zoo*, followed by *I Know An Old Woman Who Swallowed A Fly* and several other children's classics. If he couldn't think of any for a bit, he would simply sing a football song or two.

From time to time a passenger would get off and another would get on. They all seemed to know Dean, and had gossip to exchange before they either left the bus or took their seat. The bus meandered through areas of East Lothian that Jack and Margaret had never seen before, taking well over an hour to make a journey that they in their car would cover in less than twenty minutes.

The numbers on the bus began to slowly thin out. Jack and Margaret themselves were going all the way into Edinburgh, but it seemed that most of the other passengers were getting off before they reached the city. Dean looked after them all, though often teasing them brutally as they went on their way: 'Mind and find a better football team to support before I see you next'; 'See you when you look a less ugly'; and - especially for Tina - 'Are you putting on weight, Tina, or are you expecting?'

As passengers got off and the bus approached Edinburgh, it got quieter, and Margaret and Jack sat in silence. Once, they glanced at each other and smiled, and Margaret laid her head on Jack's shoulder and closed her eyes. To his surprise, Dean called back to Jack, 'Go ahead, nod off if you want, I'll wake you when you get there. You're the last two left on the bus.' Jack hadn't realised that was the case, but he was tired and gratefully nodded off.

It was Margaret who wakened. Dean was nudging her gently.

'Come on, Margaret, waken up, you have to waken up.'

She half-opened her eyes. The bus looked a little different, a lot smaller. Dean looked a little different, too, still wearing his white shirt and tie but with a green top as well.

'Come on, Margaret, we're nearly there.'

'Sorry,' she said, 'I didn't mean to fall asleep. Thanks for waking me.' She turned to look for Jack but he was lying out on a seat on the other side of the bus. She reached across.

'Jack… Jack,' she said, waking him, 'we'll miss our stop.'

Jack didn't reply.

'Come on, Jack,' she repeated, then, turning to Dean, she added, 'He's dreadful in the morning, too.' Dean didn't reply.

'Jack… Jack!'

'Margaret, he's not going to waken up,' Dean said quietly.

She looked at the paramedic, bewildered. Then she said to her husband, 'What happened, Jack?'

'We think he had a stroke, Margaret. While you were waiting for the bus. Won't have felt a thing - he'd have been dead before he hit the ground.'

'But I was there, too. I must have been there'

Dean patted her hand. 'The other passengers said you passed out when it happened. Understandable with the shock, of course. That's what they said, anyway. We'll have to check you out, but I'm sure that'll be right.'

'But we actually got on the bus. It said it was The Last Bus.'

Dean looked at her quizzically.

'Strange that. Some of the other paramedics call it that - not me, though. It doesn't seem respectful.'

'Call it what?' she asked.

'This ambulance is actually nicknamed The Last Bus. Just don't ask why. I don't like the name myself.'

Hoots Mon

Part I: Joe's Bright Idea

IF I HAD TO SUM UP JOE – Little Joe – Mackay's life in a few words it would have to be 'a man for whom most things have gone awfully wrong, but who's managed to get one thing fabulously right.'

In his early fifties, he certainly looks no movie star. He's not short, over six feet tall in fact, but he looks a bit geeky, and his hair recedes well beyond the midpoint of his skull. He's a man of no great talent, although any attempts to break that to him – gently or otherwise – fall on deaf ears. He looks like a man who's seen great sadness in his life, which he has, because once upon a time he had ambitions to be a policeman, an ambition that went horribly wrong one Friday night a dozen years or so ago when he arrested some lout who then falsely accused PC Joe of indecent assault. It took almost two years to clear Joe's name, during which time he had a serious nervous breakdown and was 'advised' that his career was over. (Of course the police supported him. After he was cleared.) Joe actually won significant compensation, but without his beloved police force he was bereft.

The thing he did fabulously right was to find Bev, the woman of his dreams – the woman of any man's dreams, to be honest. Bev, as well as being drop-dead-gorgeous, fell totally in love with Joe, seeing in her husband a naive innate honesty rarely found in the human race. She knew Joe was innocent all those years ago, because she knew he wouldn't have a clue what 'indecent assault' was. So she supported him, nursed him back to full health, and then started to look for outlets for Joe's creativity, which she was in a position to do because she herself was incredibly rich. Anyone who remembers the legendary Beverley Rome Employment Agency will recall that it was the place to be in the 1990's, so much so that she was asked to name her price by some investment trust that wanted to go into that sector and was prepared to pay megabucks to get there. So Bev named her price… then multiplied it by nine and the investment trust grabbed it.

Bev was now a very wealthy woman, and with her new windfall she did three things. Firstly, she put far and away most of it into safe investments (it really was a lot of money). Second, she bought Joe a nearby ironmonger's business as a means of giving her husband something to do – and to keep her from going mad while he lounged around the house. And finally, she created a custom-built recording studio in the back garden of their house in upmarket Merchiston, on Edinburgh's Southside.

It's in this last little theatre that our story begins. Joe has an older brother, Joshua, whom everyone calls 'Fleece' because he wears one all the time, and who's also a bit of a disaster area generally, but in most other respects is quite different from his younger sibling. Where Joe is thinnish, naive, and could do with more hair, Fleece sports an unkempt beard, is cynical and could do with losing a lot of weight. You'd never guess they were brothers, but they're surprisingly loyal to each other, so much so that Fleece – who happens to be a half-decent drummer – has a regular Sunday afternoon jam session with Joe simply to keep his brother amused. Joe attempts to play the guitar; Fleece attempts to create some sort of rhythm to go with him.

There would only have been the two of them were it not for the fact that Fleece happens to have been the best man at my wedding and I, in a moment of weakness, agreed to join them playing my beat-up old acoustic guitar, suitably amplified, and I in turn brought along an old school colleague of mine – I used to be a teacher – called Geoff Arrowsmith. Geoff *does* play guitar, rather better than either Joe or me; but he plays it very precisely according to the demands of his guitar teacher, so for the most part he needs to sight-read music which detracts rather from the rock-star look. Our line-up lacks a bass, but that's another story. For the most part we do without, although I'm trying to learn a little to help us get by. And we've already had some adventures together, but that's yet another story. There are actually a lot of stories to tell about our little band, but I mustn't get distracted.

So this particular Sunday afternoon there are just the four of us: Little Joe, Fleece, Geoff and myself. My name's Brian Reid, of course, although Little Joe and Fleece call me 'Captain' for no reason I can recall. I'm usually landed with the singing, but it's not to be my rôle this time – thankfully I play only a walk-on part in this story. But you can enter the stage along with me if you like.

Habit has it that Geoff and I arrive together in his not-quite-big-enough sports car, and when we ring the doorbell, habit also also has it that Bev greets us, ushering first Geoff and then me into their beautiful hallway. These days even Geoff gets a chaste kiss on the cheek, but as he then moves through to the back of the house, she reserves something rather better for me, a full, lingering, lips-on kiss, plus a hand placed somewhere about my person. Don't misunderstand, though, this is nothing untoward between Bev and me – she's totally in love with Joe – but I've known Bev for a long time, and for some reason she gives me special credit for once helping her husband out of his personal mire.

Bev's hand is always an important indicator for what's in store for me each afternoon. Bev has a mesmeric effect on men, which was why she was so successful in the male-dominated business world; they did whatever she asked of them. Her charms work more on some men than others, though, and I'm afraid I'm particularly susceptible. If she breathes a whisper in my ear, or if she so much as touches my arm softly, a high-voltage sensuous wave engulfs me. I'm simply paralysed.

But how Bev chooses to make contact with me also gives me a heads-up on whether or not she needs me to be particularly nice to her husband today. Usually, if her kiss is accompanied by a brush on the arm, there's not much required of me; but her arm on my waist means I have some task to perform, something to endure for Little Joe's sake. Today, Bev greets me not only with that lingering kiss, but a full-scale sensuous massage of my left buttock. It's devastating, I feel it everywhere, especially... well, you understand that I feel it everywhere. What's more, she adds a soft 'Wonderful to see you, Brian,' gasped into my ear. It means she wants something very big from me.

As Geoff marches enthusiastically on ahead of me, Bev leads me by the hand – there's that caress again – through the hall, up the back garden path, and through the door of an innocent-looking building that looks for all the world like a garage, except that there's no door for the car to enter. As I enter, Little Joe is playing electric guitar and brother Fleece is hammering his drum kit as loudly as he possibly can in the hope that he won't be able to hear Joe. I'm used to it now, though, and I simply ignore the racket.

'Captain!' roars Fleece. 'Just the man!'

'Afternoon, Fleece,' I yell back at him. 'How can I help?'.

Meanwhile Joe's in a trance, but it's a very loud trance. Little Joe has a pet project: he's convinced that the roots of Jamaican reggae music lie in Scottish rumpty-tum folk music, and in the past he's tried to prove it with some dreadful hybrid combinations. I've no idea what he's singing here but it sounds every bit as bad as everything else he's ever come up with. Probably even worse.

'Help me, Captain, just help me! Please!'

Fleece doesn't usually sound desperate, and because he's still playing the drums as Little Joe sings and plays the guitar, I'm assuming that nothing serious is wrong. It turns out that I'm very, very mistaken.

'What is it?' I ask Fleece as I start to unpack my guitars from their cases.

'You'll find out soon enough, you'll find out,' he replies, shaking his head. Bear in mind he doesn't stop drumming at all during the conversation.

'That bad?'

'Worst yet,' Fleece assures me, then he roars in laughter. Fleece continues to be overweight, unkempt and with a huge beard, which means that I have no idea whatsoever whether or not he's simply winding me up.

Geoff, meanwhile, is already tuning up. No-one has really paid him much attention, which is partly because he actually quite likes what everyone now knows as Little Joe's 'rasta-jock' music. He comes from Lincolnshire, which means he hasn't been quite as scarred by experiences listening to second-rate Scottish pub singers. (To be fair, I

---

was one of those myself once.) Anyway, he still seems to see some novelty value in Joe's musical enterprise.

The other reason why no-one speaks to Geoff is because there's a little game going on involving the rest of us, even soft-hearted Bev: who's going to be first to ask Geoff how he is? The thing is, Geoff tells you how he is. In glorious Technicolor – the word 'fine' would never cross his mind.

This week, Joe's the one who cracks. He now owes everyone else one pound.

'How are things, Geoff?' he shouts across Fleece's drumming. Fleece actually stops – the other three of us have won. Now we batten down the hatches for Geoff's reply.

'Goodness me!' Geoff replies. Geoff says 'Goodness me!' quite a lot. All the time, to be honest. 'Goodness me,' he repeats, 'I'm so glad you asked. You know, I was getting a little concerned about my left pinkie, it didn't seem to be moving so well. So what did I do? Goodness me, I took myself to the chemist's shop, you know that one in the middle of Corstorphine? Goodness me, why should you? Anyway, there's a pharmacy there and I decided to ask the woman – she was such a nice woman – a few other things as well. I got her to look at my knee, at a small spot on my left ear, and also I needed to talk about my water works and my… well, you know, my number twos. Sorry, Bev, but goodness me, we all do it don't we?

'Anyway, I was there for well over thirty minutes but she was ever so good, goodness me these people are so good, aren't they? And she was very good about my... well I suppose they're my bowel movements, aren't they? Let's be upfront about this, this is the twenty-first century after all, goodness me. And she had a good look – '

There's a chorus of 'WHAT!'

'Well, goodness me, everyone, you can't expect her just to go by what I say can you? She has to have a look.'

We're stunned. Fleece manages to say it for us. 'Geoff, you mean you dropped your trousers...?'

Geoff blinks, then rocks with laughter. 'No, no, goodness me, everyone. Of course I didn't take any clothes off. I didn't need to. I'd taken a sample in.'

There's another chorus of 'WHAT?' and I notice that even Bev can't stand this – she's turned towards the door to cover up how much she's laughing.

Geoff continues. 'You can tell so much from a sample, you know, goodness me, yes. Look it up on the internet. You see, if it's – ' He's interrupted by the crash of Fleece falling off his stool at the drums, knocking over most of the kit while he's at it. I think this might have been deliberate; Fleece can have his intelligent moments.

Bev calls out loudly. 'I think I should go and make some cheese scones. Would that be a good idea?'

'Yes, please,' I say, 'and can I come too?'

'NO!' yells Fleece, 'You're staying here!'

I give him a look that says, I don't like the sound of this. And I don't.

With Bev safely out of the way, Little Joe decides to take charge before Geoff can resume with the sordid details of his daily excretions.

'Captain! Captain! Look what Bev found!' he tells me, positively bouncing on the studio floor as he says it. In fact he's waving a cutting from a newspaper, the *Sun*, I think. On he goes.

'Captain, it's an advert! It's an advert! They're looking for songwriters!'

'Em… who's they?' Fleece chuckles.

'It's an advert from the BBC,' Joe says. 'Apparently it's in all the papers, at least all the cheap ones like the *Sun* and the *Express*. They're looking for entries for *A Song for Europe*!'

I look at Joe. This is a man whom I regard as a friend, albeit that every time I'm in his company I'm made to feel like his social worker. I decide that the best policy is to find a seat and sit on it. Geoff's listening as well, now. Fleece, meantime, is simply looking to see what my reaction is.

'Say that again, Joe?'

'It seems they're looking for new blood for *A Song for Europe*,' he explains. *A Song for Europe* is an annual pan-European TV-based contest that Britain traditionally does embarrassingly badly in. 'The BBC are so fed up that Britain keeps scoring no points that they're asking new songwriters to come forward.'

'And you think…' Privately, I'd rather not think, but I realise I'm going to have to, and soon.

'Yes, Captain… Rasta-jock!'

He passes the clipping to me and, sure enough, it's a call for new songwriters to come forward with potential entries. I pass it on to Geoff, then a couple of thoughts occur to me.

'Joe... two things. First of all, aren't the songs supposed to be Scottish? Yours are Jamaican. And second, isn't the song supposed to be original? Your rasta-jock just uses old songs to a new beat, doesn't it?' I'm thinking of some of these Scottish folk songs he's re-jigged with a reggae beat, the most recent of which is a thing called *The Jute Mill Song* which actually sounds faintly convincing as a reggae number. Joe's had death-threats playing it, though.

Joe smiles. He's got something here, and I don't like the sound of it.

'It is an original song, Captain.'

'You have a song? What do you mean – you've written one?'

'Is that so incredible?' Joe sounds quite defensive, bullish even. 'Am I so awful that I can't be trusted to write anything? Is what I write that bad? Is it?' He's getting rather wound up, but it seems a bit unfair; his brother Fleece is quite happy to tell Joe how bad his music is, and Fleece never seems to get harangued like this at all.

Fortunately, Bev's not there any more. Bev, if you didn't know, can not only operate all my sensual nerves with a mere brush of her hand, she can also invade my brain with telepathic commands which reduce me to the status of a ventriloquist's dummy. But she's far away, safely in the kitchen making cheese scones.

Brian, how could you do that to Joe? How could you? I'm so disappointed.

What? How did she do that? She's fully thirty metres away with a sound-proof wall between us. And I never said a word. Bev doesn't choose to use her new-found extra powers to explain.

Geoff, however, is interested. He's always been the one member of our band who's been prepared to encourage Joe.

'Goodness me, Joe,' he says 'goodness me! Are we planning on appearing on TV?'

'Of course,' squeaks Joe, whose voice always rises an octave when he's excited. 'There's an entry form on the *Song for Europe* website!'

'And what about the song?' I ask. 'Is it ready?'

'Of course,' he says, 'do you want to hear it?'

At this point I'd like to say 'No, not if it was the last thing on earth that would save my life,' but instead something drastic happens to me.

Of course you'd like to hear it, Brian. I know you'll ask Joe to play his song and then you'll do whatever's needed to make it as good as possible.

'Of course I'd like to hear it, Joe,' I tell him. 'You play it first then we'll see what the rest of us can add to it.' I've no idea what makes me say this at all – that's a lie, I know perfectly well what's making me say it. I'm immediately rewarded with a slow, glorious sensation which starts in my neck, travels down my spine, and… keeps going. Why bother with Class A drugs?

That's better, Brian. Good boy.

Fleece, who long ago worked out what Bev does to me, just smiles and shakes his head. Geoff smiles when he frowns, and frowns when he smiles, so it might otherwise be hard to tell what he's really thinking except that basically he's a very nice man indeed who will do anything to help a friend in need. Right at this moment his friend Joe is in dire need.

'Come on, Joe, let's hear it. Goodness me, it might be a world-beater!'

Fleece finally makes it clear where he stands. 'I've heard it, Geoff. Trust me, this is no world-beater, except as in 'beating equals torture' sense. It's not too late.'

Joe scowls. Geoff frown-smiles and says simply, 'Come on boys, let's see what it's like. It must be worth hearing once.'

'Go on, then, Joe.' I think that might have been me.

Announcing that he's playing in B minor, Joe starts to play his guitar, that ever-present chung chagga, chung chagga, chung chagga rhythm that underpins so much reggae. Fleece, either out of fraternal loyalty or more likely because he just wants to see our reaction, joins in so that Geoff and I are completely cornered. Not that Geoff minds – he's used to Joe's rasta-jock and simply plays strange augmented chords at the start of every bar – it's really only my part that's in doubt. I've been using Joe's rasta-jock as a punch-bag for my miserable attempts to play bass guitar, which effectively amount to boom, boom, boom, boom at an exceptionally basic level, so I reckon this new song of his is worth murdering, too.

But it's much, much worse than even I had ever feared. Especially when Joe starts singing.

Down in the forest where the bluebells grow
Up in the mountains in the driving snow
Over on the beach where the wild winds blow
Over in the isles the sunsets glow

Then there's a chorus – this is the bit I know we're expected to join in…

Hoots Mon, Hoots Mon
Hoots Mon, Hoots Mon

Dressed in my finest tartan trews
To go with brand-new walking shoes
I lean on the dyke and I quietly muse
Can I see more sheep or hieland coos?

Can I ever live this down? More chorus. This time I have to join in because everyone else is, even Fleece, although I know he's just doing it to annoy me.

Hoots Mon, Hoots Mon
Hoots Mon, Hoots Mon

Then a miracle, it stops. Silence. I breath a sigh of relief that I appear still to be alive.

Except that there's more to come. The silence is one of those reggae things where the band simply does a dramatic pause, and it's followed by a sort of unaccompanied – for the first line, anyway – middle eight…

When the miserable weather's the colour of heather in the skies
I'm spared by the gales of the bites of the midges and flies

After which we're off again.

Hoots Mon,
Hoots Mon,
Hoots Mon

So as I stand upon the highest ground
And take the chance to have a gaze around
Let me cogitate upon these thoughts profound
And let the drone of merry bagpipes sound

Hoots Mon, Hoots Mon
Hoots Mon, Hoots Mon
Hoots Mon, Hoots Mon
Hoots Mon, Hoots Mon

The song peters out three verses and four choruses too late, as unrehearsed jam music recorded in a garage usually does. I'm gasping for breath. No words at all exist in the English language to describe this monster of a 'song', if that indeed is a description it deserves at all. I'm frankly horrified at the thought that Little Joe thinks it's any good at all.

Eventually Geoff breaks the silence.

'Goodness me!'

'It's great, isn't it, Geoff?' says Joe. 'It's just what we're looking for.'

Geoff frown-smiles furiously. I can tell he's breathing deeply, something his wife taught him to do when he has a sudden shock. Fleece however is simply doubled up in laughter.

'Well, Captain? Whadayamakeathat?' he calls across in a fake American accent.

I take a deep breath. I'm pretty sure that Bev is reading my mind from the kitchen here, so it's important to choose my words carefully.

'It's… it's interesting,' I manage.

Brian, can't you do better than that? I'm disappointed.

This gets two negative responses. In my head, there's a curt *Try harder, Brian*, while Fleece announces that he's no intention of 'working' on it any more than he has to.

Geoff tries. 'Goodness me, boys, it's different, isn't it?' But no-one's too impressed.

I'm depending on you, Brian. Please, for me.

'How about groundbreaking?' I suddenly blurt out. 'It's groundbreaking, isn't it?'

Suddenly, Little Joe's delighted; somehow, this is apparently the accolade he's dreamed of. 'Groundbreaking. You really mean that, Captain?'

Fleece likes the description, too. 'Groundbreaking?' he roars. 'Groundbreaking? Ideal for anyone looking to dig up a road, you mean, Captain? It's fucking – '

'No, Fleece, that's what they said about Picasso. And Tchaikovsky. And Tracey Emin. And Elvis. It's just that it's new.' I'm working really hard here.

Geoff, bless him, backs me up. 'Goodness me, Fleece, of course Captain's right. Anything new like this takes a while to be accepted.'

'Captain, am I the new Elvis?' Little Joe asks brightly.

This is a very difficult path I'm having to steer here. 'It's a whole new genre, Joe. You're the new Joe Mackay. Rastajock has come home to Scotland.' Where on earth that little speech came from I have no idea.

That's better, Brian.

Fleece is not impressed. 'Your judgement is sadly lacking, Captain, your judgement is sadly lacking.'

'Goodness me,' Geoff says, 'Is it so much to ask you to support your little brother?' These are harsh words by Geoff's standards, but he often feels protective of Joe when Fleece is criticising his younger brother, which is ironic because Fleece himself is only really part of this setup because he wants to help Little Joe.

There's a brief pause while everyone digests what's going on here, then Little Joe quietly bleats, 'So, can I enter *Hoots Mon* for *A Song for Europe*?'

'Em, Joe,' I point out, 'we've only played it through once. Is this not a bit premature? And you know what Geoff's like – he needs all the notes and chords written out in full as sheet music. There's so much to do.' Geoff nods furiously to reinforce the point.

Just then there's a surprising intervention from Fleece.

'It can only get better with practice, Joe,' he says. I know what he actually means – it can't get any worse than it already is. But Joe himself takes it as a vote of approval from his big brother.

'Does that mean I can enter it?' For some reason he's looking at me, a throwback to a day when I was the band's front man. 'The closing date for entries is Friday.'

I shrug my shoulders. 'They can only say no, Joe. If you don't try…'

Joe's ecstatic. Meanwhile, I'm waiting for Bev to invade my central nervous system once more with another telepathic thoughts. Instead, I'm surprised to see her appear at the door of Joe's studio.

'Brian, I wonder if you could give me a hand with the cheese scones? I'm struggling to carry everything.'

Bev usually manages fine but I'm too well brought-up to point that out. As we step inside the kitchen door, however, she puts her arm around my waist, pulls me towards her and kisses me. I can't describe it, except to say... it's extremely sensual.

Eventually we pull away from each other; I know what she's going to say.

'Thank you, Brian. You know how much I love Joe and how much his music means to him. He needs your support so much, it's your opinion he values.'

'I know Bev, I know, but...'

'Well it's better *me* kissing you than Joe, isn't it?'

We're still laughing as we carry the coffee and fresh cheese scones back into the studio, to discover that Joe has already filled out the form, shoved it into an addressed envelope, and put a first-class stamp on it. I can see what everyone's thinking: that's the last we'll hear of it.

But it's not. Two weeks later, we're invited to come and audition in a Glasgow studios for *A Song for Europe*.

Part II: Rehearsal

JOE'S ALREADY TEXTED US to say that *A Song for Europe* has been in touch before we meet exactly three Sundays after *Hoots Mon* first saw the light of day, but it doesn't stop him from being excited. Actually 'excited' might be the wrong word – as we arrive, he's bouncing on the floor in a manner something akin to an agitated pogo-stick.

The letter – from the BBC's Light Entertainment department – is printed on fairly innocuous-looking paper, is addressed to Little Joe, and hopes that 'he and and any necessary support will be available to take part in an audition at BBC Scotland's Studio 4 in Glasgow' on Thursday 18th September. Naturally, Joe's available – he has an ironmongers' shop in Morningside Road but Bev's more than happy to man the shop for him that day. Or he could simply close it for the day, on the grounds that he rarely sells anything anyway. Geoff's retired – like me, he's a retired teacher – and although I work Tuesdays and Thursdays in a Costa coffee shop near Edinburgh's West End, I can easily swap days with a colleague. Fleece, however, is being obstructive.

'Sorry, boys,' he says, 'can't make it. Can't get time off.' Fleece is still working, a civil servant in what is currently known as the Department of Work and Pensions, the government agency that tries to find work for people and refuses them benefits when it fails.

'Come on, Fleece, surely you can manage one day,' Joe says.

'This is my final year, Little Joe. My own pension depends on me working every one of the three hundred and sixty-five days this year.'

'Come on, Fleece,' I call across to him, laughing, 'you could take a day's annual leave.'

'Leave!!' he roars, 'You expect me give up my holidays to play this unmentionable rubbish?'

'Well… yes. Why not?'

In his best deep voice, he booms, 'Because it is beneath my dignity, Captain, beneath my dignity.'

We eyeball each other across the room. 'Fleece, you have no dignity,' I say, quietly. Then a thought occurs to me. 'Tell you what, Fleece, if you play drums on Joe's track in Glasgow, I'll buy you a steak pie supper afterwards.'

Fleece, who looks like a pirate, now smiles like a pirate as well, topping off the effect with a drumstick between his teeth. 'Throw in a deep-fried Mars Bar and you've got a deal.'

'Deal.'

The thing is, I knew all along that there was never the slightest danger that Fleece would let us down, or to be more exact, let his little brother down. Like so many people who seem to tease and annoy those close to them, Fleece would do anything to help Little Joe. He's bemused – we all are – that Little Joe and 'his support' have even been offered an audition for *A Song for Europe*, but he's definitely pleased, too. Being a big, burly, bearded rugby player – he still plays for some veterans' team – he can be a useful man to have at your side. Fleece, however, likes to pretend that he's unreliable, and indeed he's often late, although he's never late for the things that matter, such when he was best man at my wedding. But this stage act of his isn't easily grasped by others, certainly not Joe himself, or Geoff, or even the telepathic Bev; only I understand what makes him tick, and when he's being serious or otherwise. So, even now, Little Joe has to ask to be sure to make that Fleece isn't winding him up.

'Fleece… does that mean you'll come?' he pleads, hopefully.

Fleece takes a big deep breath – he's about to break into some sort of Shakespearean speech, so I cut him off.

'Fleece is coming with us, Joe, yes.'

Joe usually responds with an excited jump for joy, but on this occasion it's pure relief that overwhelms him, and he feels compelled to sit down on a chair. 'We have a complete band, then,' he says quietly, as though the very notion is completely overwhelming.

'I wouldn't go that far, Joe,' I reply. 'You're expecting me to play the bass guitar. I don't think that's very complete.'

'I'm sure you'll not let me down,' Joe replies. I'm slightly taken aback by the very notion that, after all I've done for Joe over the years, after all I've put up with, he could ever accuse me of 'letting him down'. Actually, it's pretty clear what Little Joe's real problem is: he's suddenly found himself far further down this *Song for Europe* line than he ever imagined possible and he's scared of letting us down. Privately, with that awful song of his, I think he's got every reason to worry.

The reason for meeting on Sundays is to rehearse whatever act we have, and so the band quickly gets down to practice. One advantage of entering and trying to win *A Song for Europe* is that we only have to rehearse the one song; the disadvantage is that if that one song is *Hoots Mon* then we're in for a long afternoon. Bev has been in, as ever. She's arranged that she'll come back with cheese scones and mugs of coffee – her classic Sunday combination – but in two hours' time, she announces, rather than the usual one-and-a-half hours. She's going to drive us hard.

Joe doesn't really have any other way of leading a rehearsal than simply to sing the song over and over again. He himself doesn't know the words very well, which isn't much help either, so that our first ninety minutes' work is utterly excruciating – even the normally placid and supportive Geoff is starting to get irritated.

Fortunately, we have Fleece, who can always be relied upon to shine the light of perspective onto any venture.

'Fuck me, Joe, this is such shit that we don't know when it's good shit or just plain rubbish shit! It always sounds so bad to me that I can't tell when we've got it right.'

Little Joe looks like he's about to burst into tears. 'I thought you said you liked it, Josh,' he says. Joe still uses his brother's real name.

'I said no such thing! I said – '

I decide it might be a good time to intercept Fleece mid-rant before he can do any more damage to Joe's delicate ego.

'Fleece appreciates the groundbreaking value of rasta-jock, Joe.' I assure him. '*Hoots Mon* might not what he'd choose to have played at his funeral, but he's a fine drummer who I know takes a professional pride in his work, will give his all when asked, will do so without prejudice or rancour, and will provide a rhythm section that both he and you can be proud of.' It's another extraordinary speech by my standards, and all the time I'm keeping an eye on Fleece's reaction as I give it.

Actually, both Fleece and Little Joe are temporarily dumb-struck by my passionate delivery, matched in history only by the Gettysburg Address. That only leaves one person to say anything.

'Goodness me!' followed by, 'Why goodness me, Brian, how right you are! Goodness me, well said. Yes, goodness me.'

Fleece is simply staring at me, knowing that I'm daring him to admit that he's too bad a drummer to play with Little Joe... he'll never do that. Then he simply smiles. It starts as a chuckle, then he begins to shake his head, then the chuckle becomes a tremulous roar which as inevitably as night follows day culminates in him falling off his stool, on this occasion bringing down two cymbals and a hi-hat.

Little Joe is still a little non-plussed.

'Does that mean we can carry on practising, Captain?' he asks me.

Privately, I think, no, Joe, we simply can't carry on as we were doing before, but I can't think of a good way to say it to him. Then I have a brainwave, not just any old brainwave, but a five-star brainwave.

'We need an independent judge to tell us if we're any good or not,' I say. 'How about asking Bev to supervise?'

This goes down exactly as I'd expected, like a lead balloon. Fleece immediately burst out laughing again, and this time I'm worried because his face goes a puce colour that suggests he's in imminent danger of cardiac arrest. Geoff frown-smiles furiously, and even Little Joe looks bemused.

'But C-Captain,' he stammers, 'Bev... doesn't know anything about music. In fact she's...'

'She's completely tone-deaf!' Fleece roars. 'She wouldn't know a G sharp from a tin opener!'

'Goodness me, Brian, that's right, isn't it?' Geoff chips in. 'Bev would have a problem there, wouldn't she?'

I'm counting on Joe to come to his wife's defence – they dote on each other, remember – and I'm not mistaken. Now he starts to come out swinging.

'Bev's as good as the rest of you,' he yells angrily. 'How dare you suggest she's not musical.'

'Excuse me, Joe,' I say quietly, 'but I think it was my idea to involve Bev.' Joe nods a grumpy apology to me, and I continue. 'The thing is, this is... groundbreaking stuff we're doing here, so someone with very few preconceptions about music might be an ideal judge of where we are. Why don't we ask if she'll help? Joe, would you go and fetch her?'

Joe trundles off, still slightly unsure, and Geoff immediately says, 'I suppose it might work, boys, goodness me all sorts of things can work these days.'

Fleece just looks at me unblinkingly, smiling. 'You cunning bastard. You cunning bastard.' I shrug my shoulders. He knows I've simply dumped the responsibility for the whole show onto someone else.

Moments later a smiling but slightly doubtful-looking Bev follows Little Joe back into the studio.

'I find this a little hard to believe, boys,' she says. 'Music's not exactly my strong point.'

'Captain here thinks you're going to turn us from sows' ears into sows' heads,' Fleece roars.

'Seriously, Bev,' I tell her, 'we need a fresh mind here. We need someone to tell us whether we're getting better or worse. We haven't a clue – we've no idea what it's supposed to sound like.'

'The song's groundbreaking, Bev, remember?' Fleece adds, shaking his head.

I can tell Bev's mystified, and for once she can't read my mind, although she tries. *What's going on here, Brian? Is Joe being messed about here?* But I can reply honestly, *Trust me, Bev. He needs your input right at this moment.*

Bev looks at me with a look that might say she trusts me, might say she doesn't, but definitely says she hasn't a clue what's being expected of her. In fact everyone's correct about Bev: for all her many strengths and powers, she is no musician. I'm counting on the fact that Joe's rasta-jock isn't music either. So once more we set off playing *Hoots Mon*, then we play it again, then again until... suddenly Fleece screams.

'WHAT THE FUCK!'

This particular statement is in no way unusual from Fleece; in fact it's a phrase he resorts to every four-and-a-half minutes on average. But what takes everyone aback here is the sheer volume. Fleece is a loud man, but this is an ear-splitting wail, and on closer examination he might, just might be close to tears. Everyone else in the room is suitably concerned.

'Goodness me, Fleece!' Geoff says. 'What is it?'

Fleece is shaking his head, staring at the floor.

'I can't do it, boys,' he says, eventually.

Little Joe looks desperately hurt. Bev looks as angry as I've ever seen her; her wiles don't work on Fleece, and sometimes she gets frustrated that he can be so awkward – even although, deep down, she knows that actually Fleece does more for Little Joe than anyone else except Bev herself.

'Are you saying you won't be part of Little Joe's backing band, Fleece?' I ask him eventually.

'No,' he replies. I haven't a clue what that means.

'Goodness me,' Geoff says. I haven't a clue what that means, either.

'Just to be clear, Fleece, you're withdrawing from Little Joe's band, is that right?' I ask him.

Suddenly Fleece looks up with his all-too-familiar piratical grin. Of course he's been playing with us all. 'No, that's not what I mean at all,' he says, 'tempting as it might seem. I mean that I can't stand practising *Hoots Mon* or whatever it's called any more. Just let's go there and play the fucking thing. We can't make this better with practice, we can only discover new horrors.' Fleece then completes the pirate image by placing a drumstick between his teeth exactly where a knife should be.

There's a communal sigh of relief, and although Bev is still furious, now it's because Fleece has teased her and Joe. Joe, of course, still needs clarification, but a reassuring quiet word from his wife does the trick.

Geoff is frown-smiling furiously. 'Now let me get this straight, boys. Does that mean we're not practising *Hoots Mon* any more?'

In chorus, Fleece and I say 'Correct.'

'Goodness me!'

'Is that going to be a problem, Geoff?'

'Goodness me, no. In fact my guitar teacher' – Geoff faithfully attends a guitar lesson every week – 'was slightly concerned that practising rasta-jock wasn't good for the rest of my playing.'

This throws Little Joe into something of a relapse, and Bev's none too impressed either.

'What's wrong with Joe's music?' Bev asks Geoff sharply. I've never seen her quite in this mood before. I can tell she needs calming down.

'It's only a technical thing, Bev,' I try to tell her. 'Rasta-jock and blues put the stress on different beats in the bar, and it's quite difficult to switch from one rhythm to the other. And not practising will make our music fresher, more alive.' This may be utter nonsense, but remember that Bev doesn't know much about music so she's quite mollified. She even sends me a little message. *Thank you, Brian. I should have known I could trust you.* And her smile has returned.

Fleece looks across at me and removes his drumstick from his teeth. 'So that's it, is it, Captain? We can all just go home?'

'Till the eighteenth, Fleece. Till the eighteenth.'

We've all - even Bev – forgotten that cheese scones and coffee were supposed to follow our rehearsal.

Part III: The Red Light Is On

THE UPSHOT OF ALL THIS is that when we go through to Glasgow for our audition, we are hopelessly under-rehearsed, or, as Fleece has been putting it, 'fresh'. We've each worked on our own individual parts, I suspect. I certainly have, furiously trying to learn the bass line for Little Joe's curious Scottish-folk-music-cum-reggae, and fortunately it doesn't go terribly quickly.

We meet outside the new BBC Scotland headquarters at Pacific Quay overlooking the River Clyde – Little Joe's been there for ages, of course. Even Fleece looks to have had a haircut for the occasion. Reporting at reception, we're invited to sit down in a waiting area while 'Mairi' comes to collect us. Some five minutes or so later, a very tall woman with short hair and a clipboard, not necessarily in that order, turns up to welcome us. I'm convinced she's been watching us from round the corner to get us nervous, by the way. I'm sure they all do that.

'Hi there. I'm Mairi Montefiori,' she announces, then shakes hands with each of the four of us in turn as we introduce ourselves. 'I'm the producer of this year's UK *Song For Europe* show.'

'Goodness me! Does that mean you're the boss?' Geoff asks, rather clumsily.

'Yes. Are you surprised?' Mairi smiles, but her eyes say 'do you have a problem with that?'

'Goodness me, no,' Geoff blurts out, frowning furiously. Goodness me, is he nervous? If he is, then so am I.

'Our friend Geoff here says 'Goodness me' all the time,' Fleece says, trying to be helpful; as usual he's a little louder than he need be. 'Just ignore him.' Geoff frowns, not quite knowing whether Fleece has insulted him or just been helpful.

Mairi responds by ignoring all of us except to say 'Follow me' and abruptly turns so that all we see of her is a rear view disappearing down the corridor. She's not dressed the way I expect from a BBC employee, she's clearly wearing a suit from which the jacket has been removed. We shuffle off after her with our kit, frantically trying to keep up, and just about manage to follow her into a modern recording studio room which has copious amounts of public address and amplification equipment. At one end is the usual glass screen behind which the production team can try to make performers sound rather better than they really are. Or, hopefully in our case, totally different from the way we really are.

'Welcome to Studio Four,' Mairi announces abruptly, still in business-like mode. Clearly Geoff has irritated her, but there's not a lot any of us can do about that given that (a) Geoff didn't mean to and therefore couldn't apologise without possibly making things worse and (b) Mairi seems determined to extract every last ounce of pleasure possible from being offended.

'These are your two sound engineers, Mark Kelso and Tom Newbury. Do you know each other? Have you worked professionally before?' she asks, still in clipped tones.

'Er… no,' we reply. It's hardly in unison, more of a ripple. The two engineers don't even bother to acknowledge Mairi's question by looking up. After a brief and awkward silence, Mairi says she'll leave us to it and return in two hours.

Once the door closes, Mark and Tom do pay us some attention, and introduce themselves again, which allows us all the chance to start all over again in a slightly easier manner.

'I'd ask you what you did to rattle Mairi's cage,' one of them – Mark, I think – says, 'but frankly she's not worth caring about. Just ignore her.' Interestingly, they're around the same height and build and they both have designer stubble, which makes them look quite alike.

'Geoff here,' I explain, 'was being polite and friendly and she took it the wrong way, I'm afraid.'

'Goodness me,' Geoff says, 'was it my fault? Oh goodness me, boys, I'm so sorry! But what did I say?'

'You said 'goodness me', Geoff, ye daft gowk,' Fleece roars.

'Goodness me? Did I? Oh goodness me, I'm so sorry!'

'I wouldn't get too bothered, mate,' says the other engineer, probably Tom. 'She's management, she gets paid plenty, too much actually, and she has a degree in bossing people around.'

'Goodness me,' Geoff says, 'can you get degrees in that, too, these days? I thought it was strange enough with media studies and brewing.'

'Brewing is a fine skill,' roars Fleece. 'And drinking is a finer one still!'

Mark smiles, then says quietly, 'Perhaps you guys should make some sweet music. Studio time is expensive.'

'We'll let you listen to us first, then you can decide if the music's sweet or not.'

'Well that sounds a good plan,' Mark says. 'Let's get you set up then we can take it from there.'

It actually takes us twenty-five minutes to set up all of our equipment, most of which is Fleece's drum-kit, of course. The only way we can carry it is for each us to take one of his drums in one hand while we each carry our own guitar case in the other, so that when it's all laid down on the studio floor Fleece has to count everything first to check it's all there – a bit like one of those flat-pack furniture kits which people seem to enjoy making up these days. On the other hand, we've been told that we'll need no amplification equipment, and sure enough the studio is strewn with a choice of amplifiers and pre-amplifiers, as well as a state-of-the-art public address system for vocalists. Geoff is particularly impressed by the number of power-points in the room, an admittedly staggering thirty-four. Effectively, while Fleece is trying to get set up, all we have to do is to plug our instruments in to the nearest socket.

While all this is happening, Tom – who has some sort of hybrid posh London accent – is playing out a little pantomime of his own with what he calls his 'baffles' – wall screens that he can lower, tilt and angle to give a satisfactory degree of echo in the recording. As he's doing so, he explains that he wants to record each of us as separately as possible so that he can alter the balance and mix of the sound later after we've gone. And he laughs politely when Fleece suggests that he might want to consider muting Little Joe's contribution completely.

Eventually, it's recording time. Mark – who is clearly Irish, probably from the Belfast area – explains that what he wants us to do is to is to play the whole song through once as if we were playing to an audience of ten thousand. Then both he and Tom go into the sound control room, and when the red light goes on, we know we're 'recording' and ready to go. Fleece starts with a little rattle on the snare drum, I join in with my primitive bass and suddenly Geoff and Little Joe are in as well, none of which is actually too bad until Joe starts singing:

Down in the forest where the bluebells grow
Up in the mountains in the driving snow...

I'm not a very good bass player, but I've managed to reduce the bass part to something a three-year-old can play. It's just as well, because just before the end of the first verse I happen to look up to see that the sound recording engineers' box is empty – or at least it appears to be until I spot Mark and Tom picking themselves up off the floor. I do believe they've been laughing, and perhaps they still might be, except that they're doing their best to hide the fact.

Fortunately, I'm the only one facing in the right direction to see them, apart from Geoff, that is, who of course is so immersed in his sheet music that he spots nothing. Normally I'd be laughing with Mark and Tom, but I'm actually sufficiently annoyed on Joe's behalf to get my head down and pull him through all of this. How dare these two be so rude as to ask us through to Glasgow just to laugh at us? And when it's over, and the red light goes out to indicate that we're not recording any more, I quietly make my way into the engineers' box, shut the door – it's soundproofed, after all – and let them both know what I think of them. Which, if you must know, is that I think that they're selfish spoiled brats who forget that while they only have to listen to Little Joe's music once, Fleece, Geoff and I have to play along with it each and every Sunday afternoon, and this week, thanks to Mark and Tom, on a Thursday too. I walk out and quietly slam the door. Only Fleece looks at me rather quizzically; Little Joe is simply beside himself with joy and Geoff is still altering some chord fingering on the sheet music.

After a respectable interval, Tom and Mark emerge, trying to look a little contrite.

'Well, boys,' Mark says, 'it's a start.'

'Is it a good start?' Fleece asks.

'It's a start.'

Then Mark goes on to explain what he wants us to do: he's going to record us all together once more, this time listening to our first attempt through headphones as we play. We'll practise that briefly to get used to it, then they'll record each of us separately, playing our own part. Little Joe will record his vocal part all by itself, too.

It's a process that takes us all the way through until well past four in the afternoon, by which time I can tell both Tom and Mark are... well, shall we say they're getting a little tired of *Hoots Mon*? We're visited a couple of times by Clipboard Mairi, who simply calls in, listens briefly, then goes away again.

At half past four it's agreed that Tom and Mark have all they need from us, and just then Mairi appears for one final visit. She has a quiet word with the engineers, which none of us can hear but which seems to involve a great deal of head-shaking, then finger-wagging, then finally both Tom and Mark simply shrug at Clipboard Mairi with a gesture that clearly says 'don't say I didn't warn you.'

Eventually she emerges from the engineering booth and approaches Little Joe. 'You say that you wrote this... song of yours, is that so, Mr Mackay?'

'Yes,' Joe replies, slightly suspiciously.

'You do realise that you'll have to make over the rights to us at the BBC, don't you? Otherwise we won't be able to play it or to release it as a single.'

Joe looks less than certain about this, rightly so. 'How do we make any money ourselves, then?'

She smiled patronisingly in return. 'You don't, Mr Mackay. We make you famous, which in turn allows you to make a better deal with recording labels for other numbers you might come up with in the future.'

'Oh,' says Joe, deflated.

'It's standard BBC policy.' Mairi continues to be abrupt to the point of rudeness. 'It was the same last year with Nearly Lynn.' Nearly Lynn was a true low point of UK entries for *A Song for Europe*. Normally a transvestite Vera Lynn tribute act from Newcastle, she had managed to come up with a patriotic pan-European marching song, to which she had goose-stepped backwards and forwards across the stage throughout her performance on the big night. She had come last of the twenty-eight entries, the traditional British result.

'Can Little Joe continue to play it in his concerts and record it on his albums?' I ask. 'Surely he's allowed to make a living from his own work?'

Mairi turns to look at me. She angles her head backwards to that she's looking directly at me down her nose.

'You're the bass player, are you?' If it's intended as a put-down, then it's worked. 'I'm not sure if it's any of your business, Mr...'

'Reid.'

'I'm not sure if it's any of your business, Mr Reid, but I suppose the answer is yes, he can continue to play it in concerts and to record it.'

Little Joe offers me a little support. 'Mr Reid has a lot of experience in songwriting and copyright, Mairi,' he says, then turns to me saying, 'Thanks for asking, Captain.' I nod. I can tell that Mairi now hates Geoff, Little Joe and me, and straightaway she gives us a chance to make her hate us even more.

'Perhaps you would like to play...' – she has to look down at her clipboard – '...*Hoots Mon* for me, gentlemen?'

'It'll be our pleasure,' laughs Fleece. 'It really will.' He turns to us, saying, 'Come on, boys, let her have it!' and he and I launch into the early bars of Joe's masterpiece.

Three minutes and fourteen seconds later, Mairi's face is as white as a sheet. Meanwhile, while she's been listening to and watching us in the studio itself, once again I alone have been able to see Mark and Tom doubled up with laughter in their soundproof engineering room.

Little Joe is desperate for Mairi's approval. 'Well?'

'It's... different,' is all she can say in reply.

'Do you think we've got a chance of qualifying for *A Song for Europe*?' he continues.

I try to intercept. 'Joe, I don't really think we can ask Mairi that – '

But Mairi surprises me, all of us, in fact.

'Oh I think it's highly likely your song will qualify, Mr Mackay. You were the only entrant this year.'

I'm speechless with amazement, Little Joe with joy. Geoff – of course – says 'Goodness me'; Fleece – of course – says 'Fuck me.'

'Nobody wants to enter *A Song for Europe* on behalf of the United Kingdom any more. It's the kiss of death to a music career, it seems. Plus it seems to be a waste of time because everyone else in Europe hates Britain anyway and this is a good way of giving us a kicking. And of course there's all the countries that vote to support each other, no matter how bad their songs are. Most of the entries are really pretty dreadful, you know. It's just that they're in languages we don't understand so we're protected from the worst of it.'

'Is my song 'pretty dreadful'?' Little Joe asks, plaintively.

Mairi looks at him, considers telling a lie, then ducks Joe's question altogether. 'I hope you do well, gentlemen,' Mairi says. 'My job is to improve Britain's results at *A Song for Europe*. If I don't get a top-three finish I'm out of a job. Now, if you'll forgive me, I've got some work I should be doing. It's been nice meeting you,' she says. She's lying; the coldness in her eyes give it away. She not only wishes she'd never met us, she wishes she'd never set foot inside BBC Scotland's headquarters at Pacific Quay.

No sooner has she gone than Geoff says something I've never once heard him say before.

'Goodness me, she was a horrible woman, wasn't she? Goodness me, I didn't like her.'

Mark and Tom march over to shake our hands.

'We didn't know she's got to make top three or she's out – that's news to us,' Mark says. 'Sorry to have to say it, boys, but it would be great for us if we got rid of her.'

Little Joe is completely confused, but knows his song is not being complimented.

Fleece hasn't bothered to get off his drum-kit stool, so anything he says continues to be yelled across the room. 'That woman, I'm afraid, is what we in the trade call 'rubber-ducked',' he pronounces. 'And I for one thinks she deserves everything that's coming to her.' Meanwhile Geoff is still frowning and smiling alternately, and shaking his head in disbelief saying, 'Goodness me, goodness me,' all the time.

Is it only me who needs the clarification then?

'Hang on a minute,' I say to Mark and Tom, but for the benefit of my fellow band members, too. 'Are we the UK entry for *A Song for Europe* then?'

'Yes,' says Tom. 'I thought Mairi had made that clear.'

'So how do you tell the general public that we're the lucky winners? Send out postcards?'

Mark and Tom look at each other, then Mark says, 'I suppose there's no reason really why you should know the programme scheduling. On the 17th January edition of *The Ricky Rollo Show*, you'll have a slot to play your… song.'

'Ricky Rollo?' Ricky Rollo is a late-night chat show host with his own programme on Saturday nights; it has viewing figures of almost eight million weekly.

'Of course,' Mark says. 'You know he'll be the host of *A Song for Europe* as well when it comes to Glasgow in March next year? He always does that sort of stuff these days.'

'So that means… we're going to be… on television?' Little Joe asks.

Tom and Mark chuckle. 'I think that's the general idea, isn't it? Eight million viewers for Rollo's show, then – well, more than a hundred million, I suppose, for the event itself.'

Little Joe still needs to hear it said. 'Are we definitely going to be on the telly? Is the song good enough?'

'Oh you're definitely going to be on the television,' Mark says, grinning. 'You've got there by default. As for your song being good enough… well, think of all the shit we've entered before and…'

'Boom-banga-wallop,' Fleece roars from the back, rocking with laughter.

'Goodness me!' says Geoff, frown-smiling, but with more smiles than frowns; he's pleased for Joe.

'*The Ricky Rollo Show… A Song for Europe…*,' Joe repeats, numb. We're going to be famous.'

'Or infamous, Joe,' I point out.

Part IV: A Song for Europe

I NEED TO START by describing Ricky Rollo.

He's fantastically rich, on one of those BBC contracts that aren't supposed to exist any more in these times of austerity, but do so nevertheless. Ricky is coining in almost three million pounds' salary every year for his go-to presence on a number of shows on television, and one one-hour-a-week show on Radio 2. He's amazingly popular: I suppose he can be hilariously funny without being really unpleasant to his chat-show guests. He seems to be able to get them to laugh with him at aspects of their own lives. He's funny, clever, well-read and -prepared, and gay. In fact Ricky Rollo is so camp that he could house the entire British Army. Nevertheless, he doesn't make any play of his sexuality other than his outrageous dress, and there more than a few straight guys who dress in silly suits, too. We each respond to the prospect of *The Ricky Rollo Show* in our predictable ways: I'm looking forward to meeting him; Little Joe is nervous; Geoff is lost in a sea of 'goodness me's; Fleece simply couldn't care less.

So when we're asked to return to Glasgow – to the same studio, oddly, as the audition was held in – it's more than a little disappointing to discover that Ricky himself will not be there. Instead, the BBC's plan is to make one of those videos of us recording the song and to show the video instead on *The Ricky Rollo Show*. Mark and Tom are both present of course, but now there are five other people present to deal with the camerawork, lighting and – because it's technically a movie – a director. Every single one of them looks the same: the same height build, the same jeans-and-casual-shirt look, trainers, and the mandatory designer stubble beard. No women. Even I can see that perhaps, after all, the BBC is a little gender-biased in certain areas, although this is just one tiny snapshot.

Trying to show an interest in what's going on, I ask the man who appears to be the director how this will be slotted into *The Ricky Rollo Show*. He has one of these identification passes draped on a lanyard around his neck and because his name is short I can – miraculously – read it: Dave Scott.

'Oh that's the least of our problems,' Dave says breezily, 'we'll be relying on CGI a lot for this.'

'As in… computer-generated imagery?'

'Of course,' he says. 'How else would you appear on *The Ricky Rollo Show*?' Dave can see I'm a bit bemused. 'It's just a little bit risky to allow you to appear live, don't you think?'

Clearly, our reputation precedes us, but I'm still speechless.

'Do you ever watch Ricky's show?' he asks me.

'Of course.' I should include 'occasionally' there but it doesn't seem a good idea somehow.

'Well you'll remember that he often closes his show with some band or other playing them out and the credits rolling over them. It gives us a chance to do all sorts of stuff to cover up the fact that the band in question actually recorded the music the week before. It's a bit like a conjuring act, I suppose – the audience's mind is on other things so that they don't notice our little sleight of hand.'

'Really?'

'Do you ever see Ricky in the same shot?' he asks me.

'But there's an audience. And they're dancing or clapping in time with the music.'

'Not to that band's music. We have a whole library of 'audience footage' which we can adapt to our needs. We know your stuff is reggae beat so we've got lots of reggae audiences and we just slow their reactions, or speed them up, until we get a match.'

'Will that happen in *A Song for Europe* itself, too?'

'Sadly, no. That's why it's so crap. But the BBC learned its lesson years ago on an obscure show that ran on BBC3 called *The Rock And Roll Radio Road Show*. We allowed a post-grunge heavy-metal band called The Dambusters on for a single-number slot when we hadn't checked out their background properly. During the show – which went out supposedly live but broadcast-delayed by five minutes, thankfully – the band did their special party-piece of smashing their guitars into the studio cameras. Cost us a fortune. And it was the end of the show.'

'What did you do?'

'Showed an old episode of *Bilko*. I think the programmers reckoned that *Bilko* was the nearest comedy we had to crude loud rock.' He smiles. 'Anyway, ever since then it's been policy not to allow any untested bands onto live TV, so I'm afraid we're recording you here, and broadcasting you later.'

And that's exactly what happens. Three weeks later, for the first time in ages, I find myself watching *The Ricky Rollo Show* for our moment of... glory? I'm not sure I'd call it that. Ricky, dressed for the evening in a bright blue suit with yellow stars to represent the European Union flag, announces us right at the end as 'the United Kingdom's entry for this year's *A Song for Europe*' before waving to everyone and calling out who's on next week's show, so that our ever-so-subtle introduction to *Hoots Mon* is lost in the chaos. And if that isn't bad enough, we're faded out three-quarters of the way through to make way for a trailer for some Saturday-night game show which I simply never watch, so that my first move is to reach for the 'Off' button on the TV remote.

I'm not sure the screen has actually gone fully blank when the telephone starts to ring: Joe, inevitably.

'Did you see it, Captain, did you see it?' He's got that excited-little-boy-at-Christmas voice in action.

I try to be measured. 'I saw it. They made us look remarkably decent.'

'We looked great, Captain!'

'I'm not sure about 'great', Joe, but it's amazing what clever mixing and editing can do for mediocre musicians like us.'

'So you think I'm mediocre?' There's bristle in his tone.

'Well, I'm mediocre anyway,' I admit.

'Well I thought it was great. First time on live television!'

Given that we've just been sitting on our sofas watching ourselves on 'live' TV, I'm not sure that Joe's definition and mine are quite the same. But I've also noticed that he didn't correct my self-effacing 'I'm mediocre'. Instead, I try to stop Joe from getting carried away.

'We've still got an awful lot of work to do before we're ready for a final performance at *A Song for Europe*, Joe.'

'Do you think so?'

'I'm afraid so.' And I try to explain to him, as gently as is possible to a dear friend who has no idea how bad he is musically, that this might be a long haul. A few minutes later, he ends the call, rather less excited than when it began. I feel guilty, but not a coward at least.

Fleece is definitely a coward, and when we meet the following Sunday for our weekly practice at Joe and Bev's house, I take the matter up with him.

'You, you rat,' I yell at him, only partly joking, 'I saw you on *The Ricky Rollo Show*, or to be more exact I didn't see you.'

Fleece looks at me innocently. 'I can't begin to think what you're talking about, Captain old boy.'

'It was your hat.' For the recording, Fleece had been wearing a big floppy-rimmed thing while drumming, which I'd assumed had been intended to conceal his ageing features, especially his receding hair, but in fact had been pulled so low down over his eyes that he had been unidentifiable. 'You were hiding.'

'Me?' Fleece replies, still coming innocent all over. 'ME??? Do you have a good lawyer, Captain?'

'Actually, yes, he's not bad. He's the same as yours. Last time I saw him, he told me you owed him some money.'

Fleece shrugs. 'A trifle, a trifle...'

'Anyway,' I continue to rant at him, 'when the rest of us are visible, you have to be as well.'

'I have my reputation to consider, Captain,' Fleece replies.

He's hopeless in this mood; he simply refuses to be serious. In any case, I'm only jealous that I didn't think of the idea first. 'I presume you're going to do the same thing on the night,' Fleece says, trying to be helpful.

'Nothing surer. We could probably persuade Geoff to do it as well, and leave Joe to enjoy his moment in the sun all by himself,' I add.

'Little Joe Mackay and his backing band!' Fleece roars. 'As it happens...' and he then produces from a crumpled carrier bag two brand new wide-brimmed hats exactly the same as his own. 'I got the lot in SaveAPoundOrTwo.' A new shop has opened up nearby which sells all sorts of low-quality stuff you don't actually need for next to nothing.

'Thanks, Fleece,' I say, genuinely grateful. In a conversation I can't quite hear, Fleece hands one to Geoff, too, who of course replies 'Goodness me' a couple of times.

'I've just told Geoff it's our new compulsory band uniform,' Fleece explains.

At that very moment Joe himself decides to take command.

'Izzy-wizzy, let's get busy!'

It's such a stupid thing to say that even Fleece is silenced while Joe tells us what he wants us to do. He's hopeless at explaining anything, particularly anything musical, but it doesn't matter because all he wants us to do is the same as we've been doing for months – play this damned song of his. I've often suggested warm-ups, but he's not really interested, and the only thing that rescues us this time is Bev's appearance with her freshly-made cheese scones at the stroke of four o'clock.

'How's it going boys?' she asks, looking at me. Bev knows that whatever I say, she'll be able to get the truth out me. Telepathically.

'Not bad,' I reply.

I feel her reply between my shoulder-blades. *Do you mean that, Brian?*

'It'll not be for the want of practice.'

That bad?

I say nothing, hoping that the others will come to my aid. Fleece pulls his hat down further his eyes, while Geoff just stands looking rather vacant, smiling and frowning.

Oh dear, Brian, what are we going to do? Bev looks worried, although what she actually says is: 'Well, I'm sure you'll be just great on the night,' squeezing my arm with the message *I know I can trust you, Brian*. That's just the thing, Bev puts so much responsibility onto my shoulders. Why mine?

Bev finds an excuse to ease her way past me, and as she does so, she whispers, 'Because I know I can trust you, Brian, didn't I just tell you?' into my ear. This time the effect on me is electrifying, sending shivers all the way up and down my spine. She may be Joe's wife, she may be completely and totally in love with her husband, but she's happy to use her power over me to get whatever she feels he needs. Right now she feels *Hoots Mon* needs something else to lift it.

The words just emerge from my lips.

'What we need is a brass section,' I say.

Little Joe looks as if I've hit him with something. Geoff looks up from his sheet music as if I've just told him some bad news. But only Fleece, looking up slowly from his hiding place behind his hat, actually says anything.

'Have you gone fucking mad, Captain?'

'No,' I explain calmly. 'Reggae music often has a brass section. It would lift our performance.'

'It would, Fleece, it would,' Joe says. 'Captain's right.' He's starting to get excited, and I can tell Bev's pleased with me – provisionally.

'Do you actually know any brass players, Brian?' she asks.

'Just so, Beverley, just so,' Fleece says. 'Who the fuck is going to play along with us?'

'I know one or two who might help us for the sake of doing a good turn,' I tell him.

'Fuck me, Captain. You must have some nerve.'

*

The weeks pass and eventually we're given our instructions for attending *A Song for Europe*. It's being broadcast from a very new twelve-thousand seated auditorium call The Hydro and the BBC has spared no expense to make sure it goes well. Of course *A Song for Europe* was originally conceived as a means of showing off pan-European television links, but that's old hat nowadays. These days it's all about winning, or in Britain's case not coming last or getting 'nul points'. It's not entirely the fault of the singers or the songs, although in truth the things we've put forward haven't helped either.

No, the real problem is that *A Song for Europe* has become politicised. Europe has become divided into blocs: the former Yugoslav countries, the former Soviet bloc, the Scandinavian countries, the southern Mediterranean countries and so on. They're not allowed to vote for themselves, but they can conspire to vote for each other. Britain, without any friends in Europe, is isolated like the little boy invited to the party but whom no-one actually likes. So no-one votes for the United Kingdom song.

In an attempt to improve the country's prospects – and his own shortly before an impending general election – the UK prime minister has been furiously lobbying various

European governments to gain a little friendly support. But there have also been some international developments which I haven't fully understood – a trade war, a border clash, a couple of disputes about refugees, and a smuggling conspiracy. Also, there has been a huge clash over the distribution of the European Union budget, and another about the price of oil in Poland. Various governments have been making all sorts of veiled threats, and in fact *A Song for Europe* has been openly criticised in some newspapers for trying to paper over the cracks. Even the United Kingdom itself hasn't been exempt. The Irish government has been campaigning for the release of some long-standing former IRA member who was convicted twenty years ago of some bombing. Because he still maintains his innocence, he's not been allowed out of prison. It manifests itself as an Irish complaint about *Hoots Mon* on the grounds that – especially with the added brass section – it's now really a West Indian entry and therefore not European. This requires us to make a small late adjustment to our performance, and I'm ashamed to say that the idea comes from me.

'Why don't we add bagpipes as well?' I suggest.

'Bagpipes?' Fleece replies. 'Captain, we're in enough trouble as it is. Have you gone completely fucking mad?'

Patiently, I explain to everyone that the droning bagpipes will complement the cleaner brass parts nicely, that there's a reference to bagpipes in the song, and – most important of all – will reassure the organising committee that this is indeed a 'native' British song. What's more, I happen to know a piper who stays just along the road from me and owes me a favour: I put up some shelves in his kitchen recently. And he happens to be a friend of the brass players, even playing the cornet in his spare time.

But politics being what it is, the Irish are still kicking up a fuss right up to the day, so that even when we arrive in Glasgow there's a real concern that we might not be allowed to use the brass section, in which case the bagpipes would seem a little crude. It's all or nothing really.

We're told to be on site at noon, which seems ridiculously early except that a full rehearsal is planned. There's a roll-call, and then around one o'clock Ricky Rollo arrives. The private Ricky Rollo proves to be a complete surprise; he's not camp at all. In fact, he could be mistaken for almost anyone BBC employee in the entire studio, except, of course, that he doesn't have any designer stubble. (Although it looks as though he's yet to shave.) He comes over to meet us, as the host entry, shakes all of our hands and then shrugs his shoulders.

'Is it something to do with the way I look,' he asks.

'Well,' I say, 'it's just that you look so...'

'Ordinary? I hope so. All that fancy-dress stuff is just the stage act. And it means I can go shopping in Tesco without being recognised a lot of the time. It gives Trevor a breather as well.' Everyone knows his partner is Trevor Davis, a minor film director. 'Did I disappoint you?' he asks, without a hint of irony in his voice.

'Quite the reverse.'

Ricky smiles a brief acknowledgement, but he's in work mode. 'Look,' he says, 'the thing with these Eurovision things is that there's actually an awful lot of scope for things to go wrong – we're so dependent on all the different broadcasters getting everything right at once. You can make our life very much easier by keeping your own act simple. And short. How long is your song?' he asks, turning to Joe.

'Two minutes forty-three seconds,' Joe replies. Ricky chuckles.

'Which is about two minutes forty-two seconds too long!' calls Fleece from behind him, which lightens the mood, or at least lightens everyone's mood except Little Joe, who of course is hurt.

'Anyway,' Ricky says, 'you're on just three from the end, which is a big advantage. The songs at the end attract more votes because the judges haven't quite managed to forget them yet.'

'What's last, then?' I ask.

'Ireland.' Brilliant, our worst Eurovision enemy is getting the prime spot. It's also one of the pre-competition favourites; we're quoted at seventy-five to one against. But Ricky says that in recent years the bookmakers have been hopelessly wrong trying to predict which song will tickle the judges' fancy on the night.

One by one the various countries rehearse their pieces, although we ourselves hear none of them – for some reason the Eurovision Song Contest organisers have deemed it too much of an advantage to hear earlier entries. The purpose of the rehearsal is really to check sound levels for each group throughout each European country, and because only the sound engineers can hear anything, the process is stultifyingly boring for the participants. Even Ricky Rollo isn't supposed to hear anything, although one or two of the engineers let him hear a snatch of a couple of the numbers. He does make a point of listening to ours, though, announcing at the end that it was two seconds faster than Joe had promised (which Joe puts down to big night nerves). By six o'clock we're ready, and by eight o'clock, incredibly, we've been given a snack and some water, dressed and had our makeup applied (Geoff was very uncomfortable in makeup, there were an awful lot of 'goodness me's, goodness me, an awful lot), and we're ready to go out live.

Suddenly, the enormity of where we are dawns on me, and curiously the other person who's realised what's at stake is Fleece. The pair of us are standing together, well away from where anyone can hear us.

'Fuck me, Captain, what the fuck have we done here? What have got ourselves into?'

'Trust in Joe, Fleece,' I intone. 'Trust in Joe.'

'Thanks, Captain, I'll go and commit suicide now.'

'Not yet, Fleece. Wait till after our gig, then you'll have two reasons to do it.'

Fleece looks at me. 'Now I know why you're one of my oldest friends, Captain. You're never afraid to tell it like it us.' Then he adds, 'I think I know what it was like to be on the Titanic.'

Somewhere around five to nine we're sitting in our dressing room tucking into some BBC prawn mayonnaise sandwiches when it suddenly dawns on us that what we're looking at on the monitor is not a rehearsal at all, it's actually the real show. Because we're on as entrant number twenty-six out of the twenty-eight, this song – it happens to be some sort of punk-rock all-female band from Spain – is number nineteen, and our turn isn't quite as far away as we'd assumed. A cold shiver runs down my spine.

'Cheer up, Fleece, we've been in worse fixes,' I say to Fleece, more trying to convince myself than anything else.

'Name two,' Fleece replies. 'And name any where we haven't been lucky to escape by the skin of our teeth.' I give him a wry smile. He has a point. And then I see something that really does worry me – not Geoff's continued practising of the guitar music, I'm used to that, it's Joe, who appears to be trying to memorise the lyrics of the song.

'Joe,' I say, then repeat, 'Joe... what's going on?'

Little Joe has a look of blind panic on his face.

'Captain, I'm having a mental block,' he says, 'I can't remember the words. I just can't remember them at all.'

'You'll be fine, Joe,' I try to say as calmly as I can, although now I'm panicking too.

'Pity you didn't forget the whole thing a long time ago,' Fleece suggests. 'Then we'd all have been saved a load of trouble.' It's not what Little Joe wants to hear, but that doesn't matter because Joe isn't listening to anything at all, sensible or otherwise; he's got his eyes screwed up as he furiously tries to repeat the two verses.

'You'll be fine when you're playing the music as well, Joe,' I say.

This pantomime goes on for a few tortuous minutes and then we get a surprise visitor, Mairi Montefiori, the easily-offended producer we met on our very first visit to BBC Headquarters. This time she's a little easier.

'Everything OK, gentlemen?'

Straight away Geoff spots her and goes across to see her. 'Goodness me, it's you. I'm so sorry about the last time, I meant no offence, I simply say 'goodness me' a lot, at least they tell me I do. I really didn't mean – '

She cuts him off. 'Mr Arrowsmith, I'm told you're actually very nice and I was wrong to take offence. I think I'm the one who should apologise.'

'Oh goodness me, no, goodness me – '

'Please,' I say, 'Mairi, you've come at a good time. Our vocalist has an attack of nerves and can't remember the words.'

'I thought he wrote it,' she says, somewhat amused.

'Any suggestions?'

'Of course. We can put them onto an autocue. He probably won't really need them, but knowing they're there will give your singer more confidence. Don't worry, we often do it.'

'Please, if you would,' I say. Fleece turns to Little Joe to tell him the good news, although he actually has to explain it three times, Joe's so terrified. It turns out that putting Joe's lyrics on the auto cue is simply a matter of typing them into a computer keyboard somewhere, and although Fleece insists that the person doing might go blind in the process, it's done in no time.

But there is a problem with the brass section. I've been keeping it quiet that in fact it's a small sub-section of a local Salvation Army Band. They're insisting that they wear full uniform, partly because they want to show that it really is a British entry, and partly because they think it might attract new recruits. It turns out not to be a deal-breaker for any of the band – they're too preoccupied now with other things – but it nearly is for the piper, the one non-Salvationist in the wind section. The bagpiper is actually Polish, a fellow called Marek who's desperate to assimilate into Scottish culture and is now insisting that, if the others wear Salvation Army uniform, he should as well... except that there isn't any for him. Fortunately the BBC's costume department comes up with something, and although it's apparently a nineteenth-century version, Marek is satisfied.

And by the time Marek's kitted out, song number twenty-four is playing, and our producer Mairi is back to tell us we should be heading for The Hydro's enormous stage; she's smiling and trying to look relaxed, but I can see that the late upset with Marek's Salvation Army uniform has rattled her. I can tell she feels we're cutting this all a bit fine. She's every right to be bothered, but only because we're awful, not because we're late. In fact, having something to do at this stage has taken the edge off our nerves: even Little Joe's finally seen something to laugh at in the idea of a Polish bagpiper pretending to be a member of the Salvation Army by dressing up in period kit. We're ushered to the performance zone where the audience can see us, although they're under strict instructions to pretend they can't.

Ricky Rollo is in full flow. Entry number twenty-five, directly before ours, is from Malta, and proves to be a ballad sung in English and performed by a buxom woman who, we're informed, was once a Maltese superstar and film actress but these days is trying to rebuild her career after a three-year jail sentence for tax fraud. Like all the other songs in *The Eurovision Song Contest*, it's broadcast from her own country – that's the point, to show off pan-European media links – which means that not only can we hear her, we can also hear the boos as she takes the stage. Mairi explains that the Maltese public remain furious that she used her connections to the Maltese prime minister to escape a sentence three times as long. It doesn't sound good, and neither does she, frankly. When it comes to an end, no amount of background interference can hide the boos coming from the Valetta audience.

Suddenly, Ricky Rollo is whipping up an audience frenzy in the Hydro, a noise which sounds like a cross between a football match and a flock of wintering geese. It's our turn, and this is what he's good at: distracting the television public so that no-one notices just how bad we really are. He's dressed in a gold and purple striped suit with massive lapels, which glints and shimmers just the right amount so that everyone looks at him rather than us. And he's in full camp-mode.

'Ladies... and... gentlemen...! Viewers... at... home...! If you're watching, Your Majesty, now's the time to wave your Union Jack!' Everyone laughs – this is why he's so good, of course, he can do respectful irreverence so well. 'The moment has come where we present the UNITED KINGDOM entry!' People in the audience cheer, despite the fact that alcohol is banned and most haven't a clue what's about to hit their senses. 'It's... it's... it's... Joe Mackay And His Band with... *Hoots Mon!*'

Powerful searchlights suddenly descend on Fleece, hat over his eyes at his drum-kit, who responds by launching into the beat closely followed by me on bass, with an identical hat over my eyes. Even Geoff has followed the party line with one, leaving only Joe himself exposed to the world. Off he goes.

Down in the forest where the bluebells grow
Up in the mountains in the driving snow...

The great advantage of Joe's song is that it's mercifully short, and the whole nightmare is over surprisingly quickly. Joe doesn't forget any words, Geoff gets all the guitar chords right, the Salvation Army brass-bagpipe section sounds

sounds spot-on, Fleece keeps the beat perfectly, and even I don't foul up the base. It's so good that it's almost mediocre.

Ricky summons up an enormous wave of applause, cheers, whistling, and flag-waving from the twelve thousand people, who incidentally are being *paid* to attend and sound like this – it's BBC Rent-A-Crowd, or else we'd be lucky to have any more than our families there. We take three carefully-orchestrated curtain-calls and then are told by the producer to 'skip off quickly'. Immediately, Joe, who understandably is completely bouncing that he's got through this ordeal, is grabbed by two young men, one of those irritating BBC comedy acts that seems to get more exposure than it deserves... but then I suppose you could say that about us, too. They interview Joe to ask him 'how it went' ('great'), 'what do you think of the audience ('great'), and what he thinks of his chances ('great'). It allows the rest of us to slide off back towards the dressing room unnoticed.

Once we're there, Mairi pops in to say 'well done' to all of us, and particularly to Joe of course, and she spots Marek starting to remove his fake Salvation Army uniform.

'What are you doing?' she asks, alarmed.

'Kun I nutt remoof this now?' Marek asks. His English is fine, actually, but he doesn't use it enough to have a good accent, he spends too much time with other Polish mates.

'No, no, no,' she says, 'you have to stay dressed up for when the results come in. The cameras will watch your reactions, all of you. And if you win, you'll have to go back on to do it again.'

For the first time in the entire night, every single person in the room bursts into total laughter, even Little Joe. Perhaps after all he's just relieved to have survived.

'Fuck me, Mairi, you can't really say with a straight face that we were good enough to win, can you? Go on.'

'Oh, the winner won't be the best song,' she replies, straight-faced. 'It'll be whichever country has got the politics right.' Then she looks at us again. 'I guess that rules Britain out, doesn't it? Nobody likes us.'

'Not even the Irish,' I say.

'Especially the Irish,' she agrees.

The last of the entries, the Irish one, comes and goes. It's not bad, but when you've been involved in your one and only *Eurovision Song Contest* you rather hope your own song will not do too badly. Even *Hoots Mon!* All the newspapers this week have been questioning whether Britain should pull out of *The Eurovision Song Contest*, one political party demanding an in/out referendum on the subject. It's been made clear to us that we have a national duty (a) not to come last and (b) not to score zero points. It's a weighty responsibility, and I'm not sure Little Joe will be able to stand the pressure. Geoff has had to go the toilet eight times already, but that's no more than average for Geoff, who has a continuing 'problem with the waterworks' – but whatever you do, don't ask him about it.

The interval follows, which really exists to allow the first few countries a little time to decide which songs they like best It could be anything that plugs this hole, but on this occasion the BBC have managed to get an old girl band called Princesses Five to reform for the first time in years and sing a medley of their old hits. Despite the fact that they haven't performed together for years, that two of them don't really speak to the other three any more, and that several are now very, very rich indeed, Princesses Five will undoubtedly be the highlight of tonight's show.

And it's also where Ricky Rollo really starts to come into his own, joking with both the audience and this ageing 'girl band' – can you really be a girl band when none of you is under forty? – and even joining in, comically, with the dance steps of the last number. It all helps to anaesthetise the audience after all the rubbish they've just had to endure.

Meanwhile, towards the end of this interval break, we're asked to take our place on sofas at the side of the stage – Ricky's had this part set up to conform with his weekly chat show, and the cameras will be trained on us to pick up our reactions as the results come in. Ours will a public execution,

And by now the results are due. Each country will announce their votes in the order in which their contestants sang, which means the first of all is Slovenia. I'm not quite sure where Slovenia is, actually. Ever-professional in his gold and purple striped suit, Ricky creates all the usual tension.

'Good evening, Ljubljana!' And now I've just learned what Slovenia's capital is.

The scoring system for *The Eurovision Song Contest* is arcane: the song they like best gets twelve points, the second best gets ten, then eight, seven, and so on all the way down to one for the tenth choice. It takes ages to announce, and into the bargain the votes are announced in reverse order so that which country's song is to get the magic 'twelve points' isn't known until the very end. It's going to take a very long time indeed, and Ricky Rollo will earn his salary tonight if he can keep everyone from nodding off completely.

Slovenia, it appears, used to be part of the former Yugoslavia, and therefore we'd expected these countries all to vote for each other, but it turns out that this year it's not quite that simple. Bosnia, Croatia and Serbia, all former Yugoslavian countries, also all fancy their chances of winning. They all hate each other, but they don't want to make it too obvious, so Slovenia casts a few votes for each of its neighbours but casts seven votes for an execrable Icelandic piece of nonsense and four… for us! Straight away we know we're not going to get zero points.

This pattern continues with next few countries; none of them seem to like our song very much, but they'll give it a few votes to avoid having to give it to their fiercest competitors. Halfway through, we're lying in a respectable fifth place, although that takes a knock when in quick succession the French and then the Germans resolutely give us 'nul points'. The French refuse to speak in anything except French, but when Ricky responds in perfect French, they simply appear petty and rude. When next he pointedly offers to speak in German to the Germans, they equally pointedly thank him for his courtesy and insist they'll happily communicate in English.

Our position takes a further knock when it's the United Kingdom's turn to vote, because of course countries can't vote for their own entries. In fact by now it's clear that the Irish song is faintly emerging as leader, although several others are still in the hunt. That includes ours, just, although we continue to get a small run of minor points awarded by every other country and gradually our song emerges as the main challenger to the Irish one. This is despite the fact that not one single country has rated it so far in their top three – we're just almost everyone's fourth, fifth or sixth choice. The second last country to vote is Norway, whose own song remains pointless, and although they give us a few votes, they give Ireland the full twelve, all but sealing our fate.

Joe and Geoff have taken some time to grasp what's going on, but both now understand that we've had a respectable showing, and the BBC will be delighted.

'Goodness me,' Geoff says, 'haven't we done well!'

'We're only eleven points behind, Captain, we could still do it with the last round.'

Fleece is asleep, head covered by the hat, so it's left to me to break it to Joe. 'Look, Joe, there's good news and bad. The good news is that the Irish can't vote for themselves.

The bad news is… I somehow think it's highly unlikely the Irish will help us win *The Eurovision Song Contest*. Don't you remember how they tried to get your song disqualified because it was West Indian, not British?'

Joe's immediately downcast. 'I suppose so.'

Ricky Rollo is still in full swing. 'Come in Dublin!!'

A laconic voice returns his greeting, then begins, 'The results of the Irish voting was as follows…' then slowly runs through the votes, giving four votes to the awful Norway song, but, as predicted, not mentioning us at all. Until…

'…and finally, United Kingdom, twelve points.' The Irish announcer doesn't say it with any great drama, he just signs off with a 'Goodnight, Glasgow,' and that's that. We've won by one solitary point, courtesy of our biggest rivals.

Ricky Rollo, of course, is jumping up and down with excitement. Joe's song, *Hoots Mon!* is the first British *Eurovision Song Contest* winner in living memory. At first Ricky can barely speak; Geoff can only say 'goodness me', and Little Joe looks totally stunned. I have to wake Fleece up to explain what's happened.

'What the fuck?' is Fleece's predictable response, but then, at my request, he gently explains it to Little Joe that his lovingly-created rasta-jock number is ringing all around the continent of Europe. Joe himself is interviewed by Ricky, and, zombie-like, answers them remarkable sensibly avoiding any bad language or the usual long line of thank-yous accompanied by tears. Then of course, we're immediately whisked back on stage to do a repeat of our winning song, which plays out the credits Europe-wide.

As we're going back to the dressing room, Fleece and I stumble across Mairi, who's looking rather smug. Geoff and Joe are well out of earshot.

'That was a turn-up for the books,' I say to her.

'Yes,' she says, 'that all went rather well, didn't it?'

Fleece and I look her, then at each other. There's just something in the way she's said it that makes me something else. 'Who'd have thought it? The Irish vote for us to give us victory.'

'Yes,' she repeats, 'it went rather well.'

Fleece says nothing but his ears are flapping. He wants me to pursue this, I can tell. So do I, actually.

'So why did the Irish vote for us?' I ask. 'What do you know?'

'The Irish were always going to vote for you,' she explains. 'Their government needed three billion pounds loan to help dig them out of their current financial crisis. Voting for you was part of the price.'

'But the Irish tried to get us disqualified.'

'That was just a cover to keep the Irish public happy. They wouldn't be pleased if it was known their government was being too cooperative.'

Fleece and I can hardly believe this. 'Was any other country 'helped'?'

'One or two. Our government gave contracts here and there to some small countries.'

Fleece is shaking his head, and I don't blame him.

'What's in for our government, then?'

'Oh that's easy,' she smiles. 'You've just won the next general election for them.'

Fleece and I sigh in despair. Then I say to him, 'Fleece what have we done?'

'We're just pawns in their game, Captain, we're just pawns in their game.'

Mairi stops at our closed dressing room door; Joe and Geoff are inside. She looks earnestly at us.

'Will you tell the others?' she asks.

'No fucking chance,' Fleece says. 'I love my brother too much. It'd break his heart.'

'I thought you wouldn't, somehow. Blissful ignorance must be wonderful, mustn't it?'

I'd already warmed to Mairi, but that clinched it.

Hoots Mon

(from the short story of the same name by Gordon Lawrie)

Acknowledgements

The writing of these 20 stories spans almost a decade, and so many people have had an input that, to be honest, I've forgotten most of them; if I've left you out of the following list, please accept my apologies, let me know and I'll try to put it right in a later edition.

First of all, thanks to American writer Don Tassone for providing the Foreword. Don's a prolific and busy fiction writer. I recommend his work to readers: he writes fiction of all lengths, including a wealth of micro-fiction for Friday Flash Fiction, the online publication that I edit myself. Anyone can try out his style for size at his own website. Don reads his own stories beautifully, by the way.

My brother-in-law in Canada, Dougie Dalgleish, not only provided the inspiration for the Yokey-Doky laboratory, he was also kind enough to read these short stories and give honest feedback about them. That's very much appreciated: you'd be surprised how many people take on a manuscript then never bother to do anything with it.

Then there are individuals who inspired stories and characters; you have to have real people in your mind to imagine how fictional characters would respond to the events that take place in a story. Most of my characters are amalgams of people I know: A's facial expressions on B's body with C's temperament and D's turns of phrase. But there's always a danger that you're going to upset somebody by confessing you've written a character in a story around their personal little foibles and idiosyncrasies, so I won't mention any at all. Besides, some of my friends and acquaintances might be offended if I *didn't* apparently regard them as interesting enough to write about.

Acknowledgements

Instead, I'll give a nod to individuals who created situations that led to certain stories. My niece Alison Dunwell and her colleague Annabelle Cavarinho at Midlothian Libraries not only supported my early writing, between them they bounced me into writing *Ex Libris*. Emma Baird once met me in a café near Haymarket, although no orange items of clothing were anywhere to be seen. Senior education officials (I was a teacher, remember) created the meaningless nonsense that calls itself an annual staff review. We've been known to play what passes for bridge with friends in their Perthshire house, which features floor-to-ceiling windows ideal for cheating on a dark night – if only my eyesight were good enough at that distance. I'm not often invited to writers' awards ceremonies, but most of these things have the same format: food – anything from wine and nibbles to a full-on black-tie dinner, followed by interminable distribution of hardware and acceptance speeches.

A belated thanks to Elspeth and Michael Walker for a lovely dinner in June 2014 at their Gullane home, and to Dean the bus driver for entertaining us on the way home.

I wrote *The Beginning of Something Beautiful* myself, but my hospital consultant son Al looked over it for technical blunders. It's dangerous for any writer to be overly dependent on the internet – especially in the field of medical science where things change so quickly. Another member of my family, my wife Katherine, introduced me to birdwatching half a century ago, although I didn't see any waxwings for twenty years or so. You have to know what you're looking for, and where to look, as with so many other things.

And finally, of course, while I've been typing all this, Katherine has also had to endure the sight of me typing away endlessly on my laptop, with nothing to look at apart from a large lit-up Apple logo. The Apple logo might be more handsome, come to think of it.

Notes

I've never really considered myself to be a short story writer, so to discover that I'd written enough to allow me to select twenty was a bit of a surprise. I write short stories when the mood takes me; I've certainly never set out to write a series of them. When a writer gets stuck writing a novel – the dreaded 'writer's block' that we all experience from time to time – I find a good therapy is to write anything, perhaps in a different genre. I'm no poet, but essays are good, as are short stories. Each has the advantage that the writer should manage to complete the task he or she set out to do.

Novels aren't usually 'one story'. They're almost always an interweaving of different themes, plots and sub-plots that the writer has to keep a tight grip on. Short stories, on the other hand, can focus on one tight sequence of events that leads from a beginning to a conclusion. All you need is the germ of an idea and off you go. Although these stories are all fiction, they've mostly been triggered by something or other. Sometimes something has genuinely happened and I've developed it through a sort of 'what-iffery' into a short story. Sometimes it's been some sort of image. Sometimes I wanted to tell the reader a little more about characters from *Four Old Geezers and a Valkyrie*. Quite often in this volume, the stories have been centred on some random piece of music that I've composed.

Ex Libris was written in desperation. A few days before I was due to do an author event in a Midlothian public library one evening, I caught sight of a little poster inviting the public to 'come and hear author Gordon Lawrie read from his latest work.' The trouble was that there was no 'latest work', so I hurriedly bashed something down – which explains why I chose to set the events in that county.

I always felt sorry for **Tam**, a character from *Four Old Geezers*. He gets a bit of a hard time in the novel, not particularly deservedly, and has to make a hasty exit. This story ties up some loose ends.

Favour for a Friend has no real true-life inspiration, but the initial set-up is credible enough: someone helps their best friend seal a lifelong relationship with their partner, even although they themselves are strongly attracted to that person. The story asks many questions, none of which I really have answers to myself.

Anyone who's experienced an annual staff review will recognise what nonsense happens all too often in **Gorilla Warfare**. I once accidentally submitted a personal review form which was blank on the reverse of all five pages. I hadn't realised there was a reverse side to complete, so when it was pointed out to me, I was obliged to point out in return that neither I nor the reviewer had noticed that I'd left the same pages blank the previous year as well.

I'm a grandpa, and my grandchildren are great company. I've never been been fishing with any of them, but grandfathers everywhere will relate to **Fishermen**.

Can you remember the voice of a departed loved one? It's surprising how I can't recall my mother's voice, although I can vividly remember my father's laughter. **Grace Notes** explores this theme, and throws in a little piece of piano music at the same time. Sadly, I can't play it very well myself.

Bridges Burned, like *Tam*, harks back to a number of characters from *Four Old Geezers*, picking up where they left off. We've been known to play bridge with friends in their

Perthshire house, but no one takes it that seriously. Nevertheless, they have a large picture-frame window on one side of the room which would be perfect for cheating at cards, if only I had the eyesight for it.

It's What We Do is a bit of an outlier in this volume, because it was inspired by, and written for, a short story competition with a vivid black and white vector image as a prompt. The image itself was lost long ago.

I've lived in the Stockbridge area of Edinburgh for nearly 50 years, and throughout that time, shops owned by Italian and Asian families have been at the heart of life in Raeburn Place. Life hasn't always been easy, though, and occasionally they've been threatened by unsavoury individuals intent on trouble. **The Shopkeeper** is based on an amalgam of some of these characters.

I have a brother-in-law who used to be a professor of food science in Canada, and a visit to his lab many years ago gave me an insight into what the research department of Maddison's Dairy, where **Squeak** worked might look like. Readers of a certain age will recall those awful American jingles associated with fifties' advertising campaigns – but they were effective, otherwise you wouldn't still remember them.

The Beginning of Something Beautiful is almost an essay, written as a first-person narrative, although things do happen along the way.

Award ceremonies of any sort can often be a little cringeworthy, but artistic ones frequently have the added spice of jealousy. **Paradise Lost** is about snobbery in publishing and writing. Everyone is terribly polite, but they're all just a little secretly disappointed that their work hasn't been recognised. I know all about that, I'm afraid.

Celtic Conundrum started with the tune; sometimes a tune pops into my head and then I write something to go around it. The story itself is one of those pass-on-the-torch things found in Annie Proulx's *Accordion Crimes* or the old western movie *Winchester 73*. I've tried to record it somewhere, but it's quite difficult for one person to play all the instruments at the same time.

Incredibly, **The Second Best Parking Attendant** in the City is largely true. I was passing in the street, in fact, when a bespectacled Asian parking attendant set out to book a car for the most questionable of infractions. For some reason I decided I had to intervene – perhaps I knew the owner, I don't recall – but he defended himself with this 'second best parking attendant' plea. And he really did back it up by saying he booked members of his own family. Once any writer's heard something like that, there's not a lot more required to complete the story.

The two outdoor recreations in my life are golf and birdwatching. **Waxwings** are one of the hoped-for highlights of the winter, and during years of large irruptions people like me look out for notifications on social media where they can be seen. But I'm not a 'twitcher'; I just like to look at them. Waxwings really are beautiful birds, as are so many of our most common species. Geoff and Sheila are two more returning characters from *Four Old Geezers*.

Agent Orange was probably the very first short story I ever wrote. I was due to meet another writer, with whom I'd only communicated by email, off the train at Edinburgh's Haymarket Station. We did head for a nearby coffee shop, but apart from that I can't remember anything. We might have been talking about publishing one of *her* books.

I really enjoyed writing **The Audition**, one of the shortest stories. I'm particularly delighted that several readers from the Tennessee area have commented that the accents are spot-on. I like to imagine the story as a sitcom short film.

Magda is another character from *Four Old Geezers*, as are Jane and Brian. Brian, the narrator, is actually the central character in that novel, too, as well as in the final story, *Hoots Mon*. Stories involving these characters are all told in the present tense. Magda is some young woman, for sure. The story is also the vehicle for a song I really like called *The Shores of Caledonia*, written as a response to the xenophobia and racism that I think were the main driving forces behind Brexit.

Back in 2014, my wife Katherine and I were invited to a dinner party with friends in Gullane, around twenty miles east of Edinburgh. As alcohol was involved, the journey home had to be by public transport – by **The Last Bus**, in fact. The driver, who really was called Dean, clearly knew all the regulars. and he also led a sing-song just like the one in the story.

At 16,000 words, the final story, **Hoots Mon**, is almost a novella, and divided into four parts. The idea of rasta-jock – Little Joe's unique fusion of Jamaican reggae and Scottish guitar-thumping folk music – came from *Four Old Geezers and a Valkyrie*, and during author events I was often asked to let audiences hear what it sounded like. It's actually incredibly hard to play, a bit like rubbing circles on your tummy and patting your head simultaneously. However, I eventually managed to write an original song, and this is the story of what happens to it. *Hoots Mon* also sees the return of The Flying Saucers, the band from the original novel, and many familiar faces. As with several other stories, the musical score is included so that readers can take it on themselves if they feel up to it. Be aware, though, that 'rasta-jock' comes with a giant-sized warning:

**'THIS MUSIC MAY SERIOUSLY
HARM YOUR HEALTH.'**